☥ *You accept that membership in the Society is a privilege that comes with responsibilities as well as rewards. When one member fails, everyone fails.*

☥ *Society members are bound to the strictest levels of secrecy. You will not speak to Outsiders about the Society, not to family nor to friends.*

☥ *Apart from Society functions, you are not at liberty to discuss the Society amongst yourselves.*

☥ *You will leave the room if the Society is brought up in a public setting.*

☥ *You will attend all Society functions and meetings as requested. You will not be late.*

☥ *Infractions to these and further rules will be punishable by whatever means the Society's Leadership deems appropriate.*

☥ *You will accept the Society's orders above those of all others, whether church, school, or state.*

Also by Tom Dolby
THE TRUST

Tom Dolby

SECRET SOCIETY

KATHERINE TEGEN BOOKS
An Imprint of HarperCollins Publishers

Katherine Tegen Books is an imprint of HarperCollins Publishers.

Secret Society

Copyright © 2009 by Tom Dolby

www.harperteen.com

Library of Congress Cataloging-in-Publication Data
Dolby, Tom.
Secret society / by Tom Dolby. — 1st ed.
p. cm.
Summary: Three Manhattan teens, Phoebe, Nick, and Lauren, are
initiated into an age-old secret society that offers them the fulfillment
of their wildest dreams but demands their undying loyalty, while
Nick's friend Patch, an aspiring filmmaker, tries to document the
society's activities.
ISBN 978-0-06-172163-2
[1. Secret societies—Fiction. 2. Interpersonal relations—Fiction.
3. Motion pictures—Production and direction—Fiction. 4. Wealth—
Fiction. 5. New York (N.Y.)—Fiction.] I. Title.
PZ7.D7003Sec 2009   2009014572
[Fic]—dc22   CIP
                                                              AC

Typography by Amy Ryan
11 12 13 14 15 CG/BVG 10 9 8 7 6 5 4 3 2 1
❖
First paperback edition

"*Nothing is easier than self-deceit.*
For what each man wishes, that he also believes to be true."
—Demosthenes

"*The greatest trick the Devil ever pulled*
was convincing the world he didn't exist."
—Christopher McQuarrie, *The Usual Suspects*

For E.B.

PROLOGUE

Even the most seasoned walkers through Manhattan's Central Park often miss Cleopatra's Needle. The seven-story Egyptian obelisk dates back to the fifteenth century B.C.E. and stands less than a hundred yards from the Metropolitan Museum of Art.

One Thanksgiving morning, it was hard to ignore. At the base of the granite obelisk was the body of a young man, lying among dead leaves and candy bar wrappers. The figure was naked but for a pair of white cotton briefs. It was discovered by a jogger at six-thirty A.M., and by eight, no fewer than fifty onlookers had gathered. Police officers cordoned off the area, reporters with camera crews commented on the scene, and holiday tourists gawked at the spectacle.

Detectives noted the details: white male, mid- to late teens, brown hair, blue eyes.

The only identifying mark: a dime-sized tattoo of an ankh, the Egyptian symbol for life, at the back of his neck.

I

REBIRTH

CHAPTER ONE

Invitations, Phoebe Dowling realized, often come from the most unexpected places.

The last thing she thought would happen on the third day of her junior year at the Chadwick School was that an adorable, shaggy-haired guy would hand her a flyer for a party: NICK BELL PRESENTS OLD SCHOOL ELECTROCLASH AT THE FREEZER, MUSIC BY DJ APOCALYPSE. Phoebe had read about DJ Apocalypse in *Vanity Fair*, how he spun for celebs and press-hungry socialites, but she never thought she'd get to go to one of his parties. And the boy who handed her the invite? Someone had told her once that if she and her mom ever moved to Manhattan, the guys really were better looking, but she hadn't believed it. Until now.

"Thanks," she croaked, as she felt her long, reddish-brown

hair slide awkwardly over her lightly freckled forehead. She rushed to push it back behind her ear, catching it on her upper ear piercing.

"No problem," he said, rushing down the hall, his worn loafers squeaking as he dodged book bags and elbows while handing out three more glossy invites in the time it had taken her to recover. She looked at his retreating figure, at the classic, threadbare blazer askew on his broad frame.

The Chadwick School, that brick-and-stone fortress located on the northeast edge of the Upper East Side, hadn't exactly turned out to be what she had expected upon arriving in Manhattan from Los Angeles. Phoebe's old school, St. Catherine's, was known for its privileged student body, just as Chadwick was. St. Catherine's had been populated by the bratty offspring of film stars and studio execs, as well as the odd artsy student, which Phoebe herself had been. But there was something different about the students at Chadwick. They all had it so *together*. It was as if they had been shopping at Bergdorf's since they were three, as if they had had credit cards in their own names and cell phones forever, as if they didn't know what it was like to feel their freedom or finances limited in any way. Phoebe sighed as she packed her book bag. She could play the game if she had to; her mother said that if she hated it there, she could transfer next year. But for now, she had to stick it out.

Classes were done for the day, and students streamed down

the hall in every direction, a rush of khakis and plaid skirts and papers and notebooks. The school's interiors were like a Merchant Ivory film: wood paneling in the hallways, inlaid mosaics in the entryway. True, some of Chadwick had been modernized—the student podcast station, the music practice rooms—but most of it wasn't brand-new, the way everything seemed to be in California. The place had history: Phoebe could feel it as she ran her finger along the student graffiti carved into the oak Harkness tables, those large oval-shaped classroom tables that had been invented at a New England boarding school. She could sense it as she noticed the worn spots on the marble stairs that students had been climbing for nearly two hundred years.

That afternoon, she was planning on hopping on the 6 train, transferring at Grand Central, going over to the West Side, and visiting her mom at the gallery where her work was repped. She noticed the boys getting in cabs, and some of the girls even jumping into hired cars, giggling all the way. She had a creeping sensation that everyone else was having more fun than she was, was experiencing more of this grand, glittering city. Phoebe wanted to experience every version of New York: the gritty one, the glamorous one. Who held the key? That was what she needed to know. Who would make her Manhattan the one she had seen in the movies? She suspected that it was boys like the one who had handed her the invitation, boys like Nick Bell, who knew such things, who were to the manner born. Even if the manor was a penthouse apartment on Fifth Avenue.

Nick clutched his iPhone in his sweaty palm as he listened to the voice on the other end: "There's a problem with the liquor."

Even though he was jogging around the Central Park Reservoir, his sneakers pounding against the ground, he still felt his body seize up, a shiver running to his stomach. Had Amir, one of the owners of the club where he was throwing his bash that night, finally realized that the majority of his guests would be underage?

"Yeah, what?" Nick said, attempting to sound like he was in control.

"The vodka sponsor's delivery hasn't arrived yet," Amir said.

Nick felt himself relax. "We still have a few hours, don't we? Besides, is one missing brand really that big a deal? Just switch it out with something cheaper."

"I don't know, Nick—you know how this crowd gets if they don't get their top-shelf stuff during open bar."

"It'll be fine," Nick said, as he slowed down his jog to a trot. "You could put Popov in a Ketel One bottle and no one would know the difference."

"I guess you know them better than I do."

"Amir, trust me, it's the least of our worries." He cringed, hoping Amir wouldn't ask him what he meant.

He clicked off the call and went back to the Digitalism track he was listening to—not exactly the most relaxing music, but it would get him psyched for the evening. Once the party started, he had six hours of DJ Apocalypse's electronica to look forward to—that is, if he could confirm that the elusive turntablist was still coming. The guy hadn't returned Nick's last three messages.

Soaked from his run in the early September heat, he arrived home to his family's Fifth Avenue apartment and took the elevator up to the top floor. As he traipsed through the foyer of the penthouse and up the staircase to the second level, he waved away Gertie, their rotund cook, when she asked if he wanted a snack. He could hear low voices coming from behind the living room's paneled pocket doors—it sounded like his mother and his father and a male voice he didn't recognize. He paused for a moment, although he couldn't make anything out. It was unusual for his father to be home this early.

Nick thought ahead to the party as he cooled off in his bedroom, peeling off his sweaty socks and kicking his rank-smelling sneakers into a corner. He was trying not to stress, but all his usual worries came back to him: Had he invited enough people? Had he invited too many? Would the right ones show up? As of that afternoon, he was almost out of flyers—a good or a bad thing, depending on how you looked at it. He looked down at his phone. There was a text from his best friend, Patch, who had been in charge of setting up the door list for the party:

GUEST LIST MAXED AT 600. CLOSING IT NOW.

Nick texted him back that it was cool. The club held only about four hundred people, so six hundred names would be more than enough to pack the place while still allowing for no-shows. Although he had organized only a few club nights in the past, all out in the Hamptons, he was starting to feel like he was getting good at it. He grinned to himself, awash in excitement and adrenaline. Everything from the summer was coming to fruition.

It had all started when his parents had, almost shockingly, given him nearly free rein at the beach over summer break, and he had been doing what he liked to think of as "party-ing with a purpose." Club owners at the Purple Elephant in Southampton and the Chocolate Lounge outside East Hampton had said that when they decamped back to the city in the fall, they would give him his own night there—that is, if he could promise to attract the kind of crowd they knew he could bring in: young, good looking, with disposable income for bottle service and an appetite for VIP treatment. Nick knew it was a little shady to give such power to a high school junior, but that was the thing: The club owners—Amir and his partner, Costa—didn't know that he was still in high school.

As they were foreigners (one was from Israel, Nick thought, and the other from—Brazil, was it?), they weren't too familiar with the local private school scene, so when he said that he was a student at Chadwick, they had assumed he was already in college. He made a point of not shaving whenever he was going to be in their proximity, and given his recent growth spurt to a full six feet, two inches, they had no idea that he was only sixteen years old. They had seen him hanging out with the girls and guys he had grown up with; the guys were all relatively attractive (and if they did have acne or awkward haircuts, their parents whisked them off to a dermatologist or overpriced salon to get the problem fixed), and the girls— most of all, the girls—dressed older, acted older. With their expensive highlights and Marc Jacobs handbags and Christian Louboutin heels and casually smoked Nat Shermans, there was no way an onlooker could ever tell that his friends were only sixteen, seventeen, sometimes even as young as fifteen years old, never mind what it said on their fake IDs.

Nick had become a social butterfly, but the thing was— although he didn't dare tell anyone—he didn't really like most of the kids he was spending time with. The city was full of so many different kinds of people, and his parents had protected him, sheltered him from them all. It was starting to drive him crazy, drive him out of his skull. Some of his friends drowned it all out by being stoned 24–7, living in a cloud of cannabis, but that bored Nick. Sometimes, he wanted nothing more than to go back to the days when everything had been simple, when a weekend meant hanging out at the Southampton house on the glassed-in sunporch, renting bad Bruce Willis movies and eating too much pizza.

He put it out of his head as he stepped from the shower and wrapped a towel around his waist. His party was at The Freezer, Amir and Costa's cash cow of a nightclub down in the Meatpacking District, which was admittedly past its prime. It was a good entry, though, to the New York promoting scene for Nick. The bad news was that DJ Apocalypse, supposedly fresh off a flight from Paris where he had headlined at a party for Veuve Clicquot—and rumored to have fallen off the wagon since his stint in rehab for meth addiction—was still nowhere to be found.

CHAPTER TWO

The skirt was to die for.

Lauren Mortimer was standing in front of a rack of new arrivals at Giroux New York, a boutique on Fourteenth Street that she had been obsessed with since she was twelve. The skirt, by an up-and-coming London designer, was short without being slutty short and was constructed of gorgeous folds of gray chiffon. It had an almost 1960s feel to it, which Lauren loved; it would be the perfect thing to wear to Nick's party that night. She would pair it with the little Alexander McQueen leather jacket she had picked up a few weeks ago.

She lived for this, that sartorial moment when something in a store could take your breath away.

Once again, Lauren was in the Meatpacking District, her guilty pleasure, the site of so many of her sins, and she was trawling for fashion. She was the only person she knew who actually liked that the neighborhood could be so nasty. There was something exciting about stepping over slightly foul-smelling, blood-strewn streets with full shopping bags from Scoop or Catherine Malandrino or Diane von Furstenberg. It always made her feel as if she were in a shoot for French or Italian *Vogue,* that sharp contrast of fashion and filth. Lauren thought of herself as a purist: She loved the fact that designers had moved into the neighborhood, but she hated that it had driven out the nightclubs and the culture (not to mention most of the meatpacking plants). She didn't mean the bridge-and-tunnel-packed clubs that occupied it today; there were still plenty of those, filled with girls with done-up hair and sparkly tops, outfits that made them look like hookers. From everything Lauren had heard, there used to be *real* nightclubs: goth clubs, performance art clubs, that sort of thing. Not that she had ever been to them, but she knew the stories. Her mother's town car used to pull up at Jeffrey when the downtown style mecca was still the street's main fashion outpost and Lauren was about nine years old. Her mother would try on shoe after shoe while a salesclerk with a shaved head and a serpent tattoo would amuse her with sanitized, PG-rated stories of everything that had gone on the night before: the performances, the transsexual go-go dancers, the European designers out with their models, the craziness, the all-night dancing. Lauren could read between the lines: Fashion equaled excitement and sex and fun, and she wanted to be part of it.

Now Lauren went downtown on her own, in a cab or on the subway (which, weirdly, she sometimes preferred—everyone was so *normal* compared to the people in her life on the Upper East), and explored that world herself. She didn't know where she might fit into it, but what she did know was that she didn't want to be like her mother: drinking gimlets at four in the afternoon, moaning about her failed marriage, poring over photos from her days as a debutante. It was beyond pathetic. *Live in the present!* Lauren wanted to scream at her. But she couldn't, and anyway, her mom wouldn't. It was much easier, after all, to soak in the gin-laced past.

She turned over the skirt's price tag: nine hundred dollars. Would her mother notice if she put it on her platinum card? No, Lauren shopped at Giroux all the time, so what was the big deal? Even if her parents' divorce had frozen her mother's love life, it had done no such thing to her bank account.

Later that evening, Nick's best friend, Patchfield Evans III, threw on a pair of wrinkled jeans and a T-shirt as he readied himself for his friend's party. He had printed out the guest list and also emailed a copy to the club's owners, as Nick had requested. He went out to the living room, where his grandmother, Eugenia, was sitting. Her fingers danced gracefully over the keys of the old Steinway, which was, to Patch's ear, a tad out of tune. Every day, she still got dressed, did up her white hair, put on makeup, even a string of pearls, as though she might be receiving a gentleman caller.

He reviewed his evening plans with her, and she nodded as if they had been on her mind all day.

"Nick will be there?" she asked.

Patch nodded.

"Be careful, yes? If there's a problem, you call on your . . . you know."

"Cell phone, Genie, cell phone." He had saved up and bought her one several years ago, but she never seemed to use it.

"That's right." She smiled. "Cell phone. I'll be here."

"I know," Patch said, chuckling a bit. As if his grandmother would ever leave the apartment at this hour. "You want me to bring you anything?"

She shook her head. "My dear, I have everything I need." She opened a drawer and held up a stack of delivery menus, giving him an impish grin. "There's a Cary Grant marathon on Turner Classics. I'll be up late."

Patch headed back to his bedroom to finish getting ready. He shared the small two-bedroom with Genie, which he didn't mind, all things considered. Eugenia Rogers Madison was eighty-three years old and knew things about the city and about Patch's life that sometimes he didn't even realize himself. Even though they lived in a landmarked co-op building across the street from the Metropolitan Museum, their place was a far cry from the sprawling penthouse where Nick lived, ten floors above them. In Patch's apartment, which had been split up from a much larger unit, the linoleum was coming up in the kitchen, and the electrical hadn't been inspected since the 1960s (they nearly had a fire last year when his grandmother plugged too many appliances into one extension cord). Eugenia and her late husband, Patch's grandfather, had bought the apartment in 1953 for less than what a parking space in the city would cost today. His grandfather had never made much money of his own, and Patch's father had died in a terrible drowning accident when Patch was five, without ever having the foresight to purchase life insurance for the family. His mother, sadly, was in an institution upstate. One day, for no reason that was apparent to anyone, she had turned completely catatonic. Patch now saw her only a few times a year.

He sighed as he laced up his dirty Puma sneakers, glancing up to his desk at the video work in progress on the glowing monitor, a grimy old flat screen that Nick had been about to toss. Four years ago, it had been far better than the ancient one Patch had owned at the time, but now it was looking a bit shopworn.

As he reached for his wallet, Patch thought about how he and his grandmother had the oldest kind of old money: the kind that didn't exist anymore.

Patch grabbed the rest of his equipment and headed for the door. He needed to get some good footage for his vlog,

PatchWork, the type that would really impress some of the TV producers he had been meeting with. He was nervous about tonight, and he tried to think past it. He and the producers were in endless "talks" about him directing a reality show set at Chadwick, a situation that was admittedly impressive for a high school junior, but it was not enough for Patch. He had gotten the email two months ago, out of nowhere: "I've been watching your vlog. I produce television shows. Can we meet?" What had followed had been a flurry of lawyers and agents and release forms. The school was thrilled that a high profile project might be shot on school grounds. Their enthusiasm had been surprising, but Chadwick was in need of a shot of energy—and the money the project could raise for the endowment fund wouldn't hurt, either. The biggest benefit was that the headmaster and the administration thought the show might be the boost the school needed to modernize its image, to make it seem less stuffy and stuck up. Patch was in the final round of discussions with a series of producers; he wanted to sign with a team that would really get it, that wouldn't make him feel like he had sold out. He imagined what his idol, Gus Van Sant, would do. That is, if Gus Van Sant shot documentaries about private school kids.

CHAPTER THREE

Nick had shown up at The Freezer half an hour before the doors were set to open. As he entered, saying hello to the doormen, he noticed a strange man in a suit lurking a few doors down. Probably just the usual eurotrash who populated the area, but something about it bothered Nick. He had been looking right at him.

The club manager's iPod was on autoshuffle, so music was blasting, but it wouldn't be long before people started to notice that DJ Apocalypse wasn't in the booth. Nick had gone all out for this party: Patch had designed the flyers, they had sent out emails, Nick had enlisted friends, classmates, older brothers and sisters to spread the word. If all went well, the club would be packed.

The Freezer was a cavernous space on Gansevoort Street

that used to be a meatpacking plant. Multiple rooms surrounded one large dance floor, all a flight of stairs down from the street. Nick hoped that because it was underground, it would have a certain cool factor to it, the feeling of being a den of iniquity. He was disappointed to see, once he arrived, that the club was looking down at the heels. The vinyl upholstery was repaired with packing tape. The DJ booth, upon close inspection, was constructed of cheap, black-painted plywood. The distinct smell of vomit lingered in one of the restrooms. Nick asked Amir if the lights could be turned down any lower, and the club owner obliged. Maybe with the lights dim and the laser effects going, no one would notice that the place was a dump. Thank God they wouldn't be carding for drinks after people got in, and the first hour would be open bar, albeit without a full range of premium vodkas. Nothing like a few free drinks to get things going. Nick tried to push away his sense of dread. What if no one showed?

Adding to his anxiety, his parents had given him a bizarre guilt trip that evening about what he was wearing. They never seemed to care, hadn't made a comment in two years (save for the occasional request for him to tuck in his shirt or straighten his tie), and yet tonight, both his mother and father had sat him down and given him a mini lecture on how he shouldn't be going out dressed in a way that was so shabby, how he was representing his family, how he was a Bell and Bells were expected to look, act, and dress a certain way. Nick had paid them no mind and had worn his usual obscure punk band T and olive-green German army jacket he had picked up on Bleecker Street in the Village.

At ten P.M., the club's doors opened, and reportedly a line already snaked down the block. Private school kids from all over the city started pouring in, the guys flashing their fake IDs, the girls usually getting in with little more than a flirtatious smile and the air that they were far too busy to be concerned with the possibility of not being admitted. The word had apparently gotten out that this was the party to be at on the first Friday after the start of school. People were chatting, drinking, texting each other, snapping pics on their phones. Nick paused for a moment, satisfied with the turnout, before jumping to the next problem: DJ Apocalypse was clearly flaking on his engagement. Nick was relieved to spot Patch twenty minutes later, the digital video camera—his friend's ever-present social crutch, he sometimes thought—held in front of him. Nick grabbed Patch, who gave him a glare.

"What are you doing? I was in the middle of a sequence."

"You can always do a cut later. I need your help."

Patch adjusted his round Harry Potter–style glasses and swept his straight brown hair out of his eyes. "What with?"

Nick motioned to the DJ booth. "The Apocalypse. It's not happening tonight," he said, attempting a bad joke.

"Probably passed out at the Gramercy Park Hotel," Patch

said. "I told you that you shouldn't have hired him. How much did you put down?"

"Twelve hundred. Maybe I can still cancel the check." He groaned. "This is not good."

"Okay, so what do you need?"

"I need you to DJ. Do you have your iPod?"

Patch nodded.

"Good. Plug it into the laptop. It's all hooked up to the mixing board. No one'll know the difference. You've got all the good stuff on there, right?"

"What do you think I listen to all day?"

"Make it the usual: some Daft Punk, some Interpol, some mashups. Everyone'll think you're the opening act or something, and by the time they realize that he's not coming, they'll be too drunk to care."

"You're a class act, Bell," Patch said.

"Piss off. Help me out, okay? This party has to go down well. My name is on the line."

"You got it. But I'm still filming from the booth."

"Patch, I don't care if you do Stoli shots there. Just play the music." Nick cringed as he realized his gaffe: Patch had recently gone straight edge—no booze, no drugs, no cigs— after a series of particularly bad nights over the summer.

Patch nodded and headed for the DJ booth, and Nick saw from afar that he was plugging in his iPod to the laptop and getting acquainted with the system. Sometimes Nick didn't know what he would do without his friend.

Nick turned around quickly, his blood pumping, ready to troubleshoot the next problem. Amir and Costa had a reputation for romancing their female clientele as the evening wore on, which meant that their attention often wandered. Nick wanted to make sure that his party went down well, that it wasn't one of those lame club nights that sucked because the bar ran out of ice or a speaker blew out. As he turned around, he bumped into someone, a slightly awkward girl in jeans and a white blouse. Tall, pretty, long straight reddish-brown hair, looking a bit frazzled as they collided. He remembered her, vaguely, from handing her a flyer earlier that day at school.

"I'm so sorry," she said quickly, even though it was clearly his fault.

"New here, right?"

She smiled. "Yeah."

"Well, welcome to my party. It's part of the official Chadwick School welcome kit."

"Really?" She looked serious.

"I'm kidding. It's totally not. Please."

"Oh." She relaxed a bit. "I'm sorry, I feel so clueless here. I just moved to the city. God, that sounds incredibly lame."

"Don't worry about it. You want a drink ticket?"

"Sure, thanks."

Nick reached in his pocket, only to realize that he didn't have any. "Dammit. I'm sorry. They didn't give me any yet.

Wanna follow me to the bar?"

The girl nodded. Nick was about to ask her name and tell her his when a foursome of Chadwick girls, all seniors, came up to him, squealing his name.

"Nicky Bell!" one of them exclaimed, using his childhood appellation, in a flutter of perfume and manicured nails. "Your party is *so* cute! We had no idea—I mean, we came down here to stop by after dinner, but this is just darling, really. So *raw*. So *real*. Did you have them do up the place like this? I mean, the silver walls, the—" She lowered her voice. "—*cheap-looking* seating. It's *way* cool. *So* downtown!"

"No, it's sort of—" Nick faltered. "Yeah, sure, we made it work." Let them think whatever they want, right? "Do you know . . ." He turned around to look for the girl he was supposed to go to the bar with, but she had gotten caught up with the crowd. It was the part of throwing parties that he hated: You never really got to talk to anyone, and sometimes, if you weren't quick enough, you didn't even catch their names. Everyone always thought of Nick as a party boy, but it wasn't how he thought of himself. The parties were just something to do, something to pass the time. They weren't what he wanted to do with his life. Part of it was to tick off his parents. His mother and father had made it very clear that throwing downtown parties was not an appropriate vocation for someone of his, in his mother's words, "social class." He was supposed to be teaching sailing or working on his tennis game or studying an extra foreign language.

The four girls ran off. Nick was relieved to be rid of their patronizing comments. Even he found senior girls intimidating, although he had known those girls most of his life. But now, he realized, he had started to find them downright annoying.

Looking around, he saw that the girl with the reddish-brown hair had disappeared.

CHAPTER FOUR

Lauren had arrived fashionably late to the party. She saw a few girls she knew, but did the nod and "I'll catch up with you later" wave and then headed for the bar. There wasn't anything she had to do the next day, a Saturday. Her mother was headed to East Hampton for a fall luncheon hosted by a family friend, so Lauren would have the apartment to herself. Her little sister, Allison, was a freshman at a boarding school in Connecticut, and she had moved back there a week ago. Lauren felt a twinge of loneliness, although she tried to swallow it down. She had never been one of those girls who clung to their boyfriends like a life raft, and yet, at times like this, she admitted that it would be nice to have someone in her life. She had planned on coming with a trio of girls from school, but had decided at the last moment against it. The three were going to meet at a townhouse in the East Seventies to do shots beforehand, but Lauren didn't like showing up sloppy drunk at these things. Even though Diana Mortimer had been drinking more than usual lately, it was another thing her mother had taught her: Showing up somewhere sloshed was tacky. But now, as she sipped her first vodka and soda of the evening, she felt the cool crisp sense of isolation as the liquor warmed her chest. It was as if the party was happening around her, and she wasn't connected to it at all. *This is it. This is the beginning of my junior year. And I am completely, utterly alone, a princess dressed up for the ball with no one to escort me.*

Her boyfriend from last year, Robert, had graduated, gone to Dartmouth, one of the handful of schools where all nice boys from Park Avenue go, and Lauren was surprised to realize that she didn't miss him, a revelation that only saddened her more. She had lost her virginity to him, but now that he was gone, had moved on, would not be seeing or even talking to her, it was almost as if it had never happened at all. It was never right, even Lauren knew that. She wanted someone far more exciting that a cookie-cutter preppie, but still, within her his absence resonated. She thought with a groan about the kinds of people her mother wanted her to hang out with. Her mother was already lobbying for her to be part of a dreadful debutante ball called the International, even though it was more than two years away. What could be more miserable than being paired up with a guy she barely knew and being dragged to a whirlwind of superficial parties? It was the kind of thing that sounded like a blast when she was thirteen, but now, it held very little appeal.

She stood behind a willowy, long-haired girl as she looked idly among the crowd for her friends. The girl was balancing a drink precariously near the edge of the bar while trying to pull out a dollar for a tip from one of those artsy-chic wallets made from duct tape and cardboard. The drink was on the verge of falling off the bar when Lauren grabbed it.

"Oh my God, I'm so sorry," the girl said. "I am such a klutz."

"No worries," Lauren said coolly, handing it back to her. Lauren looked at the girl from head to toe, a terrible habit she had acquired from her mother. Really, it was just plain rude, but she couldn't help her desire to size other people up. "Are those ballet flats?" Lauren asked, feeling a shred of nostalgia for her long-lost days at Madame Pomeroy's studio on Third Avenue. She hadn't taken ballet since she was eleven.

"Oh, yeah," the girl said. "I know, sort of stupid, I was actually unpacking, and they were the first thing I pulled out . . ."

"No, stop—I love them. They're *genius*. And in silver! Like Lanvin. But not. I mean, oh my God. You're tall enough, you can pull it off. Please don't hate me if I copy you."

"Oh, I don't care." Who was this girl?

"What's your name?"

"Oh, um, Phoebe Dowling." The girl introduced herself

almost as if she didn't expect Lauren to offer her own name back, although Lauren did anyway.

"So you're new? Not bad to be invited to Nick Bell's party."

"To be honest, I have no idea what I'm doing here."

The girl was nothing if not candid. Lauren appreciated it. She grabbed Phoebe's hand and motioned to the other side of the room. "Come with me. We're sitting over there."

This was an entirely new side of Lauren; she had always thrived on being a bit selfish. Now suddenly the idea of taking someone under her wing, of showing someone around, seemed strangely appealing.

The evening was flying by for Nick, as people kept grabbing him into clusters of conversation. Before he knew it, it was already half after midnight. He had posed for the requisite photographs and made sure everything was in order (the right people had indeed shown up, and save for the missing DJ and alcohol snafu, things were pretty much running themselves). He was finally able to pull himself away from a group that was doing shots and go up to the booth to check on Patch.

"Everything okay?" he asked. His friend was hunched over the mixing board, his blue Old Navy hoodie almost making him look like a real DJ.

Patch nodded. "I downloaded a few new tracks . . . It's going to kill."

"People are texting me with all these requests," Nick said. "Check it out." Nick handed his phone to Patch, who copied down some of the songs that people wanted to hear. Nick saw his cell vibrating in Patch's hand.

Patch suddenly gave him an uncomfortable look. "You've got another message." He quickly handed the phone back to Nick.

It wasn't a request. Nick frowned. It was from an unknown number.

53 GANSEVOORT STREET. 1 A.M. YOU KNOW WHAT TO DO.

Nick found his hands trembling. He had heard of messages like this, but he wasn't sure exactly what it meant. He frowned again.

"What's wrong?" Patch asked.

"Nothing," Nick said quickly, hoping Patch hadn't seen the message. It was the type of thing you couldn't talk about. Patch's own cell phone was sitting next to the mixing board: no messages. Nick took a deep breath. He felt terrible lying to his best friend, but he had no choice. There were various things the message could mean, but he was pretty certain that this one was from the Society, a fabled secret group that supposedly recruited in early September each year, starting with the incoming class of New York private school juniors.

The little that he knew about the Society was that if you were invited to one of its gatherings, you went, no questions asked, and you didn't talk about it to anyone else. Besides, maybe Patch was going to be tapped. The only way Nick could find out would be to go.

Why did Nick want to be part of something like this? It was the kind of thing that said, *You matter. You are important. You belong.* Nick had pieced together rumors over the years; what he had gleaned was that the Society was a breeding ground for those who would go on to run the country, run the world. It was the kind of thing Nick had spent the past few years running away from, but now that he was in its midst, that he had received this strange invitation, he couldn't resist satisfying his curiosity. He felt like such a sellout, but he had to know what it was all about.

Nick checked the time on his phone. "I have to go," he said.

"You're going to leave your own party?"

Nick sighed. He didn't know how he was going to explain this. "There's just something I have to take care of."

He looked down at the crowd: they were oblivious, dancing, swaying to the music. They wouldn't miss him, not at all.

CHAPTER FIVE

Phoebe followed as Lauren deftly guided her across the club and over to her table. Phoebe was impressed by Lauren's social acumen. As they pushed their way across the dance floor, she made one-line quips and greetings to people she knew, ignored those she didn't with a steely gaze, and even exchanged barbs with a girl who stepped on her foot without apologizing. And all this while chattering on to Phoebe, asking her where she had moved from and what her interests were.

It gave Phoebe pause—wasn't Lauren Mortimer known as the bitchiest girl in school? A clotheshorse? The queen bee of Chadwick's popular crowd? Lately, though, people said that Lauren had become moody and introspective—Phoebe thought that sounded more like her friends. Still, she wanted to be careful; within two days of arriving at Chadwick, Phoebe had already heard most of the stories about Lauren, although she didn't know if they were rumors or fact. How Lauren had stolen another girl's boyfriend. How Lauren had scored an internship at *Vogue* using her mother's connections. How Lauren's hand in marriage had already been promised to a twenty-year-old Italian count. How Lauren never flew commercial, only in her father's private plane. Phoebe had no idea which stories she could believe, so she decided she would take her at face value: as a pretty girl in very expensive clothes.

When it came to matters of fashion, Phoebe herself had felt painfully unprepared for the evening. All her LA clothes, even the cute ensembles she had splurged on from Fred Segal, didn't seem right. But she had apparently made the cut: a simple pair of skinny jeans, an empire-waist top, and then (what Lauren had deemed so *au courant*), a pair of ballet flats that had been spray-painted silver for a school play, now flaking in parts, but basically in decent shape. Adding to Phoebe's anxiety, she had decided to come alone. She had promised herself that she wasn't going to do this at Chadwick, that she wouldn't subject herself to the horrors of showing up solo, but she knew she didn't have a choice if she wanted to go to the party. Although she had met a handful of girls during the first few days of school, she didn't really know any of them well enough to call them up and *ask*—and the possibility that they might decline was too awful to consider. She figured that if she was having a bad time, she could walk the five blocks back home. So screw it, she had thought. What did she have to lose?

They arrived at a table filled with well-dressed girls who looked bored. Lauren slid in with the confidence of someone who knew she belonged, and air kisses were exchanged. For a moment Phoebe had the horrifying feeling that she was going to have to introduce herself, but Lauren came to her rescue. "Guys, this is Phoebe—she's from LA. The cool part, not the nasty part." Phoebe was introduced to Irina, a girl with dark, smoky eyes; Chloë, a blond girl who had what looked to be a pink Birken bag, although Phoebe couldn't be sure; and Victoria, who had the sharpest cheekbones Phoebe had ever seen on a sixteen-year-old.

Phoebe liked Lauren, but the rest of them—they looked like they had walked off the pages of a magazine. She found it tiresome while also oddly appealing. She wanted to shake Lauren and say, *Do you really like these people? Don't you think you could do better?* But instead she smiled blithely and tried to follow along with the conversation, although it wasn't easy with the blasting music and flashing lights. The girls asked her all about her time in LA, and her mother's photography, and the gallery that was showing her work. It was all pronounced as "incredibly cool," which surprised Phoebe, who never thought of what her mother did as cool. She always thought of it as anguished, tortured, coming out of some kind of inner pain.

But maybe that was how it was with art. You suffered, and in the end, people thought it was cool.

She sipped her gin and tonic, lost in thought. She wanted so much for her mother, Maia, to be happy here, to meet someone. It wasn't easy to care for your mom when she went on crying jags during every free moment and didn't pick up her camera, the only thing she really loved (apart from Phoebe, of course), for months at a time. But now, her mother's career was on the rise again; she was dating. Phoebe too had the chance to remake her life, to mold it into anything she chose. It didn't matter that they weren't rich (the Bank Street townhouse was theirs temporarily thanks to a wealthy sculptor friend of her mother's); it didn't matter that they weren't famous. Phoebe's father, after all, was just another venture capitalist who had lost too much money in the last recession. When he had started to make money again, he and her mother had grown apart, and the prospect of dating a younger woman had come before their family. Now he was back in LA, and they were here, a year and a half after the initial separation, adrift on the island of Manhattan. She didn't know what to do with these feelings, and she found herself zoning out as she sat there with Lauren's friends, clutching her gin and tonic as if she hadn't had a drink in months.

These girls all seemed to have it so easy. Apart from the slightest hint of discontentedness that Phoebe sensed in Lauren, they didn't appear to be concerned with any of the things

Phoebe was: Would she get into a good college? Could she ever really succeed as an artist? Would she get a break early, or would she have to wait as long as her mom had? And if it was the former, could she hack it? Was her stuff really any good? Everything she had worked on in LA—mixed media collages combined with painting, mostly—was all packed up now, but maybe she should get them out and keep working on them—

"Hey." Lauren poked her. "You okay?"

"Sorry," Phoebe said. "I just got distracted. It's a lot to think about, moving to the city and all." She bit her lip, embarrassed that she had revealed any vulnerability. These girls weren't the vulnerable types, at least not on the outside.

"Where do you live?"

"Bank Street."

"Oh my God, I *love* that street. There's a place nearby that has the best cupcakes."

Phoebe nodded and smiled. That was what most people said when she mentioned Bank Street. It was a lovely street full of lush greenery and prewar brownstones, but the only thing people ever mentioned were those damned cupcakes, as if nothing else mattered in the world.

Phoebe felt her phone buzz, and she reached to get it. A text message, probably from her mother. She had her mom's old Razr phone, which she hoped wasn't pathetically uncool. It was cool, like, several years ago, right?

It was an unknown number, with a weird message to meet

at an address that was probably nearby. Was it another party? Some kind of prank?

She showed it to Lauren, who was peering intently at her own cell.

"Oh my God," Lauren whispered. "I got one of those, too."

"We can't go, can we? We have no idea—"

"I think I know what it is. We have to go. I never thought that tonight—it seems so *random*. Are we dressed right? Well, you look great." Lauren ran her fingers through her hair, letting it fall naturally over her shoulders. She looked fabulous, Phoebe thought, this uptown girl with gorgeous hair, glowing cheeks, and a perfectly straight nose, in a leather jacket and retro skirt. She wanted to tell Lauren, but that seemed, well, sort of pitiful. The other three girls were looking at Phoebe and Lauren strangely, as the two had been whispering. Lauren quickly went for a save. "There's this guy that Phoebe likes . . . I was just telling her what I know."

Phoebe felt herself blush a little, but it didn't matter. The three girls nodded approvingly. Interesting, Phoebe thought, how they didn't ask any more questions. It was as if Lauren had the power to tell them when to speak and when to shut up.

"We're going to get some air," Lauren said. "It's so stuffy in here, don't you think?"

"I'm fine," Chloë said, and the others nodded.

Lauren grabbed Phoebe and pushed her out of the booth.

Phoebe wasn't quite sure what to make of it all. Lauren starting whispering to her again as they walked up the staircase to street level. "I can't really explain . . . it's like this club that people are asked to join, people in our year. I've only heard rumors about it. You're not supposed to know who's in it. I knew a girl, a really popular girl who was in it, supposedly. She moved out to Hollywood after college, and now she's in the movies." Lauren named a rising twentysomething star.

Phoebe's eyes narrowed. "And this is the group that's sending us text messages? How did they even get our numbers?"

Lauren shrugged. "I don't know. That info is easy to get."

"I just, I don't know—it sounds kind of strange, like a cult or something." Now they were on the sidewalk.

"I wouldn't say it's a cult," Lauren said, still whispering.

Then why all the secrecy? Phoebe wondered.

"It's more like a group," Lauren continued. "Think of it like a private club, like the Union Club or the New York Racquet Club or Soho House or something—it's just something people don't talk about as much."

Phoebe looked at who was on the street, a pack of girls and guys who were smoking, flirting, exchanging taunts and jabs. It was as if Chadwick's beautiful crowd had been transported south of Fourteenth Street and, instead of looking out of place, had claimed it as their own for the night. The boy who had talked to her earlier was making his way through the throng of people. Phoebe glanced away, suddenly shy. It was too late.

"Lauren! What are you doing out here?" the boy asked her new friend.

"We have to go somewhere," Lauren said. "Another party. A friend of Phoebe's."

"Ah, so you have a name." He grinned, and stuck out his hand. "It's good to finally meet you. Officially, that is. I'm Nick."

"You, too," Phoebe said. She suddenly had this image of projecting her best self. This was what she would do—she would be the best person she could imagine herself to be. It was what she had read that New York always did to people: You became the ideal version of yourself.

Despite her reservations, her best self was following her two new friends to a strange address.

"I'll walk with you," Nick said. "I just need to, um, pick something up next door. Costa left something for the . . ." Phoebe noticed Nick stumbling on his words.

"Sure," Lauren said.

They started walking and then stopped, rather awkwardly, twenty paces later on the filthy sidewalk. They were shielded from the crowd's view by a Dumpster.

"It's right here," Nick said.

Lauren pulled out her cell and examined the address. 53 GANSEVOORT. This was it, two enormous double doors, covered with stickers and graffiti, locked with a deadbolt. There was a shoddy, dirty buzzer on the right-hand side.

"Um, we have to go here, too," Lauren said. She reached forward and pushed the buzzer, looking back at Phoebe for reassurance. She was a little scared, although she felt this was the right thing to do. Sometimes things in Manhattan were simply strange; she wasn't going to let some late-night meeting in the Meatpacking District freak her out. She looked back at Nick, who for the first time in all the years she had known him, seemed unsure of himself.

There was no sound, but the door opened. Before the three of them had a chance to compare notes on what was going on and what they were doing, they were ushered inside by a man wearing a bespoke suit, a monocle hanging from his lapel.

Inside was an enormous, cavernous space, much larger than the underground club next door. Everything was pitch-black except for a pathway lit by candles, wax dripping onto the concrete. Ahead of them, bathed in several pools of light, a party was in progress. The men were in black tie and the women wore evening gowns, and everyone had a mask on. A waiter appeared, bearing a tray of drinks in martini glasses. Lauren accepted one and sipped it carefully. It tasted like a lemon drop.

The music filling the air was big band swing. A black woman in a white sequined dress and a white fur stole was singing on a small stage in front of a band, shimmying along to the music. Lauren recognized the song; it was something her mother used to play when she was feeling nostalgic: "Between the Devil and the Deep Blue Sea." A song about being stuck in love.

Lauren looked at the twelve others who had entered with them, identifiable because they weren't dressed up or wearing masks. She knew a few kids from other schools. She recognized Alejandro Calleja, who was the son of an Argentinean billionaire, and Claire Chilton, whose mother was the head of the New York Junior League. Lauren wasn't particularly close to either of them. Alejandro was known to be a total player, and Claire was so uptight that Lauren suspected her ever-present headband was permanently affixed to her skull. Everyone looked apprehensive about where they were and what they were doing. After surveying the room, Lauren realized she and Nick and Phoebe were the only ones from Chadwick.

"Lauren!"

She heard her name and looked up. A woman not much older than she was and wearing a dress trimmed in feathers and a matching mask motioned her over. Lauren stepped forward, although she was starting to feel a bit woozy.

She recognized, as she looked more closely, who it was. It was a girl a year older than her who had also grown up in the city, Emily van Piper, someone who had never said more than a few words to her at a time. They embraced, and Lauren smiled.

"I'm so glad you're here," Emily said. "Isn't this exciting?"

Lauren nodded, although she didn't know exactly *what* was so exciting. It was, of course, all terribly glamorous: It was as if they were on the pages of a 1940s fashion spread or at Truman Capote's Black and White Ball. Women smoked from long black cigarette holders; men drank champagne from coupe glasses or martinis brought by waiters on silver trays. If only she were wearing something more interesting . . .

She looked down at her outfit, at her leather jacket, at her gray skirt and her little clutch, and she realized that it was perfect. She was the embodiment of downtown chic. She took another sip of her drink. She was the best dressed person there.

She turned back to find Phoebe, who was deep in conversation with an older gentleman.

"I know your mother's work," he was saying. "It's quite striking. She's going to make some real waves in the art world. Just you wait."

Phoebe introduced Lauren. "I can't believe any of this," Phoebe said. "It's like . . . well, it's like a party."

"It's like the best party you've ever been to," Lauren said.

"I wonder when the masks come off," Phoebe said.

"Oh, no," the man said. "That doesn't happen. At least not until later. Much, much later."

CHAPTER SIX

The drink, Nick had found out, was called Amnesia. From his early days clubbing and his explorations of his mother's medicine cabinet, he was able to guess that it had some combination of ketamine and Vicodin, maybe with some Xanax to smooth things out. He didn't believe in Special K—he knew that it was junk, that it would mess you up, a clubby drug derived from horse tranquilizer. And yet tonight, he was content to sip it down.

The room was wobbling, as if each step he took were on a different level, and Nick knew he should pace himself. The girls were still sipping their first drink, while he was on his second.

The man who had been talking to Phoebe and Lauren came over to Nick.

"Nicholas Bell," he said, putting forth a hand for Nick to shake. "I think the Society needs no introduction. Do you accept?"

Nick nodded, a reaction that was so quick, it surprised him. He had never thought of himself as the type who would be part of a secret society. But this party, this initiation—it was pretty cool, he had to admit. And if they were tapping people like Lauren and this girl Phoebe, it couldn't be the buttoned-up institution he had thought it was. Maybe this was the moment he had been waiting for, to integrate his current life with the life his parents wanted him to lead. If the Society was meeting down in the Meatpacking District, then it was a very different type of group from what his father had made it out to be.

There had been a conversation with his father, Parker Bell, over the summer, with all sorts of oblique references, but he had dismissed it; it had been more awkward than discussing sex. But now that it was happening, it made sense. Of course he would be asked. His family was one of the oldest in Manhattan; his father was the president of the Bell Trading Company, which manufactured the parts that made up the infrastructure of cities, everything from steel pipes to subway tracks. His father used to say that half of Manhattan had been built using Bell products. His mother was on numerous charity boards. His parents were frequently seen and photographed in all the right places: benefits for the Met, the opera, the ballet, the Museum of Natural History, and the Bell Foundation, of course. There was no reason he wouldn't be tapped. This must mean that his father was a member, too. It wouldn't be any other way. He didn't know who these people were or what they stood for, but he knew the name of the Society, and that was enough for him, for now. For once, he had been told that he had made the cut, that they wanted him exactly as he was. It was a delicious feeling—was it real, he wondered, or a result of the drink? He didn't know, but even as this thought flitted through his mind, he savored this sensation of excitement and adventure and acceptance as he followed the man through a dark corridor and down a staircase.

Once downstairs, Nick gasped. He was in a room filled with what looked like coffins, not the wooden kind, but sarcophagi, decorated with Egyptian motifs, images of deities, animals, sacred offerings. Candles flickered off the raw, unfinished walls of the basement. Meat company logos were still visible through peeling paint. A complicated chain-and-pulley system ran around the room, with hooks every few feet. An old slaughterhouse, this was where they were having a party. He saw a rat scurry across a beam and into a hole in the wall. Nick shuddered. He had thought next door was so raw, so gritty, but this was the real thing . . . and now he was suddenly tired, so tired. . . .

A woman came up to him, wearing a mask like the others. "You'd like to rest?" she asked.

He nodded, barely able to support the weight of his head. Two men stepped forward and placed him in the nearest coffin. Normally he would have thought it was creepy, but it seemed the most natural thing in the world. All he wanted to do was to drift off, and he was being placed in the most comfortable bed he had ever slept in. The woman took a dab of something and put it on his forehead; it smelled like lavender. He allowed the lid to shut over him.

Phoebe was spinning around, an exquisite aura enveloping her. Here was everything she wanted to achieve in New York . . . this party, the gothic setting, the jazz band. . . . It was inspiring. . . . Words and images and sounds were coming to her. . . . She wanted to go home and start making some art. . . .

She must have blacked out at a certain point, because she woke up and found herself in darkness. She was in a box lined with velvet. It smelled of tuberose, like her grandmother's perfume. She was about to scream when the lid opened and she saw she was in a room, somewhat like the one upstairs, with a cracking ceiling. A friendly hand—young, female, with nails polished an attractive shade of red—reached forward to her, and Phoebe took it. She still felt groggy, as if she were underwater. Everything would all flow along, if she could hold it together. . . .

She looked at the face. The woman was wearing a mask, the thin plastic kind you could see someone's features through. Printed on the mask, though, was another face. Phoebe focused more closely and felt a cry welling up inside her, although she was too stunned to make any sound.

It was her own face on the mask.

The woman's features were merging with her own. She raised a finger to her lips. "Silence, now," she said. "It will all make sense later."

Lauren's mentor stood with her; they were about the same height. Lauren had had the same reaction as Phoebe: surprise, then wonderment at her own face being projected on Emily van Piper's. She was to be Lauren's mentor through all this, like a big sister, Lauren reasoned. Emily handed her a list, calligraphied on a sheet of what looked like papyrus or some sort of ancient handmade paper:

☥ *You accept that membership in the Society is a privilege that comes with responsibilities as well as rewards. When one member fails, everyone fails.*

☥ *Society members are bound to the strictest levels of secrecy. You will not speak to Outsiders about the Society, not to family nor to friends.*

☥ *Apart from Society functions, you are not at liberty to discuss the Society amongst yourselves.*

☥ *You will leave the room if the Society is brought up in a public setting.*

☥ *You will attend all Society functions and meetings as requested. You will not be late.*

☥ *Infractions to these and further rules will be punishable by whatever means the Society's Leadership deems appropriate.*

☥ *You will accept the Society's orders above those of all others, whether church, school, or state.*

"Do you accept these rules as the tenets for membership?" Emily asked.

Lauren nodded. She felt that she had little choice in the matter, that if she had not been meant to be part of the Society, she would not have been asked, would not have come to the warehouse, would not have accepted the drink that had made her so tired. "Yes."

"You'll need to remove your necklace."

Lauren felt around to the back of her neck and quickly unclasped the charm she had been wearing, a small trinket she'd bought at a vintage store and had put on a chain. She looked for her purse, but couldn't remember where she had left it. Emily handed it to her, and she put her necklace away.

She was led to another room, where the initiates were being given what looked like a tattoo at the nape of their necks. Lauren shuddered for a moment. She had never gone for tattoos, always thought of them as a passing trend. "I don't believe in—"

Emily turned around and lifted up her beautiful chestnut locks. "Look closely."

Lauren peered at Emily's neckline. "I don't see anything."

Emily stood still. "Look again."

Lauren looked more closely. Finally, she saw it in the dim light, a tattoo the size of a pinky fingernail, at the nape of Emily's neck. It was nearly invisible in this light and, during normal hours, would be hidden by Emily's hair or clothing.

"What is it?"

Emily pointed to the top of the page she had handed Lauren, where there was a symbol, a cross with a loop at the top of it. "It's an ankh. The Egyptian symbol for life. It bonds all of us together. Once you get it, you are initiated into the Society. I was scared, too, but now I think it's pretty."

Lauren nodded. It was pretty, and besides, no one would ever see it unless they were standing right behind her. "Does it hurt?"

"No more than getting your ears pierced," Emily said. "Come."

There was an empty chair in front of them, and Lauren sat down. A figure, a man in a black leather mask, was handling the tattoo gun. Her hair was lifted up, and she felt a series of tiny pinpricks in the back of her neck. It didn't hurt at all; she wondered if the drink earlier had made her numb. The man, whom she realized was wearing latex gloves, took a bandage and applied it over the area where he had been working. Emily then gently placed Lauren's hair back down her shoulders.

"It's all over now," Emily said. "Welcome."

Down the street, the party was still going on. Patch, however, wasn't in the DJ booth and hadn't been for hours. He had set the mix to play six hours of music, which was more than enough, and he had locked the door to the booth, labeling it with a hastily scribbled *No Entry* sign. He had seen Nick's cell phone while he had been copying down the song requests, and he knew what it meant. It was the Night of Rebirth, the Society's initiation night. His grandmother had dated a Society member in the 1940s, so she knew that this was the time of year when new initiates were tapped. Genie had warned him about this night, had warned him to be careful.

Five hours after escaping the DJ booth and crawling through an air duct that led into the next building, he was still being careful. Careful enough to have packed extra batteries and multiple memory cards for his camera. Careful enough to have brought an infrared night-vision filter, one he had specifically ordered online for tonight's shoot. And after it was all over, careful enough to guard the five hours of footage that he had in his backpack as he walked across town, the sun rising, to the Lexington Avenue Express, the train that would take him home.

CHAPTER SEVEN

Phoebe was frantic as the fifteen of them—Lauren, Nick, and her, plus the other twelve initiates—filed out to the street. Lauren was giving her dirty looks and motioning for her to be quiet, but she didn't care. "I can't believe this," Phoebe whispered. She couldn't control the words coming out of her mouth. "How dare they!" She reached around to the back of her neck and felt the bandaged spot where the tattoo had been placed. What had she been thinking? She would never get a tattoo! Had it been safe? Couldn't you get diseases from dirty needles? They were out on the street now, the three of them huddled in a group, apart from the others.

"Shh!" Nick hissed at her. "We'll talk about it later, okay?"

"I mean, you accepted, right?" Lauren said.

Phoebe nodded. "Yes, I did, but I drank that stuff—I mean, that's not the way these things are supposed to work, is it?"

"I think it's pretty much the way the Society works," Nick said.

"What do you mean?"

The sun was starting to rise, a bluish-pink glow slowly washing over the streets. It was a little after six A.M. The light slowly revealed the area's grit, its true nature.

"Look, I can't talk about it now," Nick said. Phoebe couldn't believe the next thing she heard, but the whole evening had been so incredible, she didn't know what to expect anymore.

Nick grabbed her arm. "Meet me later today, after you've gotten some sleep. At the Viand. It's a coffee shop. Across the street from Barneys."

Phoebe nodded slowly.

"Oh my God," Lauren said. "Those are for us."

Phoebe looked up. There were fifteen black Mercedes sedans, lined up with drivers waiting, ready to take each of them home, their engines idling and sputtering fumes. There were a few people on the street at this hour, stragglers from nearby clubs, but no one paid the group or the cars much attention. The man hosing off the puke and cigarette butts on the sidewalk in front of Pastis didn't even notice. Phoebe wanted to forget the entire night, to rid herself of the memory that it had ever happened.

"This is absurd. I'm walking." Phoebe pulled away from the group before anyone could stop her, her ballet flats slapping against the sidewalk as she stepped over smatterings of broken glass, a beer bottle that had been smashed on the ground. There was no way she was letting a town car take her five blocks home; there was no way she was getting in any car at all. She took deep breaths of the chilly morning air, more confused than she had been in a long time.

Lauren woke up late that afternoon in her apartment, in her blue birdcage of a room: iron canopy bed, Pratesi linens she was afraid to spill anything on, French toile wallpaper with its sparrows staring at her in mock glee. Today, she felt the most amazing sense of contentment, as if everything was going to be fine. After such a late night, she would usually mope around the apartment, nursing her hangover with orange juice and a greasy omelet. But today she was fine, despite the three vodka-and-sodas she had drunk, not to mention whatever they had given her at the initiation. She wanted to go out, to enjoy the last hour or so of real daylight before the sun went down. She dressed quickly, throwing on a long sweater coat over jeans and a T-shirt. She hurried to the elevator, passing the gorgeous flower arrangement that sat in her mother's front hall and was refreshed weekly, although it was currently dropping petals onto the polished Biedermeier side table. The building was strangely silent as she rode downstairs in the wood-paneled elevator. She said hello to Rory, her favorite cute young doorman, who was manning the desk in the black and white lobby. Lauren looked around, as if it were all new to her, the standard-issue Park Avenue botanical prints and gilt mirrors.

"Package for you, miss," he said, in his Irish brogue. He went into the package room that was to the left of the doorman station. Lauren's heart skipped when she saw the signature aqua and chocolate brown shopping bag, tied in satin ribbon. It was Giroux New York's fall look; the store was renowned for changing its bags' color scheme each season. People in Japan collected and sold the bags on eBay, fetching hundreds of dollars for them.

Lauren looked inside. Wrapped in tissue was a black Chloé handbag she had briefly admired in the window the previous day, before buying the skirt. It was a classic bag, with its gorgeous stitching, its buckles and padlock, and they were known to be nearly impossible to obtain; although there had been one in the window, Lauren had heard that there was a long waiting list for certain colors, particularly black.

It also retailed for more than twelve thousand dollars.

A card was included with the package, on the Giroux stationery, which simply read, *With compliments*.

"Thank you," Lauren said to Rory, in an attempt to act as if this were a package she had been expecting. She didn't quite know what to do. Take the bag upstairs? Leave it at the doorman station and pick it up later? No, there was only one thing to do: She took out the bag, pocketed the card, and asked Rory to dispose of the wrapping. She swung it casually over her shoulder in the late afternoon light as she noticed the weekend nannies with their charges, families with children, young couples out on Park Avenue. As she passed awning after awning, all flanked by doormen standing in front of the iron or brass double doors, she decided she would walk over to the park. There was something bright in the air, not the usual weekend haziness, a crispness that belied the Indian summer. The bag made her happy, and for a few moments she felt simple, material satisfaction.

As she walked through the park, though, past the various monuments and landmarks she remembered from her childhood—the Angel of the Waters fountain, the Bandshell, the Lennon memorial at Strawberry Fields—she felt sad. Her mother would be coming home tomorrow afternoon from the Hamptons, and her dad—well, who knew where he was? Probably on business somewhere, if not in his apartment on Central Park West with his nasty new girlfriend. Lauren had no plans tonight. The girls were going out to a Yorkville bar that evening to flirt with college boys and procure free drinks, but she didn't feel like going. For one thing, she would have to explain her mysterious disappearance the night before. She would see them in school on Monday anyway; by then, they might have forgotten. Lauren thought about this new girl,

Phoebe, the one whose mother was an up-and-coming photographer. That made her Society material, Lauren assumed. It was sweet of Nick to take her out; she had overheard his offer that morning. Lauren had known Nick forever, and they had always been friendly, but never close. Although Nick was cute, she had never really liked dating guys her own age.

She looked down at the bag. It was pretty; it felt nice hanging on her shoulder. But she had done nothing to earn it. It wouldn't answer any of her questions. Still, she clutched it tightly as she wondered who exactly had sent it to her, what she had done to receive it, and, most important, what was expected of her in return.

CHAPTER EIGHT

That afternoon, Phoebe sat with Nick over Cokes— regular for him, diet for her—at the Viand Coffee Shop, which was bustling with Madison Avenue shoppers: families with kids, teens, old ladies with dyed hair, who looked like they'd been coming here for years. She had agreed to meet him after he had texted her a reminder. (Did the entire world have her number? She was starting to wonder.) It wasn't the best place to talk about everything, but they were keeping their voices low.

"Okay, you've got to tell me what happened last night," she said, as she crunched her straw wrapper into a ball. "It seems more like a dream than a series of cohesive memories. Like, I don't know, a Kubrick movie or something. You seem so cool with it. Is it just me?"

He paused for a moment. In this light, she could see his fine features, the little bits of hair between his eyebrows, his handsome Roman nose, the scruff on his cheeks.

"I know what you mean," he finally said. "It was surreal. It's just that I've heard stories through the years and so, well, I wasn't terribly surprised."

"'Stories' meaning . . ."

"The Society is something that has been connected to New York life for hundreds of years. Most people think it's an urban legend, like the baby crocodile that got flushed down the toilet and lives in the sewer, or the Loch Ness monster or something. Anyway, the Society exists for the good. I know it was creepy and weird last night, but you've just got to believe." He leaned forward, speaking quietly. "You see, people haven't been taking it too seriously in recent years. It used to be the kind of secret you kept until you died. But now some people think it's a joke. People have even said no to it. There was an artist, one of those renegade types—people said he was the new Damien Hirst. Was in the Whitney Biennial at seventeen, galleries were dying to rep him. The Society tapped him. He showed up, out of curiosity, but once he was inside, he bolted."

"What's he doing now?"

Nick scratched his chin. "I don't know. It was maybe two years ago, something like that. He would be in college now. I guess that's where he is. Wait, I remember: He was supposed to go to Brown, but they rejected him. Said his grades weren't good enough. Guy had been on the front page of the *Times* Arts section, and he gets dissed from an Ivy. He was supposed to be world famous. And then, just like that: He turned the Society down, and he became a nobody."

Phoebe cringed. "How on earth do you know all this? I thought it was all so *secret*." She detected the sneer in her voice.

Nick grinned. "Come on, you're from LA, you know how these things go. Like how everyone knows who's going to get nominated for an Oscar before it happens. Or how everyone knows which TV star is gay. It's one of those secrets that people can't keep. If you're in the Society, you have to keep it. But people have talked. There was a journalist a few years ago; he was writing a book on the whole thing, although I think it never went anywhere. So it's not like it's *that* secret. The truth, though, is that no one *really* knows what goes on inside it, at least no one who's on the outside. I mean, what happened last night: No one knows about that."

"But you seem like you have some kind of inside knowledge about it all."

Nick shifted uncomfortably in his seat. He looked like he'd been caught. "My father got drunk over the summer, when we were out at the beach. He didn't give me the whole picture, but he helped fill in some of the blanks for me. Only in the broadest terms. At that time, I didn't even think I'd be asked. It didn't sound like it was for me. But last night—I was surprised."

"So what does it all mean?"

Nick looked at her intently, and she shivered. She couldn't remember the last time someone, not to mention a guy, had looked at her with such incredible intensity, his pale blue eyes boring into her. "It was made very clear to me last night, Phoebe, that I shouldn't turn this down. Just by piecing together what my dad had said and what I saw. And I don't think you should, either. I'm sure there's so much that you want from Chadwick, from life, from your junior year. And they can help you get it."

"But that's ridiculous—we should be doing that stuff on our own."

"We do have to do it on our own. I mean, they can't get you into college or whatever for sitting on your ass. But they can help open doors for us. And think of the competition. Every teenager these days seems to be writing a novel or making a film or posting an award-winning blog. Don't you want to be one of the ones who gets noticed?"

"I guess so," Phoebe said. It still creeped her out. She couldn't help it. Maybe she was old-fashioned. But there was something about Nick that she trusted. The army jacket, the wavy curls that grazed his neckline: She could see it was all a pose. She could see that underneath it there was something deeper.

She didn't know what she was saying, but the words started coming out. "Okay. I'll do it. But I can't do this alone. I need, like, a partner, to be there with me. Someone I can rely on. Someone I can go to if things aren't working out. And you seem to know the most about it all. You promise you'll be there for me?"

At that moment, a little boy in the booth behind Nick spilled his chocolate milkshake all over the table. A busboy ran over with a rag, and Nick was temporarily distracted by the commotion. Phoebe couldn't ignore the sinking feeling that she had committed a major faux pas; she suddenly felt pathetic. It was as if she were asking him to be her best friend or, even more horrifyingly, her boyfriend. She meant nothing of the sort. All she wanted was to know that someone would watch her back.

Nick didn't seem fazed by any of this, not by her request nor by the screaming kid behind him. He continued looking right back at her, stirred his ice with a straw, took a sip of his soda, and smiled.

"Of course I will," he said.

At that moment, Phoebe's cell phone buzzed with a text message. She noticed Nick squirming to pull out his as well. She flipped open her phone, a nervous feeling in her stomach.

Midnight. South of Dendur, games are played. Black and white, don't dare be late.

Phoebe showed it to Nick and frowned. He had received the same message.

"Any idea what this means?" she asked.

Nick shrugged and thought about it for a moment. "South of Dendur. That's the temple in the Met. So it's south of the museum. But 'games are played'? That could be anywhere in the park."

Phoebe glanced over at the floor's scuffed black and white linoleum tiles. "Black and white, Nick. A game that's played on black and white."

Nick slapped the table. "It's obvious," he said. "The chess tables in Central Park."

"So you're going to go?" Phoebe asked.

Nick pulled out a five for their sodas and looked at her with amusement in his eyes.

"You're not getting it yet, are you, Phoebe?" he said. "We don't have a choice."

Patch had been holed up in his bedroom since returning home at six A.M. He had worried about Nick spotting him in the lobby, and so he asked the doorman not to say anything about his whereabouts. Once he was safely in his bedroom,

Patch still couldn't sleep. He looked at himself in the mirror after taking off his filthy jeans and T-shirt. He was a mess: bags under the eyes, glasses smudged, his hair a rat's nest, his forehead breaking out into an angry rash of zits. He would have taken a shower, but he was afraid of waking up Genie. It was like the worst kind of caffeine high, when you want to sleep but you can't, and so you spend the night or morning tossing and turning, every sound, every thought, every glimmer of light a provocation.

He knew he had no other option.

He put the first memory card in, and started to watch.

CHAPTER NINE

Nick woke at eleven from a dreamless sleep, his phone ringing with the ominous chimes of the alarm he had set. He had walked home that afternoon in the waning light after parting with Phoebe at the Viand. He hadn't been hungry for dinner—he had felt only an incredible tickle in his stomach, as if he might throw up. It was all too much: his club night, the initiation, the lack of proper sleep. But mostly, more than the secret society stuff, it was Phoebe. There was something about her, that despite her shyness, she was too cool for him. Downtown girl. Los Angeles. Bank Street. An artist. The most beautiful reddish color of hair he had ever seen. What would she want with a guy like him? He was a child of privilege; he was probably the type of guy she hated at her old school. But whatever—maybe they could be friends.

Don't dare be late. The directions had been clear. He scrambled out of bed, not having much time to think about what he was getting into, remembering that he had agreed to meet Phoebe at the park's Sixty-fifth Street gates. He wondered how everyone else would know where to go. They would probably meet up with one another along the way. Or they had broken another Society rule, as he and Phoebe already had, and were talking to each other about Society business. He had to wonder, why all the cloak-and-dagger secrecy? He couldn't take it that seriously, although it did frighten him a bit: the coffins, the basement in the Meatpacking District, the man with the tattoo gun. Who wouldn't be scared by all that?

He left the building at twenty to midnight, giving a nod to his doorman. His parents weren't home, still out at the beach house for the weekend. His older brothers were away at school. No one would know he was gone. Having slept most of the day, he now felt a jolt of energy.

Phoebe was a dark, shadowy figure, motionless like a small sculpture near the park gates. She turned to meet him, and he thought he saw the glimmer of a smile. The leaves on the walkway shifted in the breeze; the waxing moon illuminated the grassy embankment. There were a few couples out strolling, but for the most part, the park was empty.

"Hey," she said. They had seen each other only eight hours ago, but it seemed like ages. She had changed clothes, he thought, or maybe she hadn't—he realized that his mind was a bit of a blur.

Nick greeted her back, giving her an awkward pat on the shoulder. He hadn't spent any time thinking about what to say, and Phoebe's reticence wasn't making it easier.

People assumed it was so simple for him, but it wasn't. Figuring out girls was as difficult for Nick Bell as it was for everyone else.

Lauren had Googled "black, white, games" to see what came up. After browsing through a few pages, the chess tables riddle finally made sense. A deep tiredness had come over her since she had received the text. She had moped around in her bedroom, not wanting to face the fact that she was ignoring voice mails from her friends asking where she was. She had texted Chloë to say she wasn't feeling well, that she was going to stay home. She was already lying. Lauren knew to watch out for two situations: when she had the urge to lie and when she had the urge to drink too much. Both usually meant she wasn't doing the right thing.

A cab dropped her off at the entrance to the park. She walked quickly along the path to the Chess and Checkers House, which was surrounded by a bower overgrown with wisteria. Underneath it were the outdoor chess tables. The Society's fourteen other members from her initiation class were milling about aimlessly, chatting, and trying to figure out what to do. Aside from Claire and Alejandro and a few others, she hadn't really caught people's names last night. Everyone looked tired, and still a bit hungover. Lauren wondered if she should have had more than hummus and crackers for dinner.

One guy, Thaddeus Johnson, motioned everyone over to one of the tables underneath the pergola. "Check this out," he said. "It's a set-up board." He pointed to a table set up with silver pieces that were inlaid with ivory and onyx. Although Lauren had only met Thad last night, she had heard he was some kind of math genius—she was now remembering what someone said, about how his parents weren't rich, but he had already taken the SAT and gotten a perfect score. For a math whiz, she couldn't help noticing that his taste in clothing was impeccable.

One girl picked up a pawn, looking at it carefully.

"Don't touch it," he snapped at her, and she put it back, as if stung.

He started mumbling something to himself.

"What's up?" Nick asked.

"It's a code," Thad said, his eyes scanning the middle part of the board.

"It's a game that makes no sense," said a guy with curly dark hair and caramel skin, who was wearing, of all things, a bow tie. He offered a hand to Thad. "Bradley Winston."

Thad nodded, briefly shaking his hand, and then turned back to the game. "Each position on a chessboard represents a letter and a number. This could be the kind of code where a pattern comes out of randomness, depending on what you're looking for. You have to ignore everything that doesn't apply and hope that what comes out of it makes sense."

"Okay," Claire said. "And that leaves us where?" True to what Lauren had suspected, the girl was turning out to be a bit of a pill.

"Do you have any better ideas?" Thad said.

Claire looked down, saying nothing.

"Somebody remember this. The letters go from A to H. The numbers, one through eight, go up this side." He pointed to one side of the board.

"How do you know they go in that direction?" Bradley asked.

"The numbers and letters start on the lower left hand corner of white's side. That's just the way it works."

A few members of the group were hanging back, waiting to see what happened, while the rest of them stood in rapt attention, as if watching a magician perform a trick. Lauren stood with the group at the table, curious about what Thad would come up with. A wind rustled through the leaves on the bower.

"Okay, so let's try the center of the board, going right to left: You've got two pieces on fours. Then, two spaces. Then we can see the next three numbers are five, six, and six. I'm going to guess that the five is actually an E, which refers to the horizontal axis, assuming that this is an address—"

"Wait—how do you know it's an address?" Bradley asked.

"It has to be. I mean, we're looking for a place to go, right? If you add up just the letters, it makes ABEFG, which tells us nothing. And if you look at the second group of numbers, you get five-six-six, which we all know isn't a street. But if you turn the five into an E, you've got East Sixty-sixth Street—"

Nick continued, "And then you add the two fours—Forty-four East Sixty-sixth Street. There's your address."

"Exactly," Thad said. Lauren was impressed. Forty-four East Sixty-sixth Street was between Madison and Park, a short walk from here. Everyone started getting their stuff together and walking toward Fifth Avenue. Phoebe, Nick, and Lauren lingered behind, as Thad continued to examine the board.

"What are you doing?" Nick asked.

"Despite all the moves that make no sense, it's actually a good game they've got going here," he said. "It's almost at its end. I know what the next move would be."

"What's that?" Lauren asked.

"The queen is about to put the king into checkmate."

CHAPTER TEN

Phoebe walked the several short blocks to the specified address with Nick, Lauren, and Thad. Their new friend apparently went to The Whitford School, over on the west side. She was still getting used to the names: Dalton, Trinity, Spence, Nightingale-Bamford, Horace Mann. These kids were from all these schools, the types of schools she had been hearing about for years. Phoebe had read the appalling stories in various magazines, about how parents had tried to buy their kids' way out of trouble. How kids had made up Facebook and MySpace pages that ripped apart their teachers. How scandal after scandal would erupt and then die down. She wondered how many of them were true, if these kinds of things really happened—and particularly if they happened at Chadwick, to people like the ones she was meeting now.

The four of them approached the front door of the Sixty-sixth Street townhouse along with another group of five. It was a classic Manhattan brownstone, with a sandstone exterior and imposing façade. Would this be like last night's initiation, some freaky ritual in a basement? Phoebe wasn't up for any more tattoos—she was still getting used to the one from yesterday. It felt sore, and she was afraid to remove the bandage, although she knew she would eventually have to change the dressing. Thankfully, her hair covered it up.

The door opened, and Phoebe heard the sound of drinks and conversation. A warm light spilled out from the entryway, and Phoebe saw hints of the interior. Voices came from what looked like a drawing room in a fashionable neighborhood in London's Notting Hill. Or, for that matter, New York fifty or one hundred years ago.

A pretty young woman in a cocktail dress greeted them. It was Emily van Piper, whom Lauren had told Phoebe about last night. "Lauren! Hi! Hi, you guys." She introduced herself. "Come on in and meet the other Conscripts."

"What are the Conscripts?" Thad whispered to the group.

"It's the class above us—above us Initiates," Claire said, seemingly pleased with herself that she knew this already.

Phoebe was confused. The tone was so different—if last night was mysterious and clandestine, tonight was like a gentleman's smoking lounge circa 1955. In the corner, a skinny guy mixed drinks for everyone in a silver cocktail shaker, while the rest of the group was scattered around two clubby rooms. Phoebe's eyes ran over the floor-to-ceiling book-shelves and wood paneling with portraits of stern-looking men and women. On a tiger maple credenza against one wall, someone was actually playing records, although the music wasn't that old; a group clustered around, admiring this exotic anachronism. The girls were dressed stylishly, but not terribly formally—only Emily and a few others wore cocktail dresses; the rest were dressed casually, some even in jeans and heels. Except for the setting, it could have been any other party.

As the Initiates got drinks, a few of the Conscripts lit cig-arettes and cigars, tapping them into crystal ashtrays. Phoebe and Lauren tried not to cough—they had spoken the night before about how neither liked to smoke. Lauren said she was nearly certain that the secret to a good complexion was to avoid cigarettes.

"Phoebe?" A voice behind her sounded familiar. Phoebe turned around and recognized the source of the voice, although she wasn't exactly sure why. Then it hit her: It was Anastasia Lin, one of the youngest artists ever to be accepted into the Venice Biennale. Her video installation, *A Brief History of My Life*, in which she read from her diary, alternating between English and Cantonese, while riding the F train, had been praised by everyone from *Artforum* to the *New York Times*. Phoebe was mildly jealous. That was what she should be doing, instead of recovering from a hangover: working on her art.

She also realized why Anastasia looked and sounded familiar: She had been Phoebe's mentor last night, from the few brief snippets of the initiation that Phoebe could actually recall. Now, Phoebe remembered that Anastasia had never introduced herself, that she had only seen her face through the semiopaque plastic of the mask.

"So," Anastasia said, "the Folly begins."

"I'm sorry?" Phoebe said.

Anastasia smiled and brushed her short black bob away from her face. Before she could answer, another member, someone from the class above them, brought Phoebe a drink, and motioned for her to sit down. He was a tall, handsome guy, dirty blond hair spilling over his forehead. He fit right in, with his argyle sweater vest, Oxford cloth shirt, and corduroys. "Gin and tonic, right?"

"How did you know?" Phoebe asked.

He grinned, almost demonically. "We know these things. You're the kind of girl who drinks a gin and tonic in September."

Phoebe cringed. "Okay, come on . . ."

"Relax! I just asked your friend over there"—he motioned to Lauren—"what you might like."

Phoebe smiled and sat back in the leather club chair. She didn't really feel like drinking tonight; she wasn't used to drinking this much in general. Her mother didn't have a problem if she went to the occasional party or had a glass of wine or champagne on a special occasion, but drinking G & Ts two nights in a row? She wasn't sure how Maia would feel about that.

She wasn't sure how her mom would feel about any of this.

Nick waited by the bar as a scraggly guy with dark brown hair fixed drinks for everyone. He looked up from the cocktail he was making for Nick. "Oh, wait, you're Nick Bell, right?"

Nick nodded.

He stuck out a pale hand. "I'm Jared Willson. I'm supposed to be your mentor, you know, to, like, help you through stuff. I can't remember if I mentioned that last night, at the Night of Rebirth."

Nick gave an embarrassed grin. "I'm afraid I don't remember much about last night. I actually didn't even know it was called the Night of Rebirth."

"Don't worry, you'll get the lingo. So your mentor is basically like a big brother. I wasn't able to make the meeting when they explained it all, but that's the general idea."

"Wait, you missed a meeting?"

"Yeah, I totally shouldn't have. Had a messy night. They were really peeved. That's my first bit of advice: Don't miss meetings. Old Kitty doesn't take it too well."

"Kitty?"

"Katherine Winthrop Stapleton. They call her the Administrator; I call her the Battleaxe. Runs everything for the Elders—"

"Wait, sorry, what are the Elders?"

"They're everyone above us. Above all of you Initiates and all of us Conscripts. You become an Elder after you've been through the appropriate period of conscription. Kitty manages all that. Keeps all the records straight, does the finances. Has apparently been doing it since she became a member back in the fifties or whatever. It's her life. So you don't want to mess around with her. She knows everyone's business. She prepped us on all of you—where you go to school, what your hobbies are, your families, that kind of stuff. I mean, with you, it was pretty easy. Your family's famous around here."

Nick nodded uncomfortably, shifting his stance. "I guess so."

"I'm basically here to answer any questions, help you figure out whatever you need to. If you play your cards right, the Society can open doors for you."

"What kind of doors?"

"Anything. College admission. Introductions to famous people. I have a feeling that there's a way that you and I could really make something happen."

"What's that?" Nick said.

"Let's talk about your club night. The Freezer, was it?"

Jared took a sip from a drink he had fixed for himself.

"Oh, it went really well," Nick bluffed, not wanting to admit that he had run out on it. "Totally sold out. Packed the place. Everyone loved it." The truth was that Nick had barely even thought about his club night since he had crossed the threshold of 53 Gansevoort the night before. Since then, he hadn't heard from Patch at all. There had been a message from Costa that he had listened to, but it was only a congratulations and an invitation to hold another party whenever he wanted.

It felt good, but he wanted something more.

"I popped my head in last night—you did a nice job. How would you like to do a night with me at Twilight?" Twilight was the newest—some said most exclusive—addition to the Meatpacking District's collection of nightclubs.

"Are you serious? At Twilight? No way."

"Carlo would be thrilled."

"Carlo, as in Carlo Ferdinand?" Carlo Ferdinand was one of the best DJs in the business, in a league far above what Nick had promised to his guests the night before.

"That's right. He knows the scene needs some new blood—it's usually the same old tired promoters with the same old tricks. He likes your work. He sent me over last night to check it out, and I told him that what you did at The Freezer wasn't half bad."

"Carlo Ferdinand? Well, sure. Yeah, of course." Nick felt

himself blabbing. He took a sip of his drink, as if that would make him more coherent. This was truly excellent news— a connection like this might not happen over the course of years in the business, might not happen ever. But now here it was, dropped in his lap.

CHAPTER ELEVEN

Anastasia took a sip of her martini, leaving a dark-red lipstick print on her glass. "Here's how it works. Basically, the Society can help you—but you'll only get out of it as much as you put into it."

"Okay . . ." Phoebe nodded, still a bit confused. "Like how did it help you?"

"The Society helped me get funding for my last show. I got studio space, I got sponsors. There's so much connectivity going on."

"Connectivity?"

"You know, connections: You've heard of the famous six degrees of separation, right?"

"Sure." Phoebe nodded. It was the theory that every person in the world is connected to every other person by, at a maximum, four other people. Add yourself and the final person in the chain, and you had your six degrees.

"Well, membership in the Society is estimated to reduce that number to something more like three degrees—which means that you are connected to everyone you'll ever need to know by, at the most, one person."

Behind Anastasia, Charles Lawrence, the handsome senior from Chadwick who had brought Phoebe a drink, came over, carrying his own gin and tonic and smoking a cigar. Phoebe's mouth went dry. It was strange being the center of so much attention. She wondered if the other new members felt this way, this out of place.

"So, Phoebe, is Anastasia using the old 'six degrees' philosophy?"

Phoebe nodded. "I guess so. Seems to make sense."

"It's one way of looking at it all. But I prefer the slightly more"—he cocked his head—"shall we say, *complex* description."

Anastasia rolled her eyes playfully, batting her long eyelashes at him. "And what's that, Charles?"

He started speaking directly to Phoebe. "Have you taken sociology?"

Phoebe shook her head.

"It doesn't matter. There's a social theorist from the nineteenth century, a French guy, Émile Durkheim. He came up with this theory of collective consciousness. You've probably heard of the collective unconscious, right?"

Phoebe nodded. "Yeah. Like, um, Jung and all that?" They had done a unit in English on Jungian symbols of the unconscious. Jung was a Swiss psychologist who believed that people shared symbols in their dreams without actually knowing it.

"It's the idea that there's always a unifying group of ideas and values that people subscribe to. In the past, it was usually religion. But these days, everything is fractured. People don't go to church, they don't go to town hall meetings, a lot of them don't even vote. So the Society's purpose is to bind together a bunch of like-minded people who can help one another. Each class helps the other, and each member will eventually provide support to the group. In the beginning, it's mostly benefits you enjoy. The idea is that first it gets you launched, gets you started on the right track. For example, who do you have guiding your career right now?"

"Guiding my career? Do you mean, like, my work at school?" She thought of her mother, who was almost always too busy with her photography. It didn't feel like her mom was guiding her at all. And her dad was several thousand miles away.

"Sure," Charles said. "But more like your life, overall. Think of it this way: What do you really want from the next two years?"

Phoebe came up with the automatic response, typical of any high school junior who was asked this question. "I guess I want to get into a good college."

Charles chuckled. "Come on, Phoebe, you can do better than that! A good college! So the magic genie comes along and grants you a wish, and all you want to do is get into a good college?"

Phoebe felt her face grow warm. He was right. It was an utterly pedestrian thing to wish for. She started stammering. "That and, of course, to work on my art. To, maybe, get a show or something. Let people see what I can do." She noticed Anastasia smiling.

"That's more like it. And don't you think you deserve some advice, someone to help you out?"

Phoebe nodded. "I guess so." She felt a bit rattled and took a gulp of her drink, hoping it would cool her. The room suddenly felt hot and stuffy.

Anastasia piped in. "We can make anything happen. Well, almost anything."

"I doubt there's much the Society can't provide," said Charles. "That's what we're here for. But tonight we're just here to have a good time." He clinked glasses with Phoebe.

There was an awkward pause, as Phoebe wasn't sure what to say. Something came to her as she glanced around the room, noting the twos and threes that were huddled together in conversation.

"Wait a second," she said. "You claimed that we were all like-minded. Isn't that sort of a sweeping generalization?"

He laughed. "Oh, I don't mean like-minded in every way. Just in one."

"What's that?" Phoebe asked.

Charles took a puff on his cigar. "You all want to succeed more than anyone. And if given the right opportunities, you have a damned good chance at doing so."

Lauren sat with Emily in a quiet corner, both sipping their second vodka tonics. "Here, read this," Emily said, as a scroll was passed to her from a silver tray that was going around the room. It was beautifully printed on parchment paper and tied with a blue ribbon. Lauren started to open it, but Emily stopped her. "Read it later. When you get home, or tomorrow. Here's the most important thing. You have to destroy it when you're done. No one can see it."

"What happens if you don't destroy it?" Lauren asked.

Emily shrugged. "I don't know. No one's ever kept it."

Lauren put it in her purse, the new one that had been given to her that afternoon.

"Nice bag," Emily said.

"Thanks—it was a gift."

"Ah, the gifts."

"What do you mean?"

"Things are going to start happening for you, sometimes in a mysterious way. But you can't question it. You just need to go with it. That's the only way you'll succeed. Take it as it comes, and accept it willingly."

Lauren nodded, attempting to hide her unease.

"Don't worry. You'll get the hang of it." Emily glanced at her watch, which, to Lauren, looked expensive. "Oh my God, it's late. We'd better get the second part of the evening going. I have an audition tomorrow afternoon with a major casting director."

"On Sunday? Is he a member?" Lauren asked. She hoped she wasn't prying.

"I don't know," Emily said. "But he certainly knows people who are. See, that's the thing. Aside from you guys and the class above us, we never really know who the members are. They can introduce themselves, so I know a handful of them well, and have met tons more at events, but there's no published directory. It's all networking. That's how you get to know people. The older members attend some of the functions, and you start to get into the flow of it all."

Lauren nodded.

"It's really a miracle," Emily said, her eyes wide. "I mean, this casting director is visiting from Beverly Hills for one day and he has thirty people he's seeing. No spots are open. And then he decides to see me on a Sunday, to make a special exception, which is so cool."

"Are you nervous?"

Emily ran her fingers through her hair. "I wouldn't say *nervous*. More like excited, you know? These things have a way of working themselves out." She looked at Lauren and smiled. "Don't you worry—before you know it, things will start working out for you as well."

CHAPTER TWELVE

Patch had woken at nine that evening, having passed out after watching the first three hours of the footage he had taken of the Society initiation. Since then, he had holed himself up in his room, emerging only to use the bathroom or to refill his bowl of microwave popcorn. It was all too strange, everything he had captured. The previous night, after seeing the address on Nick's phone, all of Patch's suspicions about what Genie had told him had been confirmed. He knew he had to get footage of what was going on. And he had to admit, he felt a bit stung that he hadn't been invited himself. His parents, after all, had been important people in New York, before his father's death and his mother's hospitalization. He deserved to be a member as much as anyone, that is, if it really was the fantastic thing that people made it out to be. But now he wasn't so sure.

He also knew there was some kind of secret Genie was hiding from him about the Society, although he had no idea what it was. He could have rifled through her papers to search for it, but she was nearly always at home, except for during the day, when he was at school. Besides, she would have noticed his snooping, and he didn't feel right about it. What kind of creep would go through his grandmother's things?

The previous six times he had left and come back to his room that Saturday night, Patch had locked the door behind him, but this time he had forgotten. He heard a quick knock and a turn of the doorknob. He leaned over to try to switch off his monitor, but instead only managed to knock over the stainless steel bowl of popcorn; it clattered and spilled all over the floor. On his screen was a frozen shot from the Society initiation. There were some fuzzy lines on the image, which was the grill of the air duct he had managed to crawl through, giving him access to five different locations. But aside from those lines, the action behind them was clear: a man in a leather mask giving what looked to be tattoos to some of his classmates, Nick included. It made Patch sick to his stomach.

His grandmother stood there, her arms folded at her chest, a scowl on her face. "Well, aren't you going to play it?"

Clearly, she knew something.

"Genie, I can't. I don't think—"

"It's my fault you got into that mess." She put one hand on the doorframe, as if to steady herself for what she was about to say. "Goddammit, Patchfield! What on earth were you thinking? I told you about the Night of Rebirth because I wanted you to be careful, because I was worried that they would get to you."

He nodded. "I know."

She looked at him dryly. "As it turns out, it seems like they had every reason not to ask you."

"Genie, don't be that way."

"You think that camera allows you to waltz in wherever you please? There are rules, Patch. Rules that must be followed. You don't mess with an organization like that." Her voice lowered to a whisper. "You don't even *talk* about it. You don't know what you're dealing with."

"Genie, I know. I saw. It's creepy stuff."

"Oh, that's all smoke and mirrors. That's not what it's really about. It's the same as it was fifty years ago. The tattoos, now I admit that's different. It used to be—" She shuddered. "It used to be absolutely vile."

"What do you mean?"

"When I was growing up, tattoos were something that sailors got. When you were admitted to the Society, you didn't get a tattoo of an ankh."

"What did you get?"

"You got an ankh on the back of your neck, all right." She

paused, her eyes shining fiercely. "You got an ankh branded right into your flesh."

Emily van Piper clinked her glass with a cocktail stirrer. "Okay, everyone, get up! We're going to the roof!"

Phoebe looked up, astonished. What could possibly be next? Emily led everyone up the main, kilim-carpeted staircase. They followed her up another staircase, past a dozen closed doors, hallways adorned with paintings—landscapes, portraits, all in aging gilt frames. Memorabilia was displayed on the walls: medals, trophies, plaques, photographs, framed letters from presidents and senators. They got to the top level, which had a white marble floor and a tiled dome ceiling. Blue light flickered on the carved wall panels.

"Okay, everyone," Emily said, "close your eyes."

Phoebe did as she was told. She heard the sound of a pair of doors sliding apart.

They were instructed to open their eyes. Before them was a swimming pool covered with a glass roof that looked right up into the sky. Tall palm trees in black ceramic urns adorned the sides of the pool, blocking any view of the city.

Phoebe blinked at this surreal sight. A swimming pool on a rooftop in Manhattan? She had heard of such things, but never imagined them really to exist.

The girls were motioned to one side and the boys to another, where there were swimsuits waiting for them and bathing cabins in which to change. Was this the kind of perk they were talking about? Phoebe wouldn't mind a place to swim laps after school.

After changing into their square-cut trunks, Nick, Thad, and the other boys dived in and started splashing around. Phoebe couldn't help sneaking a glance at their bare bodies, Nick's especially. It was lean and taut, a runner's torso with broad shoulders, as she had suspected. His chest was smooth, with the slightest bit of hair running down past his navel. It felt strange to look at him this way after everything they had been through in the last twenty-four hours, but by this point in the evening, she was too tired to care. She noticed Lauren and the Argentinean guy, Alejandro Calleja, horsing around by the edge of the pool, flirting, and she wondered if they had known each other before tonight.

Phoebe stepped into the warm water. Surprisingly, she didn't feel body conscious at all; maybe it was the alcohol, or the odd circumstances. She realized, actually, that she looked pretty good, as good as the other girls, almost as good as Lauren with her long legs and toned stomach. The bathing suits they had been given were all the same, simple black one-pieces, as if they were members of an incredibly austere swim team. It didn't matter—something felt transcendent about the experience. Lauren paddled over and gave her an affectionate squeeze on the arm.

Phoebe let herself float in the water. Everyone's shadows

danced against the palms lining the sides of the pool. Voices echoed in and out. She turned her attention to the sky, looked up at the stars. One could almost never see the stars in Manhattan, but tonight she saw them clearly. Maybe it was some kind of optical illusion, a projection.

She was reminded for a moment of a line: "We are all in the gutter, but some of us are looking at the stars." Oscar Wilde had written it more than a hundred years ago; an English teacher of hers had emailed it to their class last year while they were reading one of his plays.

She wasn't exactly in the gutter, not even on the sidewalk anymore. It was almost by magic, how fast she had risen. Was that the way with Manhattan? One afternoon you're wondering if you'll ever fit in, and the next thing you know, you're swimming in a private pool, looking up at a starry night?

It occurred to her that she had forgotten to ask what the Folly was. She would have to remember at the next meeting.

If, that is, she found out when the next meeting was.

Lauren shivered a bit as she wrapped herself in a towel that someone had handed her. She had noticed the brand name on it, and it certainly wasn't the nicest towel she had ever used. It was similar to those used at old-school athletic clubs, like the one her father belonged to. Clean, but not terribly soft and a tad ratty, as if it hadn't been replaced in the last ten years. Probably good old-fashioned WASPy thriftiness, Lauren surmised. It fit in with the old money decor of the place, that deep-seated odor of cigars and spilled whiskey.

She got dressed and said her good-byes; the swimming, even in the heated pool, had sobered everyone up, at least enough to realize it was time for the night to end. She stepped out through the entryway, noting that the detritus from the drinks party earlier—cigar butts, empty glasses, sticky cocktail napkins—had already been cleaned up. As with the previous night, cars were waiting for them outside.

On the steps of the brownstone, Lauren shared a glance with Alejandro Calleja. Earlier, she had been drawn in by his eyes, dark and brooding, a vivid contrast to his easy manner.

"So is this everything you ever dreamed of?" he said with a shy smile, as he tied his sweater around his shoulders. She couldn't tell if he was joking or serious.

"Sure," she said, nodding.

"I hear it only gets better."

"I can imagine." Lauren saw that Phoebe was next to her. "See you later?"

"Of course," Alejandro said. He gave her a squeeze on the shoulder.

"Ride with me?" Lauren said to Phoebe, even though they were going in opposite directions.

Phoebe nodded.

It was four-thirty A.M. Lauren wanted to go to a diner or something, to compare notes with Phoebe, but she was too tired, and the driver was already heading up Madison. How did he know where she lived? She leaned forward and peered into the front seat. On the passenger side was a folder, open to a page that had all of their photographs—the standard-issue yearbook photos that Chadwick published—and their home addresses, which were certainly not public knowledge. Weird.

"My mom is going to kill me if she hears me coming in," Phoebe said. "She thinks I've become a total party monster."

Lauren laughed. "As if mine would even notice. I think she's happy for me to go out. All she ever wants me to do is find a new boyfriend." She realized that Alejandro wouldn't be a bad candidate.

"Not sure mine would even notice," Phoebe said.

"Mine might not either. Too busy hitting the sauce."

There was an awkward pause. Too much information? Lauren usually wasn't so candid. She wanted to invite Phoebe up, but decided to hold back. She gave her new friend a quick hug and a peck on the cheek, and then jumped out of the car.

CHAPTER THIRTEEN

The next morning, after waking up at a normal hour, Patch sat in his bedroom with another paused scene on his monitor. He thought about the branding of the ankh, the tattoos, the idea that his classmates—even worse, his best friend—were all stuck with this mark, and they didn't even know what they were getting into. He had thought he would be better than it all, that he would do a vlog posting about it on Monday morning, that it would be some kind of joke, the type of thing that would get tons of comments, a link on Gawker, and then everyone would forget about it in a few days.

He realized now that it was no joke, not even close. Even worse, he had upset Genie. She had refused to tell him anything more when he had pressed her, simply saying that he didn't deserve to know about it if he couldn't act in a mature manner.

By mature, he understood what she meant: that silence was the price he would have to pay if he wanted more information.

Then again, maybe Genie had it wrong. Maybe it was all nothing more than a bunch of fraternity-style antics. Tattoos? Yeah, sort of extreme, but he knew at least ten people who had them, even though it was illegal to get one before you were eighteen. He didn't know what to think about it. He wanted to believe that if Nick was involved in something, it would be okay.

That was the most important thing to him: that Nick was safe.

Patch was pretty sure the Bells were in Southampton and that Nick would be alone in the apartment. Not wanting to disturb—or, for that matter, deal with—Genie, Patch crept out the back entrance near the kitchen that led up the building's service stairs. Ten flights up and he'd be at Nick's apartment. He was barely sweating, thanks to his on-and-off running habit, when he reached the top. He pulled a metal file from his back pocket. The service doors in the building were so easy to jimmy open, it was laughable. The building was the type that had such good security on the outside—closed-circuit cameras, two doormen and two porters, key-controlled floor access in the elevator—that no one ever thought it was necessary to provide much protection on the inside. For as long as he could remember, he had visited Nick's apartment this way. It made no sense, after all, to go down to the lobby, buzz Nick's penthouse, get permission, and then go all the way up again—and Nick didn't seem to mind that Patch practiced his lock-picking skills whenever he could. He inserted the file and a thin screwdriver, felt the pins click, and turned the latch. He was in.

Nick's apartment was like a tomb. He wondered if his friend was still asleep. He looked around at the kitchen with its expensive appliances, inside the pantry, down the long hallway that led to the rest of the apartment. He spied a stack of mail sitting in a basket and stepped forward to see who the top envelope was from.

That was his problem, he thought. He was too damned nosy.

"Patchfield."

Patch froze and looked up. Parker Bell, Nick's father, was standing at the entrance to the kitchen. He had come in as quietly as a slithering snake and now towered over Patch. He was an imposing man, tall with silvery gray hair. His history had always impressed Patch: He had served in Vietnam and then had taken part in antiwar protests after coming home. But since those days, he had turned into a typical Upper East Sider.

"I thought you were out at the house."

"No, Georgiana and I decided to come back early this weekend. Just got in."

"I was looking for Nick."

"Of course you were. I believe he's still asleep."

"Sure. Sorry to bother you."

"Not a problem, son." He flashed a smile, revealing his perfectly straight teeth. "But next time, I think the front entrance will suffice."

As soon as she had arrived home, Phoebe collapsed into bed. This time, unlike the previous night, she had decided she wouldn't think about anything until she had slept, at least for a few hours. On Sunday morning, she woke at ten A.M, the previous night's events gnawing at her. It wasn't only her confusion about the Society's purpose and origins. It was Charles's comment about her doing anything to get ahead. She felt like she used to be a high achiever, before Chadwick, before high school. In eighth grade, she had won the spirit award for putting in the most hours on the school newspaper. But recently, all she had been was another good student, with no honors, no accolades, not even a perfect GPA to add to her name. Where did that put her in the college race? Nick was right about the way things were. Every teenager was doing something extraordinary; if you didn't, you fell in with the pack. It made her angry. It used to be good enough to have a normal childhood, to be happy. Now you had to start thinking about college before you even started high school.

She looked at the light that was coming through her tall bedroom windows, refracted from the leafy trees outside. She reached to the glass on her bedside table and took a sip of water. The scroll that Anastasia had given her was sitting next to it.

When she had glanced at it the night before, before bed, it seemed like more jargon, so she decided she would look at it later. According to Anastasia, the sheet explaining the Society's philosophy had been prepared by the class of Conscripts. Some of it sounded like language passed down from year to year, while some of it sounded newer. The gist of it was that the Society was started several hundred years ago in Ivy League universities—Yale, Harvard, Princeton, Dartmouth—as a breeding ground for what they called the "sons of privilege." It claimed ancient Egyptian roots, although the details were a little murky. In the 1950s, at the time of the "youth culture explosion" (as the scroll called it), the group decided to start recruiting in the junior year of high school, to give its younger offspring a chance to start earlier. But Society membership wasn't always transferred by blood; members could be recruited from the outside. Phoebe thought of some of the Initiates; surely they didn't all have parents who were rich or who had been Society members themselves. She thought about herself, of course—her mother and father were not members of any such group, as far as she knew.

She read over the page once again, but it was so vague, she didn't really know what to make of it. She went to her laptop and tried searching for all the possible combinations of words that might bring up information about the Society. Phoebe came up with a few sites, mostly makeshift pages of fact and fiction about the group. The rumors were all over the place: that there was a secret crypt under the Temple of Dendur at the Met, where meetings were held once you got to a certain level . . . that there was a Society trust composed of hundreds of millions of dollars, which supported the Society's activities . . . that the Society had been losing power and that was why it had started recruiting younger . . . that its methods were violent. She cringed at the last fact, but the webpage itself seemed so hysterical, red type on black, filled with misspellings, that she didn't want to believe it. The page had animation, which crashed her browser. After she restarted her laptop, she didn't return to it.

Phoebe knew what she had seen over the past two nights. She liked the people who were there. She would have to decide for herself.

Nick woke up just before noon on Sunday. He had forgotten to let down his room's fabric shades the night before, so the midday light was streaming in. He looked around his bedroom, at its high ceiling, at the blue striped wallpaper he had been allowed to pick out when he was ten. This morning, unlike the past two nights, he felt comfortable, safe, as if nothing could touch him—until he heard someone walking down the hall outside his door. He popped his head out to see that it was his mom and dad, back early from their trip to the beach house. He wondered if he would have to tell his dad about the Society stuff—or maybe his dad already knew? It was so confusing.

He was hungry, not having eaten in nearly sixteen hours. Nick threw on some sweatpants and a T-shirt and wandered down the hall to the breakfast nook off the kitchen, the one with the fantastic view of the apartment's wraparound deck. His mother, Gigi, had done the decor to look like they were in the South of France, which Nick always thought was a bit absurd in the middle of Manhattan. But today, he enjoyed it, the idyllic sunlight-spattered patterns on the Pierre Deux tablecloth, the Provençal ceramic dishes, the topiary plants on the deck. His parents were having brunch together, as if they did this every Sunday. In reality, most weekends they were in the country; if they were in the city, they were usually attending some sort of function or his father was working.

"Sweetie, do you want some lunch?" his mother asked. She was wearing skintight jeans, a white blouse, and very little makeup, because she didn't need it. Her fiery red hair spilled down her back.

Nick nodded and started filling his plate.

"You must have been out late last night," she said.

Nick grunted an acknowledgment. "Yeah, me and, you

know, some friends, we went out."

"With some new people, I hope?" his mother asked. "Not, you know . . ."

"Mom, why do you care about how much time I spend with Patch?"

"I just think that a friendship with him is somewhat . . . well, somewhat limiting. You need friends who are on your own level."

His father seemed eager to change the subject. "We want you to have a good time. Enjoy it while you can," his dad said. "With school and college plans and everything starting to heat up, I don't want you getting too stressed out."

This was so unlike his parents. All they ever used to do was get on his case to be someone different, to achieve, to accomplish whatever they had in mind for him. And now suddenly they were being so easygoing. Except, of course, for the Patch thing. His mother had never liked Patch, although he couldn't figure out why. Nick took a bite of his bagel after piling it with lettuce, tomato, and Gertie's famous tuna salad. His mother smiled at him, and his father continued reading the paper, tortoiseshell glasses perched on his nose, as if it were any other Sunday.

Nick ate his bagel, staring at the Manhattan skyline beyond the deck. He wasn't sure if something wasn't right, or if maybe, just maybe, things were finally turning out the way he had always imagined they should.

CHAPTER FOURTEEN

On Sunday afternoon, Lauren and Phoebe met up at Giroux New York. Lauren wanted Phoebe to see her favorite store, but more important, she wanted to find out who had given her the purse. She and Phoebe gushed over the shoe department—the styles were gorgeous, spot-lit, and displayed on Lucite shelves as if they were works of art. Even Lauren didn't find them terribly practical—but, oh, if only to look . . . she loved that part of it. She was showing Phoebe a snakeskin stiletto when she heard a voice behind her.

"Miss Mortimer?"

She started before turning around. It was Sebastian Giroux himself; she recognized him from numerous articles in the *Times* Style section and *Women's Wear Daily*.

"Yes?" she said.

Mr. Giroux looked down at Lauren's bag. "I see you received my message," he said.

Of course—it was starting to make sense. "Yes, thank you so much. It's so generous of you. You didn't really have to—I mean, my God, I don't buy *that* much here! I mean, I wish I did, but you know, the prices are a little bit . . ." Her voice trailed off. She didn't even know what she was saying.

"Sometimes you have to pay for quality," he said.

"Oh, I didn't mean to imply—" Lauren blushed a little.

"Not to worry. The bag was a gift, but it was also an invitation."

Lauren raised an eyebrow at him.

He looked at her outfit, the way she was wearing a sweater dress over tight jeans, the Hermès scarf of her mother's that she had tied around the handle of the bag. "You, my dear, have style. I can tell. Just like your mother. How would you feel about working as an intern for me?"

Lauren gasped. "Oh my God, I'd love to. I mean, you know I'm still in school, right?" What was she thinking? She would skip school for this, if she had to.

"Of course, we'll work something out. You can work in the afternoons. How does that sound?"

Lauren grinned. "It sounds amazing." She turned to Phoebe. "Oh, this is my friend Phoebe, by the way. I can't—I can't believe this. Thank you so much!"

"My pleasure," he said. "You deserve this."

"Okay," Lauren said to Phoebe, as the two of them sat over coffee nearby at Pastis. "What on earth just happened there? I've never met the man in my life, never told anyone that I—okay, wait, that's not true. I posted on my Facebook page like a million years ago how much I'd love to work at that store. I told Emily last night that I'd like to be in fashion someday, but I didn't think it would happen so quickly."

Phoebe nodded. She wasn't creeped out by it; she was actually feeling a terrible sense of jealousy. God, could she be happy for someone else for once? It wasn't only that, though—it was this feeling that even if she were part of the Society, she would always be the underdog. Lauren hadn't even been a member for two days, and she had already gotten an internship. Nick had been offered a club night by his mentor, Jared, right on the spot. What had she gotten? She had mentioned to Anastasia that she would love to put together a gallery show, but Anastasia (who, Phoebe had to admit, seemed like a bit of a flake) hadn't done anything or offered her any advice. Maybe she was being silly. It had been fewer than forty-eight hours. Success wasn't supposed to happen that quickly. Still, she couldn't shake the feeling that however quickly it might happen for her, everyone else's ascent would be speedier. Earlier that day, she had rifled through the college catalogs she had started receiving in the mail, based on her PSAT scores, which, while good, were not amazing. She had unpacked her mixed media pieces from their boxes. She needed to get to work on them. What was she so afraid of?

"It's great," Phoebe said, hoping her lack of enthusiasm wasn't overly apparent.

"You don't seem so sure," Lauren said, taking a sip of her espresso.

"No, I just—well, I'm still a bit confused by it all. Some of it seems clear. It's like that perfect job interview that we all imagine, where someone says, 'You're great, we love you, we want you.' But then there are these strange things about it. Like, they haven't really spelled out to us what *we're* supposed to be doing. I mean, I seriously doubt that all this comes for free. It's like, at what point do we have to start paying them back for all these privileges—the majority of which are still unclear to me."

"The feeling I got was that first we get to take advantage of being part of it," Lauren said. "I mean, it's not like we can really do anything for anyone anyway, right? I don't have any real connections, I can't get someone a job or whatever. I think the idea is that you succeed and then you help the next group, as payback for the older classes who helped you. Which is kind of the way life works anyway, right?"

Phoebe corrected her. "Life for some people. I mean, whatever happened to just doing things on your own?"

"We still have to do stuff on our own. The Society can help open some doors for us. It's not like I won't have to fold clothes in the backroom for the next six months, but the point is, that's what I want to be doing. And no one would have ever known if they hadn't told Mr. Giroux."

Lauren's clear-eyed view of everything calmed Phoebe a bit. Her dreams would come through; she had to give them time. Right now, she should be enjoying herself: no dues, no real responsibilities. Show up to a few meetings, be pleasant, and doors would open, right?

"Emily gave me this little speech last night," Lauren said. "It was basically like, 'We're hard workers, we're the ones who make things happen, we pull the strings.' You know, all that stuff."

"They're certainly quite proud of themselves, aren't they?" Phoebe sat back in her chair.

Lauren smirked. "God, and I thought I was the cynical one!"

"I know, I'm awful," Phoebe said.

"I think they can help you. If you want to do your art, that takes money, right? And you need to be noticed. You need to be the one that people pay attention to, not some sniveling, angst-ridden gallery groupie who prides herself on reading one-dollar bargain books from the Strand." Lauren pulled a lip gloss from her bag and started applying it, as if the matter was clearly settled.

Phoebe laughed. *She* liked to read one-dollar bargain books from the Strand, but she wouldn't tell Lauren that.

That afternoon, Nick needed to clear his head, so he decided to go for a run. He bounded up Fifth Avenue to the Eighty-fifth Street entrance to the park, toward the Reservoir.

It was one of those runs when the same thoughts circled around in his head in an endless loop: the last two nights, Phoebe, lying to Patch, his parents, Phoebe, the school year starting. . . .

There was no clarity to be had today.

On the way back, he was exiting the park to the north of the museum, when he saw Patch.

"Hey!" Nick shouted.

Patch waved to him, rather tentatively, Nick thought, as if he were a person he didn't know anymore.

Nick sprinted over, his Yale T-shirt soaked and his hair a greasy mess. "Hey," he said again.

"What's up?" Patch said.

"You want to grab something to drink?"

The closest option was a hot dog stand in front of the Met, so they bought sodas there and sat on the steps. It was a familiar location for them; it felt as if they had spent half their childhood at the Met. They would play hide and go seek in the arms and armor wing and enjoy free hot chocolate in the Petrie Court Café.

"So what gives?" Nick asked. "You're so quiet."

Patch was silent for a moment before finally speaking.

"Nick, I know what's going on. I know about it all."

Nick felt a shiver. "Know about what?" he said carefully, as he moved closer to Patch on the steps.

"Everything that happened on Friday night."

Nick knew that couldn't be true: There was no way Patch could know *everything*.

Patch continued, "I know about the Society. About you being in it. You and Lauren and that new girl at Chadwick. It's creepy stuff, Nick."

"I don't know what you're talking about."

"Come on, Nick, don't mess with me."

Nick flipped up the tab on his soda can, breaking it and tossing it to the ground. "I'm not. I don't know what you're talking about." How had it, once again, become so easy for him to lie to his friend?

"Nick, I have a video. And I'm, well, I'm really scared by it."

Some tourists walked by them, so Nick lowered his voice, hissing at Patch. "How the hell did you get video of it?"

"I saw the address on your phone. I knew what was going on. I snuck in through an air duct and I taped the whole thing."

Nick froze. This was bad. Really, really bad.

"I may have to run it at some point on the vlog."

"Patch, you cannot do that. I don't think you understand. This isn't some little hijinks where you can blur out the faces and show people partying or whatever. People could get really hurt here."

"So why don't you tell me what it's really all about?"

Nick looked down. "Patch, I can't. You have to trust me on this. I need you not to run anything, not to tell anyone about it. Can you promise me that?"

"Why should I?"

"Because you're my friend."

Patch scoffed. "A real friend would have told me what's going on."

"Goddammit, Patch! Don't you get it? I can't talk about it. There are things . . . things I can't explain." Nick didn't know what he was saying, but he needed some way to get Patch off his back. He couldn't tell him about what had happened, about what he knew—little as it was. The Society had made that much clear.

Patch stood up.

"Where are you going?"

"Screw you, Nick."

Nick got up and followed him. "Come on, Patch, don't!"

Patch crossed the street in front of their building, running in front of traffic, and Nick followed him as two cabs blared their horns. Patch stopped under their building's awning. He sneered at Nick, who stood there, not knowing what to do.

Patch reached forward and flipped up the back of Nick's hair. "Did they give it to you? Do you have the mark?"

Nick looked nervously at one of their doormen, but he was busy helping a mother and her children out of a cab.

"Do you have it? Do you have the ankh?" Patch badgered him.

Nick shoved him away, and Patch shoved him back.

"Oh, is that how it's going to be?" Nick said, as he felt his face flush.

He heard a voice behind them. "Boys!" Nick's father stepped out of a black Mercedes that was idling at the curb. "Guys, cut it out! What are you, children?"

Patch spat the words at Nick. "You suck." He turned and stormed back into the building.

Nick's father looked at him. "Are you okay?"

He nodded. He was fine, physically, but he was unnerved. He and Patch had experienced their tiffs over the years, but it had never been anything like this. This wasn't something that would be easy to smooth over.

Nick's father put his hand on Nick's shoulder. "These things will happen. You can't let it bother you. You're growing up. You're picking sides. You promise me you won't let this upset you?"

"I guess not." Nick looked at his father begrudgingly.

"Good. You've got too much at stake to let something like a childhood friendship get in the way." Nick's father looked intently at his son. "Friends come and go, but you will always be a member of the Society."

CHAPTER FIFTEEN

The next day at school, everything with the Society was so far from Phoebe's mind, it was as if none of it had happened at all. What had changed, however, was that Lauren asked her to go out to lunch at a nearby café with her and her friends. Was it really this easy? Suddenly Phoebe felt like she had friends at Chadwick—admittedly, she didn't know these girls well, but she could hang out with them, gossip with them. The girls treated Lauren somewhat indifferently, and Phoebe sensed that there might be tension. She wondered if Lauren had told them anything about the weekend.

More than anything, Phoebe wanted to know more about the Society. It kept eating away at her, this idea that she was entering into something she really didn't know very much about, and yet it also seemed like such a clear, natural progression of things. She had always wanted to succeed, and now here it was, being handed to her on the proverbial silver platter.

She had already scoured the Internet the previous day, reading everything from the paranoid to the scholarly on secret societies. For every completely crazy webpage (and there had been at least three), there were at least five more praising the work of the Society, talking about how it gave anonymously to charity, how it was a breeding ground for future leaders in politics, business, and even culture. She decided to go to the Chadwick library and see if they had anything there.

The school's library was a beautiful facility on the north end of campus, connected to the main building by a series of hallways. It had deep burgundy carpeting, large Palladian windows, and oak refectory tables where you could study in between the stacks. She went to a terminal and typed in several combinations of words to bring up a string of books. Most were in the 300s, the social sciences section. After finding the right row, she pulled out a few and flipped through them. No mentions of the Society, from what she could tell. She really couldn't check them out, anyway, she realized. Phoebe had no idea about how private the Chadwick library database was, but she knew she didn't want any record of her having been interested in the topic. It was too risky.

Was all this right? she wondered. If it were so secret, didn't that make it sort of, well, wrong? But there were plenty of secrets that weren't wrong. No one knew much about her life before she had arrived at the school. No one knew she had never had a relationship that had lasted more than a few weeks. That was a secret, of sorts. Maybe this was nothing more than a group of people who were keeping a set of secrets. Was that so wrong? She thought of that Diane Arbus quote that her mom often repeated: "A photograph is a secret about a secret."

The world was full of secrets. Wasn't it better to be on the inside, knowing them, than on the outside?

On her way out of the library, still in the social sciences section, she passed the end of the 300s. Phoebe stopped cold. A book about Egyptian customs sat on the shelf, and right on its spine was an ankh.

That evening, when Lauren came home, her mother was lying on the celadon linen chaise in their living room, drinking from a highball glass. Her purse and two shopping bags of fabric samples had been dumped on the floor next to an ottoman. A classic movie was playing quietly in the background on a flat screen television that was usually hidden within a travertine console; Lauren recognized the dance number with Frank Sinatra and Bing Crosby as one of her mom's favorites.

Even more familiar was the sound of ice clinking in a glass and of her mother's slurred words.

It was six P.M., and Diana was already toasted.

"Sweetheart, come over here," her mother said.

Lauren sat primly on a settee nearby. The more sloppily her mother behaved, the more Lauren wanted to have her act together. Lauren looked at her: her tanned skin, her blonde hair, her thin-as-a-wisp figure. Sometimes her mom looked beautiful, and sometimes she looked like she was wasting away.

"Mom, what happened?"

She glanced at Lauren and then took a sip from her glass. "I lost another client. I had come from shopping at the D&D, and I was loaded down with fabric samples like a pack mule. Ann Moss, the wife of the hedge funder, gives me this speech, right over lunch. Tells me she doesn't think I have it anymore as a decorator. That she's decided to work with someone who promised that she could get into *Architectural Digest*. So she fires me. And says she wants the remainder of her retainer back, that she'll sue me if I don't reimburse her. And then she stuck me with the check for lunch!"

"So let her sue you. You don't need her."

"After the divorce, I can't afford another lawsuit. At eight hundred dollars an hour, these lawyers will clean you out. I wrote her a check right there. It was only a few thousand. But the principle—it was humiliating!"

"And you've been sitting here ever since?"

"No, I went to Bemelmans," she said, referring to the bar at The Carlyle. "Figured no one would know me there, that it would be tourists. Well, I'm on my second martini, when who do I run into but Jack Dunleavy, our accountant. I said that I had just finished having a drink with a friend. Oh, Lauren, I want so much better for you."

"What do you mean?"

"There is such a short window of opportunity in your life for success—the kind of success you really deserve. And a woman today—well, she's expected to get married, to have children, and to have a spectacular career."

"Mom, you seem to forget I'm only sixteen." Lauren poured herself a glass of Pellegrino from a tray that was sitting on a drinks cart.

"I know, but it's just so hard. When you're in college, you're busy. And then you're thrown into the job market. You have to find a husband. And you have to find a way to distinguish yourself from your peers. Don't do what I did."

"What do you mean?"

"I came out at the International Ball." Lauren had heard this story a hundred times. "Every young man wanted to go out with me. Unfortunately I picked your father, who after twenty glorious years, decided that he'd had enough."

"Mom, I know. Dad sucks. But there's nothing you can do about it."

Her mother continued, "I never had time to develop my talents. At your age, you need to take advantage of every opportunity."

Lauren wanted so badly to tell her mom about her internship, but her mom's advice was so contradictory. She would tell Lauren to take every chance she had, and then she would chastise her for not doing well enough on her schoolwork. She wouldn't approve of the internship, would dismiss it as nothing more than working in a shop.

She wanted to ask her mom about the Society, to see if she was a member. But from the sound of it, her mom had no clue. Besides, she had promised the Society that she would keep it all to herself.

Her mom was in another world, anyway. "It's so good that you have friends," she said. "Stick with your friends, honey. They're the ones who will really support you."

Lauren excused herself to use the powder room—she needed a break from her mother for a moment—and when she returned, Diana had fallen asleep on the couch. Lauren draped a beige cashmere throw over her mom, deciding to let her sleep. When she dimmed the lights, the glittering windows of Park Avenue shone through the sheer, gauzy drapes, illuminating her mother's petite frame.

That evening, Lauren set her alarm early, in case her mom slept through the night and needed to be woken before the household staff arrived.

Lauren knew one thing: She would never be like her mother. She would do everything within her power to make sure that didn't happen.

II

THE FOLLY

CHAPTER SIXTEEN

It all started with the ankh.

Late that night, Phoebe was at home, looking at her canvases again. She had stopped by the gallery after school, as her mom needed her to pick up some papers, and the owner, Michelle Schrader, had come out to speak with her. She said she'd heard that Phoebe had been working on a series, and she'd be interested in taking a look at it. Did she have any images she could send?

Phoebe felt short of breath. How had Michelle heard about her art? Maybe her mother had told her.

She rushed home and started looking at her pieces, laying them out on the floor and strategizing what to do with them. They were mixed media pieces, combining abstract painting, collage, and screen printing. They had potential, but they needed something else. Her book from the library—she figured she could take the Egyptian one out without attracting suspicion—caught her eye. The ankh. Her hand went up to the bandage on the back of her neck. Still healing, she assumed.

She went to her laptop, did an image search, and skimmed through a number of the sites. The ankh symbolized immortality, the union between male and female. It could protect against bad luck or attract good fortune. She even learned its Latin name, *crux ansata*, meaning "cross with a handle." But no mention of the Society.

It didn't matter; it was better that the ankh wasn't publicly associated with the Society. She looked back to her artwork. She was inspired by the Egyptian imagery, by the possibilities it might allow her.

She got out her sketchbook and started planning a new piece.

Down in Soho, Nick waited nervously for Jared Willson at a new lounge, Persepolis, that had a vaguely Middle Eastern theme. Although the idea of doing a party at Twilight was exciting, it also made Nick uneasy. Jared wanted to do the party on Thursdays, the prime night in the club hierarchy, as Fridays and Saturdays were thought of as being for amateurs.

Nick wasn't sure, though, that he could trust Jared. He had heard the rumors: that Jared was a hard partier, that he was on drugs, that he was a dealer. But Nick thought about all the awful things he had heard people say about him and how they weren't true. He couldn't believe mere gossip. Besides, Jared's family was well known in Manhattan, and he went to a school that was as respected as Chadwick.

Jared greeted Nick and then downed his drink and ordered another from the bartender at Persepolis, who seemed to know him.

"Dude, we'll make it all happen," he said to Nick. "You have to promise me you can get some of that young crowd, right?"

Nick nodded carefully. He didn't like to promise anything in terms of promoting. You never knew when a club would be hot one minute and not the next; if it would rain, affecting how many people went out that night; or if another, more important event would come up.

"Do you have someone in mind for a DJ?" Nick asked. He wondered if Patch might appreciate the gig. It would actually pay, as opposed to last time, for which, he now realized, he had never thanked Patch. Despite the fact that Patch had screwed up royally by filming the Society initiation, people had still raved about how fantastic the mix was that evening. And Nick wanted some way of letting Patch know that he would forgive him. He had been ignoring Nick ever since their blowup in front of the building on Sunday afternoon. "My friend Patch might be interested in doing it."

Jared stirred the ice in his glass. "I don't know . . . is he a member?" The question surprised Nick. He thought the Conscripts were supposed to know who each and every Initiate was.

"No, he's in my class at Chadwick. He's my best friend," Nick said. Or was, he thought.

"I don't know if that's a good idea," Jared said. "We need a name brand, you know, someone people'll recognize."

Nick nodded. "Of course. I understand."

"Carlo will have someone in mind, I'm sure."

As Nick sipped his Coke and the two reviewed the rest of the details of the evening—guest list, bottle service options, door policy—it was as if the meeting were a formality, as if Jared didn't really need Nick at all, as if he had just needed to sniff Nick out and figure out what kind of person he was. Nick was used to marathon brainstorming sessions with other club promoters, using his creativity to get around problems and challenges. Now it was as if the whole thing were happening like clockwork.

"Nick!"

Patch took two steps at a time to meet up with Nick the next day. Nick was sitting in front of Chadwick's entrance, looking out at the traffic on York Avenue; his book bag was slung over his shoulder, as if he were about to get up.

"I need to talk to you," Patch said. It was the most formally he had ever addressed his friend. Patch was dreading this conversation.

There had been some new developments with his TV deal. Two days earlier, Patch had been quoted in the *New York Observer* in an article about teen vlogs, and his agent had called him to let him know that one company had come out on top in terms of bidding for the rights to produce Patch's show. That morning, Patch had met with Simone Matthews, a producer for the reality TV production company Eyes Wide Open, in order to discuss the creation of a pilot episode. It was the second time he had met with the tall, thirtysomething African-American woman with an infectious smile; the first time had been at his agent's offices, before they bought his show.

This time, they had met for an early breakfast at Sant Ambroeus, the Milanese espresso bar on Madison, to discuss how to make PatchWork into a television series. She wanted edgy stuff, she said, if they were going to make this work. She already had interest in *Chadwick Prep* (which the show was going to be called) from countries as far away as Japan. All this was based on a five-minute "sizzle reel" that the company had put together. Simone promised Patch total access in terms of venues; that had been a challenge with the vlog sometimes, when a bar or club would tell Patch he couldn't film (Bungalow 8 was notorious for blocking him because of its high celeb clientele—although his being underage never seemed to be a problem). Now he felt the pressure to produce really amazing stuff that would wow the TV buyers—the show, after all, still had to be sold to a network or cable channel.

Now, Nick looked up warily. Clearly their fight was still fresh in his mind. "Yeah?"

"I met with a producer this morning. You know, the one I had been telling you about? Anyway, they want to do the show—or at least to make a pilot. But they want stuff that's really over the top, really incredible. I sort of—well, I let it slip about the footage that I have."

Nick stood up and his voice dropped to a whisper. "Patch, are you insane? I told you that you *cannot* air that footage."

"What are you so worried about?" Patch knew he was testing his friend, but he wanted to see what Nick would say. He was furious at how Nick acted like Patch needed his permission. Inwardly, though, he wanted to have his friend's blessing.

"I don't know. Look, if you value everything that we have—our friendship, everything, just please, please don't show them that stuff. Tell them you lost it or something."

"Nick, I can't do that."

"Why not? You've got plenty of other footage."

"Nick, I don't, okay? She said, 'No one is that interested in seeing scene after scene of a bunch of preppies going out drinking.' They want something more."

Nick shook his head. "So don't do the show."

Patch felt his anger flaring. This was so easy for Nick to say. "Nick, you don't get it. My life isn't like yours. I don't have carte blanche into any college I want. I don't have a credit card with no spending limit. I have to work for what I get."

Nick looked at him as if he'd been slapped. "Screw you, Patch. You know I work hard."

Patch was silent. There were so many vicious things he could say—how he knew Nick had every advantage, how Nick might not even be at Chadwick if it weren't for his family. But he held his tongue, turned around, and walked away. He didn't know what to say, so the fight, he decided, was over.

CHAPTER SEVENTEEN

Lauren walked home that evening, exhilarated after the first day of her internship at Giroux New York. The start of it was exactly as she had imagined: She had shown up and was greeted by Sebastian Giroux himself. He asked her a bit about school and then passed her on to Sabrina Harriman, the well-known creative director, who was frequently quoted in the press on style trends. Sabrina, a severe-looking woman with a hawklike nose who favored black clothes and horn-rim glasses, had been pleasant but businesslike, and Lauren sensed that they weren't exactly going to be best friends. She plunked Lauren down in the stockroom to unpack some Giroux private label dresses that had come in from Italy, a job some would have considered menial. Lauren didn't care; she was thrilled to be there. She set about unpacking the dresses and hanging them on the rolling rack as if she had been given the most important task in the entire store.

An hour or so had passed when she came upon one dress whose label had become undone. She was about to go get a needle and some black thread to tack it back on again when she noticed something strange: On the back of the label, sewn in reverse thread, white on black, was a very small ankh. Lauren flipped over the other labels, which required some maneuvering, as most were sewn down tightly. All of them had the small sign. Lauren felt a heaviness in her stomach, not knowing what it meant. She knew she had gotten the job through some sort of Society connection, but she didn't know the exact details. Was Sebastian Giroux himself a member? Was the store owned by the Society? She decided she couldn't let it bother her. She had the internship she had always wanted, and she wasn't going to let her imagination take over.

As she left that day, the most thrilling thing of all happened. She was saying good night to Sabrina, who was talking to the cleaning people about something. "Wait a second," Sabrina said to her.

Lauren cringed. Had someone seen her looking at the labels?

"Come closer," Sabrina said. She held out a hand toward Lauren's neck and touched the necklace she was wearing.

"Your pendant. It's stunning. Who made it?"

Lauren had forgotten she was even wearing it. It was

another vintage piece of costume jewelry she had bought at the Chelsea flea market over a year ago and then had reset. She had a thing about jewelry; she hated almost all mainstream styles. While she loved contemporary fashion, she felt that contemporary jewelry looked like it should be sold at the mall.

"I don't know," Lauren said. "It's vintage. I mean, I had it reset, and I added a new chain."

"I would kill for something like that in the store," Sabrina said, smiling. Her voice lowered. "You know, I thought you might be another one of, well, one of Sebastian's *connections.*" She rolled her eyes. "The usual socialites he likes working in the store."

Lauren laughed. "I'm hardly a socialite."

"That's what they all say. But I'm impressed with you. You worked for three hours downstairs without taking a single break, you didn't shop at all, and you have fantastic taste in jewelry." She patted Lauren on the shoulder. "See you next week."

Lauren floated home on that praise. When she got back to the apartment, Sabrina's words sparked an idea. She ran to her room and pulled out the sketchbook in which she sometimes played with ideas for jewelry. They were retro-inspired, not gaudy—simple, classic designs with a little bit of whimsy. She had never really thought of them as something people might be interested in; drawing them was just something she did for fun.

If Lauren wanted to have a career in fashion, she knew she'd have to go to FIT or Parsons. She needed something to set herself apart from the other applicants—particularly if she needed a scholarship, which might be necessary if her mom or dad said they wouldn't pay for it. Tuition was expensive. She would need to have a portfolio of her designs.

She began to work on more ideas.

"Phoebe, I want you to come down and meet Daniel."

Her mom was calling her to the kitchen to meet the guy she was dating—again. There had been three previous dates, and Phoebe had conveniently come up with an excuse each time not to be in the house when Daniel picked her mom up or dropped her off. It unnerved her a bit, the idea of her mom going on dates. Although she wanted her to be happy, she didn't really want to meet some new guy who was taking her out. But this time she didn't have a choice. She would have to meet Daniel, the famous art collector from Park Slope.

She plodded down the back stairs to the sleek, all-white modern kitchen. It didn't seem to fit with the rest of the house, but Phoebe liked it. The kitchen was like a blank canvas where she could let her mind wander.

Letting her mind wander was exactly what she had been doing lately. Instead of the lonely afternoons she had imagined she might be spending in a new city, she had become obsessed with her portfolio of artwork, pouring herself into her research and sketches. The Egyptian book had fascinated her: It was all about symbology, the meanings of different signs. She decided she would incorporate some of it into the series; she knew she probably shouldn't because of the Society, but she figured it would be subtle. Besides, wasn't edge what people were looking for in art today? One of Anastasia's performance pieces involved a black-and-white film of her sitting on the toilet and reading Rilke's *Letters to a Young Poet*. Even though Phoebe thought it sounded a bit inane, people had raved about how great it was, how it referenced Duchamp, Warhol, the celebration of the everyday.

Daniel Fullerton, her mother's date, was a little bit older than her mom, handsome and graying at the temples. Supposedly, Michelle Schrader had introduced them.

"Phoebe! I've heard so much about you." There was something about his voice that sounded familiar.

"Nice to meet you," she said, holding out her hand.

"Daniel's an alum of Chadwick," Maia said.

Daniel laughed. "Yeah, I graduated so long ago, it wasn't even coed back then. So I hear you've been working away at your paintings?"

"Yeah, they're more mixed media pieces, I guess." She had been experimenting with more silkscreens, a little bit of collage; the workroom upstairs where her mother's friend usually did her sculpting was a complete mess.

"I'd love to see them. Have you shown them to Michelle?"

Phoebe blushed. "No, I haven't. Not yet. I should, though, right?"

"Absolutely," Daniel said.

"We'd better get going," Maia said.

"Good meeting you," Phoebe said.

"You, too—keep it up with the paintings!"

As Daniel gave her a good-bye wink, a shudder went through Phoebe's body. She realized where she had heard that voice, so warm and inviting: Daniel had been at the Night of Rebirth.

CHAPTER EIGHTEEN

On Saturday afternoon, Phoebe and Lauren were sitting together at a round table in an upstairs ballroom at the Colonial Club, a private social club on Park Avenue that dated back to the original Astors. Security had been tight; their names and IDs were double-checked against a list, and two burly security guards stood on each side of the doors to the paneled ballroom. On a small placard was printed:

BRADFORD TRUST ASSOCIATION FALL LUNCHEON

The invitation had come in the mail, on Thursday afternoon, which was a surprise, since everything so far had been text-messaged. Phoebe was also starting to realize that the Society didn't like to give much advance notice about its events. She and Lauren had needed to pick up new dresses on Friday afternoon for the luncheon.

Most of the people at the lunch were much older, and the majority didn't introduce themselves. There were several announcements, one of which was that every Society member should save the dates between Christmas and New Year's for the annual retreat. The presentation itself was all about community service and the importance of giving. Phoebe didn't need a room full of stuffed shirts to tell her this. They had announced at the luncheon that the Society would be making an anonymous donation to the Metropolitan Museum's Egyptian wing to refurbish some of its galleries. It was a worthy cause, of course, but there had been something smug about the whole thing that Phoebe didn't like. Claire Chilton's mother, who was apparently an Elder of the Society, had given a talk about philanthropy. Again, all good, but something felt bogus about it. They had gone on and on about how they were building a generation of young leaders, helping to bring out everyone's true talents, but they hadn't actually *done* anything. All they had done was write a check. It bothered Phoebe, so as they all picked at their lemon tarts with raspberries, she finally had to say something.

"Your mother gave such a lovely talk," one girl said to Claire.

"Thank you." Claire smiled. "I think we should all be so proud of ourselves."

"Okay, help me out here," Phoebe said, putting down her fork. "Your mom's talk was great. But how can *we* feel good about this donation? We didn't raise the money. We started in this group, like, what, a week ago? I just don't really feel like it's our contribution to be proud about. We're all sitting around and drinking mimosas and toasting to the fact that someone we don't even know wrote a check."

"I beg your pardon," Claire said. "Lots of people worked really hard to raise that money."

"I totally agree," Phoebe said. "But let's do our own thing. Let's raise our own money."

Bradley Winston scoffed. "What, and have a *bake sale* or something?"

Phoebe blushed. Bradley Winston, for all his prepster ways, was the son of a brilliant Columbia professor who had written a bestseller on the politics of race. Being mocked by someone with such a pedigree stung all the more.

"No, she's right," Lauren said, thankfully coming to Phoebe's defense. "We can't rest on the laurels of the group."

"No one's *resting* on any laurels," Claire said icily, in Phoebe's direction. "You're new to this group. I'm not really sure it's your place to be commenting on things you don't understand."

Claire was probably right. Phoebe was speaking out of turn, although silently she couldn't help wishing that Claire's headband would cut off her circulation.

There was an awkward silence at the table, until someone changed the subject to the renovations on their parents' house in Newport.

Later, as they were walking home, Nick jogged to catch up with Phoebe and Lauren. Phoebe felt a warmth as he approached; she hoped he might ask her out again.

"Thank God that's over with," Nick said. "I thought I might pass out from the smell of mothballs in that place. I heard what happened at your table. I hate these charity events where no one does anything, but they all sit around and feel good about someone else's donation."

"I don't know," Lauren said. "You need to be careful, Pheeb." She looked behind them to make sure there were no Society members behind them. "There's something creepy about this whole thing—and I don't mean the secret society rituals, all that hoopla. I can't figure it out. I told you about the ankh labels, right?"

"Couldn't that mean anything?" Phoebe said. She didn't want to appear too judgmental; she felt she had already come off like a total bitch, and she didn't want Nick to think that was what she was like.

Nick took his coat and tie off and loosened his shirt-sleeves. "Come on, you guys can't let all this get to you. It's supposed to be fun."

Although Nick casually swung his jacket in the breeze, Phoebe wasn't so sure.

As they walked home, Lauren wasn't really thinking about the speeches at the luncheon. She was thinking about Alejandro Calleja. There was something about him—his confidence, his swagger—that she found appealing. It felt like he might allow her finally to have a little bit of fun, not to worry so much about what people thought. She doubted her mother would approve of Alejandro—after all, he was known to be a bit of a playboy. Lauren didn't care; she was flattered that he had taken an interest in her.

When she got home, Diana was reading Saturday's edition of Page Six while having a late lunch in the sunroom. "Did you read this about one of your classmates?" she asked, holding up the paper.

"What's that?" Her mother was always going on about how so-and-so was doing something, and Lauren should really be part of it.

"This young man, Patchfield Evans, has a new television program that he's filming. It's called *Chadwick Prep*. They're doing it at your school. Darling, why don't you befriend this boy?"

"Mom, I know him. He's been at Chadwick since kindergarten."

"Ask him to film you for his show. You need to do something that will single you out from your classmates if you're going to get into a good college."

Lauren considered what her mother had said. She had chatted with Emily van Piper that afternoon; Emily had been offered a role in an indie film by the casting director she had met with. Everyone else always seemed to be doing so much. Lauren thought about her sketchbook of designs. She had started fleshing them out, filling in the colors, making them look more professional, more like the illustrations of jewelry she had seen in books. She couldn't imagine herself drawing anything else, but somehow with clothes and jewelry, it came naturally. She didn't know what the next step was.

And then, that night before she went to bed, she realized the next step was obvious: She would show her sketchbook to Sabrina at Giroux New York.

Phoebe spent the rest of that weekend working on her art. She moved around bits of the collages, layered screen print upon screen print, until she was really confident that they were something worth showing. She took digital pictures of the four pieces and emailed them to Michelle at the gallery. She was nervous; to her, they weren't merely a step on the ladder to being a successful artist. They were a reflection of her entire aesthetic, everything she believed in.

She decided to tell her mom about it in the kitchen over dinner, lasagna that Maia had made.

"Do you really think you want to do that?" M

mean, you're so young. The pressure. Do you think you can handle it?"

"Mom, I've always wanted to work on my art. I just got distracted—by the divorce, by the move, by everything." She knew this was a low blow to her mother, but she couldn't help it. What right did her mom have to tell her that she couldn't be an artist?

"Sweetie, I want you to have fun. You're working so hard on everything else. Do you really need to throw something else into the mix?"

"This distracts me a bit, which is a good thing," Phoebe said. "I need you to support me with it."

"Of course I support you," Maia said. She paused, taking a sip of water. "Now, tell me, what did you think of Daniel?"

"Um, he's great," Phoebe said. "Really handsome."

Maia gave her daughter a funny look. "That's all?"

"Yeah, um, I think it's great that you're dating." Phoebe didn't want to tell her mother her suspicions, and what would they mean anyway?

She wished she knew.

CHAPTER NINETEEN

On Monday at school, Patch heard his name and turned around to find Lauren Mortimer, who barely ever gave him a second glance, running down the hall to talk to him.

"Hey," she said, slightly out of breath. "I know this is really random, but I have a favor to ask you. Do you have a second?"

Patch nodded, as Lauren rested her book bag on a windowsill.

"I read about your show. It's so exciting. I mean, I love the vlog, but a show—that's really cool. I was wondering if you'd be able to film my seventeenth birthday party? It's in a few weeks."

Patch looked at her skeptically. What kind of show did she think he was doing? This wasn't going to be some bogus reality show about girl stuff. Or was this party some sort of Society gig? If so, maybe that was a good thing. Maybe that would get him more of the footage he was looking for.

Lauren laughed at his confused expression. "I'm sorry. I should explain what it's all about."

By the end of her explanation—everything from the party's location to its theme to the guest list—he was sold.

The next day, while she was in the library, Phoebe got an email from Michelle: "I love your pieces. Do you want to come in and talk about them?"

Was this really happening? The bell rang for next period, and she realized she needed to respond. Phoebe wrote back that she would drop by later that afternoon.

She packed up her books and headed to class. Was it really this easy? Maybe it could be, if she would only let herself do what she was good at, if she didn't always allow her worries and doubts to get in the way of her dreams.

Later that day, she took the train down to the gallery, finding its white walls and concrete floors almost familiar. A frosty *gallerina* (the art world's fancy name for "receptionist") was sitting behind a desk and talking to a young woman who was holding a large black portfolio. The gallerina smiled at the woman curtly and said, "I'm sorry, Ms. Schrader isn't viewing new submissions right now."

"When will she be looking at new work?" the young

woman asked. Phoebe guessed she was newly out of the fine arts program at Parsons or Pratt.

"I can't really say. We're completely booked right now."

The woman thanked her and then turned around abruptly and left.

The gallerina turned to smile warmly at Phoebe. "Phoebe, Michelle told me all about you. I'm Sophie."

Phoebe smiled awkwardly as they shook hands, and Sophie led her into the gallery office. She had never paid much attention to Phoebe the past several times she had been in the gallery; apparently, now that had changed.

"Phoebe!" Michelle came around a corner into the main office, shoving a stack of papers into Sophie's arms. "I'm so glad you could come in. Let's talk about your work. Sit down. Sophie, get her a water, okay?"

Phoebe sat down at the oval marble Saarinen table that served as a meeting area.

"So talk to me about the work," Michelle said. "These four pieces." She slid open a laptop and clicked on Phoebe's four images. "They're fantastic. So fresh. It's exactly the kind of thing I'm looking for. I'd need to see them in person, of course, but I'm getting a good feeling about them from these photos."

"Right," Phoebe said, thinking back to the exchange she had witnessed at the front desk.

"What was your inspiration?"

Phoebe took a breath. "Those four pieces are about how the media has totally infiltrated our lives. How we can't get away from it."

"Can you do some more?"

"How many were you thinking?"

"I would say, twelve to eighteen. If you can produce that many, I have an opening for a show in November. An artist whom we had booked had to drop out."

Phoebe gulped. It struck her as highly unusual to get a show based on four paintings. Did the gallery have some connection to the Society? She didn't know. More important, she feared she wouldn't have time to complete so many new works, but if she wanted this show, she'd have to. The four she had created were all derived from ideas she had already worked through, stuff she had spent months thinking about. Could she come up with enough ideas to sustain a show of twelve to eighteen works? She didn't know. But it would be foolish not to accept the challenge.

"Sure," she said. "I can do it."

CHAPTER TWENTY

Over the past few days, Lauren had searched for inspiration for her new jewelry line and had done a dozen more sketches. It was all retro-inspired, the types of pieces worn by Lana Turner and Grace Kelly in old movies. She scoured the flea markets in Chelsea and Hell's Kitchen, the jewelry dealers at the Brooklyn Flea Market in Fort Greene, the little shops in Midtown and the Village.

A week later, she had assembled a portfolio of eight finished sketches to show to Sabrina at the store.

At Giroux, she knocked on the open door of the basement office, where Sabrina was flipping through designer look books for the coming season.

"Lauren," Sabrina said, "come on in. What do you have here?"

Sebastian Giroux popped his head in. "Sabrina, do you have a sec?"

"Of course. Sebastian, you might want to see this. Seems Lauren has some designs she'd like to show us."

Lauren felt herself reddening.

"Ah, a budding designer! That's what we like to see. What's going on?"

Lauren handed him her sketchbook. The first was a pendant, then a bracelet, then a pair of earrings. He peered at them intently, examining the details. "Well, well, well," he said.

Oh, God, she thought. She was so stupid to think she could do this. Phoebe was the one who had the artistic talent, not her. She had heard about her friend's gallery success and was a bit envious.

Sabrina gently pulled the book from his hand. "Ooh! I like. Could we make this?"

"It's very Tony Duquette," said Sebastian, referring to the legendary, over-the-top designer. "But modern. Wearable."

"Salable," Sabrina said.

Lauren wasn't sure if Sabrina's question had been a rhetorical one. Maybe they couldn't be made. Not all the designs might be feasible.

Sebastian scratched his temples. "You know, I think we could." He looked at Lauren as if it were the first time he had acknowledged she was in the room. "Can we try a prototype?"

"A prototype?" Lauren said. "Of course! I mean, sure."

"You would be involved, of course."

"Right." Lauren nodded, still reeling from the praise.

"When can you have them ready?" Sebastian asked Sabrina.

"Maybe two weeks, if we put a rush on it," Sabrina said. "The workshop in Brooklyn, I think, would be the best place for it?"

Lauren had a brainstorm. "I have an idea—I'm throwing a party. I think we could get some press from it. Like, you know, have the waitstaff get all dressed up, model some prototypes, that kind of thing? It would be different, right?"

"I like the way this girl thinks," said Sebastian. "You could make a splash. We could invite some buyers from other places, stores that carry Giroux."

Lauren nodded knowingly. This was turning out better than she had expected.

Simone, Patch's producer, had given him an editing suite over in the far West Thirties to work on the pilot for his show. They were roughing together an opening sequence that would introduce all the characters in the traditional format of reality television. There were several Chadwick students who featured prominently, including Nick, although Patch wondered if he would be able to get enough later footage in order to include him. He knew Nick had to be part of it—that was what made all the footage of the secret society initiation so relevant. Patch wondered if he would ever be able to fix things with Nick to the point where he could be part of the project without having an issue with the Society stuff.

The opening sequence of the pilot showed them going to school, going out at night, playing sports, shopping downtown, and even at home with their families. The footage Patch had so far hinted at fights and drama, but the difference was that if the show were produced, Patch would have full access to people's lives. It wouldn't be only snippets—it would be total access to five different Chadwick students, complete with their signed consent.

He didn't know if Nick would be one of them.

Patch found Simone extremely persuasive—she had produced hard-hitting documentaries on teen pregnancy in the Midwest and crystal meth labs in New Jersey. Patch imagined she thought prep school kids would be a cakewalk.

"All right, look," she said to him one night, "I've been watching the rough cut you made. You need a story, a throughline. It's not enough to have a bunch of random kids partying and going to school. If we're going to make this happen, I need to see something better. Something crazier."

Patch cringed. He hoped she hadn't remembered his comment about the Society footage—in their second meeting, he had mentioned that he had some material of a club initiation that he thought would be compelling. But maybe she had forgotten that by now.

Since their meeting, he had kept it stored deep on his hard drive, protected by a password. Unfortunately, though, he realized that, legally, she had a right to it—he remembered that line, after all, in his contract: "In the creation of the pilot episode, Eyes Wide Open Productions has access to all footage taken of Chadwick students by Patchfield Evans."

CHAPTER TWENTY-ONE

A week later, Phoebe and Lauren were getting blowouts together at a cheap salon on First Avenue. Phoebe loved that even though Lauren could probably afford to get blowouts from Frédéric Fekkai himself, she opted for the inexpensive, simpler solution. People didn't know this about her: that underneath the veneer of fashion, she was, at heart, a practical girl who appreciated forty-five-dollar blowouts as much as the next person.

Her practicality was one of the reasons Phoebe suspected that Lauren hadn't been hanging out with her friends Chloë, Victoria, and Irina. Those girls wouldn't know a bargain if it jumped out of their Birkins.

Or maybe it was the fact that Lauren had been chosen for the Society and the other three hadn't. Phoebe had noticed how Society membership separated people. If you knew someone wasn't a member, you were a lot less likely to want to hang out with them.

That afternoon, they were getting ready for Nick's new club night at Twilight. She supposed she should have been excited by it, but Phoebe was exhausted by the social whirl. There had been a party at the Beatrice Inn, a downtown hotspot, and also meet and greets with alumni from Yale, Princeton, and Brown, all organized by the Society. She was starting to feel like one of those overscheduled kids she read about in articles, the type who never have a moment to enjoy the fact that they're sixteen and don't have to pay taxes or work. She was sick of her entire life in the past month revolving around Society events—after all, how many times could she hear about how much real estate everyone's families owned?

She asked Lauren if she ever got tired of the whole social game, particularly the Society stuff. She knew they shouldn't be talking about it in public—they technically weren't supposed to talk about it at all—but it didn't matter at the salon, as their voices would be drowned out by the sound of the hairdryers.

"Sure," Lauren said thoughtfully, while chewing on a fingernail, "but we don't really have a choice. It's mandatory attendance, you know."

"Don't you think that's sort of bogus?" Phoebe said, though

she remembered a story Nick had told her about the ostracism you could face if you didn't attend every event. Kitty Stapleton, the Administrator, kept tabs on exactly which events people had attended, right down to whether or not they had been on time.

"Yeah, I guess so. I don't know."

"You seem distracted."

"What? Yeah." Lauren gave a shy grin.

"Let me guess . . . it's a certain smoking-hot Argentinean you're thinking about."

Lauren smiled. "He texted to ask if he would see me tonight."

"Did you write him back?"

"Not yet," Lauren said, with the weary attitude of someone well versed in being chased by boys.

"You really like him, though, right?"

"Yeah," Lauren said. "I think I do. He's really sweet. And he's not what people think he is."

Phoebe nodded. Lauren could have been describing her own feelings about Nick. She wondered, though, if things would ever reach a level where she could let him know how she felt about him.

Nick was getting ready for his club night at Twilight, all the while thinking about how things had gotten so messed up with Patch. He had sent him several emails letting him know about the night and had made sure to put him on the list "plus party," which meant Patch could bring as many people as he wanted. The only people who ever got such a designation were celebrities or important socialites.

When he got to the club, it was a contrast to his last experience at The Freezer. Twilight was a slick, multilevel venue, complete with tables for bottle service, several lounges, VIP rooms, and even secret VVIP rooms. In New York, it seemed there was always a better room to get into, and now Nick had access to them all. He had seen the club once before during the day, but at night was when it really sparkled. The glossy black walls had been polished to a shine, and the cream suede banquettes looked like they were brand-new.

"Hey, Nick, my man!" Jared slapped him on the back as he greeted him.

"So what do we need to do?"

"Dude, grab yourself a drink—you don't need to do a thing. The cleaning people finished up this afternoon, the lighting's all set, the DJ's in place, I just got authorization on our insurance certificate, and the guest list has been checked, rechecked, and alphabetized. The doormen know the rule— two ladies to every guy—because we all know it's the chicks who bring in the guys, and it's the guys who keep ordering the bottles. You know what I mean?"

Nick nodded. It was all a bit much—the bottle service, the "chicks" (a word he never used himself). He wasn't sure his crowd would be into this. They liked things to be more relaxed.

"You seriously don't need me to do anything? I'm a little more used to having to clean up last night's vomit or make sure the club got the shipment from the liquor sponsor." He was joking about the vomit, but Jared, looking at him in horror, didn't seem to get it.

"Relax, you're good. It's all on autopilot."

Autopilot. Even though autopilot might be easier, it wasn't as much fun. Nick had always liked the problem-solving aspect of his club nights. After all the build-up to this night, all he had to do now was stand around and drink?

Jared handed him fifty or so glossy black cards. "Here's a stack of drink tickets. Give those to the important people, you know?"

Jared wanted all Society members to have a good time. If they had fun, they would spread the word to their friends, and before they knew it, Thursday night at Twilight would be a must on everyone's calendar. Nick looked at the crowd of investment bankers and models who had already started trickling in. This was nothing like a night at The Freezer, and for a moment, he truly missed that club's shabby appeal.

CHAPTER TWENTY-TWO

When Lauren arrived at Phoebe's house that evening and met Phoebe's mother, Phoebe and Maia cooed over the necklace she was wearing: It was the first prototype that Sebastian Giroux's manufacturer in Red Hook had made, an onyx stone within a simple silver setting. Lauren loved it, but she was particularly excited that Phoebe and her mother liked it, too.

At Twilight, soon after the girls had ordered drinks, they were approached by a nightlife reporter, who asked them what they thought about the evening. Phoebe looked at Lauren, as if to make sure it was okay, and Lauren nodded that it was. They chatted for a few minutes about the night and the crowd. The reporter, a pretty girl in her twenties wearing a simple black dress and cat's eye glasses, motioned to her photographer, who snapped a few shots and took their names.

"And you are a . . . ?" the reporter asked Phoebe.

"Oh, um, I'm in—"

Lauren interrupted her. "She's an artist. Her show is going up next month at the Schrader Gallery."

The reporter nodded, impressed. "And you?"

"Jewelry designer," said Lauren. "This is one of my pieces."

"Can I take a look?" Lauren lifted up her hair to offer a better view of the vintage-inspired chain and ornate clasp. The reporter stepped to Lauren's side to peer at the back of her neck. Lauren realized at that moment that her ankh tattoo was probably visible just above her collar.

"I thought so," the reporter said quickly, before walking away. "Good luck, girls."

In front of Twilight, a line stretched halfway down the block, and the doormen were relishing the fact that few were getting in. Patch had carefully hidden his camera inside his messenger bag so no one would see it. As a peace offering, Nick had emailed him, promising that he was on the VIP list and that he would have clearance to film. Patch went to the front of the line, as he had been instructed. A huge bouncer, a tall guy with a shaved head, looked at the list. "What's your name? Patch, you say?"

Patch nodded. "That's right."

The bouncer scrutinized the list. "And it's just you?"

"Yes."

"I'm sorry—I'm not seeing it."

"Can I look at it?"

"You're going to have to step to the back of the line." Were they treating him this way because he wasn't wearing the right clothes? Because he didn't have an expensive haircut? He had to admit that his hair had gotten a bit scruffy, that it had been at least two months since his last cut.

"Are you joking? I'd be out here for three hours. Let me call my friend. He's the promoter. Nick Bell."

"Yeah, sure. Everyone says they know Nick Bell."

Patch pulled out his phone and scrolled to Nick's name. It went straight to voice mail. Patch left a short, annoyed message.

"You need to step away," the bouncer said. "People are trying to get in."

Patch stepped back two feet, as three women escorted by a banker type were shown past the velvet rope. His face started growing hot. He couldn't believe Nick had done this, invited him to his party (multiple times!) and then forgotten to put him on the list?

"Screw you," Patch said to the bouncer, and walked away.

Phoebe and Lauren relaxed at their table, and Nick joined them, asking a waitress if she could get them set-ups for bottle service, all of which would be comped by the club. He rolled his eyes at Phoebe as the waitress put out the bottles of vodka, mixers, ice, and glasses. Nick had told her earlier that he wasn't a believer in bottle service—he, like many others, thought it had ruined New York nightlife. It had made club owners interested only in how many bottles of premium vodka you could sell, which meant you had to pack the place with a bunch of rich guys in suits who could afford the thousand-dollar tabs. And besides, Phoebe thought, what was so special about going out if you had to mix your own drinks?

"Nice spread, Mr. Bell," Phoebe teased him. "You never cease to amaze."

He shrugged. "Whatever. You want something to eat? They have food here, too."

"We're good," Lauren said. "Phoebe's mom ordered in pizza for us. Which I totally love! I don't think my mom even knows pizza delivery exists. She would be like, 'So I don't understand . . . where does it come from? Do you get it from Mario Batali?'" Lauren's shrill imitation of her mom was perfect. Phoebe had met Diana Mortimer only once, but it was dead-on.

"I can't believe I let my cell battery die," Nick said, holding up his phone. "I am so pissed."

Lauren handed him hers. "Use mine to check messages."

"No, don't worry about it. I need a night off anyway. Apparently there's nothing for me to do here."

"What do you mean?" Phoebe asked.

"It's 'all taken care of,' as Jared keeps saying. That's not what this was supposed to be about. These nights are fun because they *are* challenging. Because you don't know how they're going to turn out."

"So go underground again," Phoebe said, nudging him.

"Maybe I will."

"You might get some coverage for the party," Lauren said.

Nick shrugged. "That's cool." He thought about it for a second and then smiled. "Yeah, poor me. Successful club night, great crowd. Whatever. Let's get some more drinks."

Alejandro came up behind them and covered Lauren's eyes. She giggled and allowed him to give her a kiss on the neck. Phoebe admired how she acted as if she were embarrassed but secretly loved the attention. And Phoebe had to admit that Alejandro was hot. He sat down next to Lauren, across from Phoebe and Nick.

Nick whispered to Phoebe, "He is so high."

"What do you mean?" Phoebe always felt like she was clueless about what substances people were using. Half the time, she couldn't even tell if people were drunk; a girl in her European history class was supposedly drinking during the day, but Phoebe had never noticed a thing.

Nick continued, making it look like the two of them were sharing a private moment—which Phoebe wished they were. "Look at his eyes. Totally dilated. And see how his hand is shaking. I heard he's a cokehead."

Phoebe felt stupid for not noticing, but more than that, she felt bad for Lauren. She figured, though, that her friend would know how to deal with it. Nick and Lauren seemed to have done most of their experimenting when they were younger, and had deemed most of it pretty extraneous to their enjoyment of Manhattan nightlife. Lauren had said a few weeks ago that it caused more problems in her life than it had solved, so these days she stuck to the occasional cocktail as her poison of choice.

Still, as Lauren and Alejandro were nuzzling each other, Phoebe wondered if her friend knew what she was getting into.

Later that night, Jared pulled Nick aside. "We have a problem. The envelope of cash that I had for the DJ disappeared." He wiped his nose, which seemed to be running. Nick wondered if Jared was lying.

"You're joking. How much was it?"

"Three thousand dollars. It was for the whole night."

"Three thousand in *cash*! Why was it in cash?"

Jared shrugged. "You know how these guys can be. It's all off the books."

"So get the money from the club."

"Can't do it. We had an incident last winter—someone sued the club because their fur coat was stolen, and they had to cover the deductible on their insurance. It was like ten grand. How stupid is that?"

Nick shook his head. "What should we do? Can we ask the Society for the money?"

"Who would we ask? The Administrator? She'd report us before she'd cut us a check."

"You're right. How much did we take in at the door?"

"We took in two grand. But we need that for next week's party. With all the comps, we didn't make as much money as I would have liked. If we don't pay Carlo's buddy, we're screwed. He'll never work with us again—and he'll tell everyone in the business that we stiff people. Is there any way you could get the money from your parents?"

Nick shook his head. "I don't have access to that kind of cash. And I can't just ask them. Why is this my problem? Shouldn't you pay for half?"

"Nick, you were supposed to take care of stuff like this."

"What are you talking about, Jared? That was never discussed."

"You can figure something out. You have more access to resources. I know you can make it happen. We have until tomorrow at noon." His phone buzzed. "Listen, I gotta get this. Let me know, okay?"

Nick suddenly had a headache. He had thought the whole point of being part of the Society was that he wouldn't have to worry about things like this. He couldn't ask his parents for the money, and he had certainly never stolen money from them. Well, maybe the odd twenty taken from his mother's purse, but that wasn't a big deal, was it? And he didn't even do that anymore. He thought about where his dad kept his checkbook, in the right-hand desk drawer in his study. It would be easy for him to write a check out to cash, go and get the money, and no one would ever know. He could make up something, say it was for repairs on his Jeep or something.

He thought of the alternative. Could he walk away from this promoting gig? This was everything he had wanted, but it had been nothing but a letdown.

Much later, when Nick got home, he crept into his father's study. It was dark save for the streetlamps out the windows on Fifth Avenue; he flicked on a small Tiffany reading light on his father's mahogany desk. The right-hand drawer was unlocked; their employees had been with them for so long that the Bells never had a household in which theft was an issue. Nick carefully rifled around in the drawer to find two checkbooks, neatly encased in leather covers. He looked at the first one: "Georgiana and Parker Bell—Household Account #1." That was the one he would use. Then he looked at the second one. Same bank, same type of checks: "The Bradford Trust Association—General Account."

Nick remembered where he had seen that name: on the placard at the Colonial Club.

The Bradford Trust Association was another name for the Society.

CHAPTER TWENTY-THREE

Lauren had to admit that she may have gone a little bit overboard in the planning of her seventeenth birthday party. She had found an old supper club in the West Forties that was about to be closed, and she had been able to rent it out for a pittance. A caterer was brought in, and an event designer arranged for palm trees, vintage movie projections on the walls, black-and-white tablecloths, and hundreds of votives that would make the shabby club into a chic, retro hotspot. The night would be glimmering, glamorous, and totally not of today's New York. Lauren wanted it to be like the Stork Club or the Copacabana or El Morocco, all of which she had heard about from her grandmother—a night that harkened back to New York fifty or sixty years ago and also represented the aesthetic of her jewelry line. Even Diana had gotten in on the planning, as she finally saw how Lauren's entrepreneurial efforts could help her get into college. Of course, Lauren didn't tell her mother that she wanted to study fashion, not business.

She did worry that tonight would be the first time Diana met Alejandro. Although they weren't officially dating—Lauren wasn't sure what they were doing—she wanted her mother to like him.

Lauren arrived early to the venue, and was pleased to see that all the female waitstaff, wearing simple black A-line dresses, were modeling her jewelry prototypes, their plunging necklines drawing attention to the bold stones and whimsical shapes of the designs. She overheard them chattering about how cute the pieces were, which thrilled her.

For Lauren's own outfit, Sebastian Giroux had designed a dress for her that he said was "very Audrey Hepburn in *Sabrina*, after she returns from Paris." A take on the Givenchy classic, it was a cream organdie pouf dress, embroidered with black and white flowers on the skirt and bustier. For jewelry, Lauren wore the signature piece of the collection, a rough cut emerald Swarovski crystal on a silver chain.

As guests started arriving, Lauren worried that it was all too much, that she had gone too far—with the party, the jewelry, the retro dress.

It wasn't until Alejandro arrived that she felt better. He gave her a kiss on the cheek and then whispered in her ear,

"You look beautiful—like a forties movie star."

She smiled, as she felt her pulse quicken. It was exactly the effect she had been going for, and he was the first to notice.

Guests started spilling in, as the Lester Lanin Orchestra—the band renowned for playing everything from presidential inaugural balls to deb parties—played old-fashioned standards. At first, Lauren was concerned people might not be into the older music, but her friends were getting into the spirit of the night, seemingly relieved that they didn't have to attend yet another party with thumping house music.

When Sebastian Giroux arrived, photographers swarmed around him, taking pictures of him with Lauren, with her mother, with other socialites. Diana had extended the invitation to at least fifty of her friends, and Lauren sensed that the whole thing was as much for her mother as it was for her. Diana had even gotten Lauren's little sister, Allison, out of boarding school for the weekend so that she could attend the party. Lauren was fine with it all: After everything her mother had been through, she wanted her to be happy.

Phoebe felt a bit glum that Friday night at Lauren's party. She had been working on her gallery show for weeks, becoming completely immersed in it. She had even passed on Lauren's invitation to get their hair done together. Phoebe's series needed something more; she still had four more canvases to complete, and she had run out of ideas. The Egyptian thing combined with media images could take her only so far, and her November deadline was less than two weeks away. When she got to the party, she grabbed a drink and made her way through the crowd.

Near the dance floor, she ran into Patch, who was filming. She knew that he and Nick had recently had a fight, but Nick had spoken of him fondly, so she didn't think there was anything wrong with talking to him.

"Hey," she said. "I need to ask you something. Can you turn the camera off?"

He looked at her warily and then carefully put down his camera. "Sure, what?"

"I need your help. I'm wondering if we could, sort of, I guess, collaborate."

"What do you mean?"

"I need something . . ." She faltered for a moment, not wanting to admit that her work wasn't going well. "I'm doing a collage-type series of works. Incorporating images, appropriating stuff from all over. But I need something more. I know you have all this amazing footage. Like, do you think you would be able to let me use some of your stills—you could pick them, of course—and I would give you credit in the installation?"

Patch leaned against a ballroom chair. "Sure, I guess so." He paused. "Yeah, I think I like that idea. Maybe email me what you have already, so I can get an idea of what you're looking for."

"Do you want, um, compensation? Maybe I can pay you if a piece is sold, something like that?"

Patch shook his head. "Don't worry about it. I mean, I don't think Andy Warhol paid for the newspaper photographs that he made into paintings, did he?"

Phoebe laughed. "I'm hardly Andy Warhol."

"Same difference," Patch said, giving her a playful nudge. "Maybe someday you will be."

"This must be Alejandro!" Diana Mortimer was squealing, much to Lauren's embarrassment, and Patch was capturing it all. Patch could see that Lauren's mom had planned this all along, that she knew exactly who Alejandro was but was pretending to be oblivious, not to know that he was the notorious son of an Argentinean financier, that he had already been in the gossip columns several times for his antics, that he was frequently photographed at parties. There was a look on Lauren's face as if she were worried that her mother wouldn't approve, but it was clear that her mother did more than approve: She encouraged it. Alejandro kissed Mrs. Mortimer on both cheeks as if the two were old friends.

Alejandro then motioned to Lauren to come with him to the dance floor, as Patch followed them with his camera. The two swayed arm in arm to "The Girl from Ipanema," which got everyone else dancing. As the song continued, it started morphing into a pop version, and a curtain on a raised platform behind the band opened to reveal a gorgeous dark-haired woman in a red velvet dress. It was the up-and-coming Brazilian bossa nova singer, Isabel Mendes. She was singing the lyrics to the song, as the band played a faster tempo and a synthesizer was added to the mix. A roar went up from the crowd as people realized who she was; that week, her single had reached number six on the pop charts, and her first music video had recently debuted on the web.

"I didn't know about this!" Lauren said, laughing. Patch moved in closer to catch their dialogue.

"It's my surprise for you. Her parents are friends of my family. She flew up from Brazil this morning." He paused. "I asked your mother if it was okay," he said, almost as if concerned it might not be. "I hope you like it?"

Lauren didn't say anything. She leaned forward and kissed him.

Around them, cameras flashed, more champagne was poured, and Patch was there to document it all.

CHAPTER TWENTY-FOUR

The next day, the images arrived in Phoebe's inbox: They were breathtaking, intense, and stirred in her a series of dreamlike memories, although she couldn't place them. They were images of a party in progress, blurred and abstracted. A woman singing, shot from above. A close-up of a sequined dress. Champagne being poured. Cigarettes smoked from thin silver holders. She had no idea how Patch had gotten these images; they were almost like surveillance cam stills or grainy pics from a black-and-white movie. This was the missing piece, the missing link her work needed, the imagery that would take her show to the next level.

A week and a half later, a van came to transport Phoebe's pieces to the gallery. Michelle had already visited her several times while the works were in progress and offered critiques, but Phoebe was still nervous about the show. She had stayed up all night putting finishing touches on them and was now completely wiped out in class. Her mother had stayed up late with her, bringing her coffee and snacks, and had told Phoebe how proud she was of her.

That afternoon, Phoebe went over to the gallery to meet Michelle and watch the show being hung. The walls had been painted to match the narrative of her show, and placards and an artist's statement had been printed up.

She couldn't believe that it was all happening so quickly.

When, by early evening, the show was nearly ready to be seen, Phoebe walked slowly by each piece, as if memorizing its exact location. For a first show, she thought, it wasn't bad at all.

"Lauren! Come here quickly!"

Lauren's mother was at the breakfast table, where she was poring over the morning's *New York Times*.

"What?" Lauren said sleepily from the other side of the kitchen, as she poured herself a cup of coffee.

"There's a write-up about Phoebe in the Arts section. 'Thirty Under Thirty in the Art World: Phoebe Dowling's raw canvases are electric with anger and possibility. The show, which opens tonight at the Schrader Gallery, demonstrates that Dowling is a talent to watch.'"

Lauren grabbed her phone and texted Phoebe a simple message: "!!!!"

"I'm so thrilled that you're associating with the right sort of people," Diana said, as she spooned herself a wedge of grapefruit. "As they say, it's not what you know . . ."

As much as Lauren was happy for Phoebe's success, she felt a twinge of jealousy. How was it that Phoebe had been in the city for less than three months and was already experiencing this level of success? Lauren had gotten an email the previous night: The buyer at Barneys had passed on her line, saying it was too specialized. *Screw them*, she thought. Giroux's store was carrying it. But it needed to succeed on a bigger scale. There had been nearly a dozen mentions of her birthday party in the gossip columns and social blogs, including a few close-ups of some of the jewelry. But there were thousands of different lines out there. She needed something that would set her apart from the rest.

CHAPTER TWENTY-FIVE

The night of her gallery opening, Phoebe stepped out of a cab with her mother. People were already crowding into the entrance, and Phoebe and her mom were too polite to push anyone else out of the way. They waited their turn and slipped on in, without anyone realizing that the artist was in their midst until Michelle started gushing.

"There she is!" Michelle shrieked, rushing over to embrace Phoebe and her mother.

Heads turned and Phoebe smiled shyly. She hadn't even gotten a chance to examine the installation when people started swarming her and asking her all sorts of questions: What was her inspiration? Where did she work? How did she manage to balance school with her art? Could she explain her technique? How did she feel about the *Times* write-up?

Her mouth was parched, and while she would have loved a water, she was handed a glass of champagne instead. She thought her mother was lost somewhere in the crowd until she spotted her chatting with Daniel, whom she was now seriously dating. Phoebe was okay with the dating part; it was his connection to the Society that made her uncomfortable, that he hadn't let on who he was. In another corner, she saw Nick with some friends from Chadwick, and she wished he would come rescue her.

Michelle rushed by with a clipboard. "You're not going to believe this. Half the pieces in the show are sold already!"

Phoebe nodded, a bit taken aback. She finally had a moment to look around at the walls, many of which were blocked by the guests crowding in to see her pieces. "I don't— I don't see them all here."

"Oh . . ." Michelle leaned forward, talking to Phoebe in a hushed voice. "There was a client several days ago who saw a preview of the show. He wanted to remain anonymous. He insisted that the pieces he was purchasing be taken down and the show be reorganized, so it wasn't obvious that they were missing."

"I don't understand. Why did this happen?"

"Let's discuss it later. Tonight is your night—just enjoy yourself."

Her night. It wasn't anything like her night. The faces swarmed around her, offering praise, accolades, congratulations. Anastasia said how proud she was of Phoebe and apparently was taking credit for having discovered her. But it all felt empty, as if she were viewing life from the bottom of a swimming pool, barely able to breathe. It didn't feel real.

The thing that felt the least real of all was the missing pieces.

She saw Patch artfully making his way through the crowd with his camera, scanning the monochromatic canvases one by one, taking in each one's individual colors: blues, greens, yellows, magentas. And then she realized, perhaps at the same time as he did, that the missing works were all the ones that contained his mysterious images.

Later that evening, Phoebe sat with Nick on the roof of his building. They could hear the Fifth Avenue traffic below and see the top of a Jeff Koons sculpture in the Met's roof garden, but aside from that, it felt like they were in a world apart.

Nick had been impressed by the show; he felt like he had known Phoebe as a friend—or maybe, as something more— and then suddenly she was being treated like a celebrity, having her photo taken and getting written up in the *Times*.

"There's something messed up about all this," Phoebe said, as she bundled her coat close to keep out the November chill. "It's like a fantasy or something, like someone is pulling the strings."

Nick didn't want to make it seem like Phoebe got the

show only because she was in the Society; he knew that would make her feel lousy. "You need to stop doubting yourself," he said. "Your paintings are amazing. The *New York Times* thinks so."

"I feel like my work hasn't had any time to develop, to mature, you know?" Phoebe said. "I mean, what am I supposed to do next?"

Nick smiled. "Go make some more art," he said. "Or don't. Give yourself some time off. But either way, don't stress about it."

"I'm sorry," she said. "I'm being such a downer."

"Not at all." He brushed aside his shaggy hair and moved a bit closer to her. "You know, I remember feeling this way when I realized that it was a pretty tough thing to get into Chadwick—even when you're six years old. I know some people think I only got in because I'm a Bell. I'll never know, but all I can do is be myself. It's like, lots of people don't even have this much fortune in their lives, am I going to go and cry about it because I do?"

"I know what you mean. My mom was, like, thirty-two before she got her first gallery show."

"You have things to say. That means more than real estate and money and all this other crap. Everything the Society claims to be about, success and all that—what you've got is so much better." He laughed. "And on top of that, you're the only person I've ever heard of who's lied to the *New York*

Times about her age, *upward*."

"I thought seventeen sounded better. Stupid, I know."

"No," Nick said, "not stupid at all." He patted her on the back.

A breeze rustled the treetops below them, and there was an awkward pause as the two of them looked out at the park. Nick was about to lean in toward her when Phoebe's phone rang.

"I should get this," she said, looking at the caller ID. "It's my mom." She answered the phone, rolling her eyes.

When she was finished, she put her phone away. "I have to go," she said. "I'm sorry."

CHAPTER TWENTY-SIX

The trouble started at Chadwick when a senior pulled out a copy of *New York* magazine that she had picked up from a newsstand that morning. There had been several more weekly editions of Twilight Thursdays, and Nick had put in face time, but little more. The fight with Jared had subsided, although Nick was angry that he had been forced to forge a check on his parents' account, despite the fact that he hadn't been caught. He was still confused about the other mysterious checkbook, but was afraid to ask his father about it—there was no way, after all, that he could admit he'd been poking around in his dad's desk.

The girl, who had jet-black hair and a silver stud in her nose, read the review loudly in the hall to a group that had gathered: "The most exclusive new night in town is Twilight Thursdays, where prep school students Jared Willson and Nick Bell—whose teachers at Whitford and Chadwick apparently aren't noticing that their students aren't quite as attentive on Friday mornings—host a raucous crowd of vodka-swilling models, i-bankers, and underage scenesters."

The crowd laughed, as Nick cringed. He hadn't expected the press to reach this level, and he certainly hadn't known that his name would be used.

It took exactly three class periods for the headmaster to call a meeting of the entire school in the recently renovated auditorium. Dr. Wilkins, who had previously been a dean at a small college, was known for his adherence to the school rule book. While some of the younger board members, particularly those in media and entertainment, had given him a directive to lighten up Chadwick's image, the headmaster drew the line at issues of drugs and alcohol.

He stood on the stage behind a podium adorned with Chadwick's seal, a coat of arms. Nick was sitting with his class in his assigned seat, while Phoebe and Lauren were a few rows behind him. The classes buzzed with anticipation as the headmaster called the meeting to attention.

"I'm sure you're all familiar with our sixth rule," he said, after greeting everyone. "It's about 'compromising the good name of the school.' Now what does that mean? It's been made quite clear to you that drinking is not permitted on campus or during school hours. But what some of you don't realize is that that extends to after hours as well. This has been an issue for some time, although not until now has it come to a head."

There was a collective groan in the room. Nick felt his neck grow hot, as he feared Dr. Wilkins might call him out by name. And then the worst happened: The headmaster held up the copy of *New York* magazine. Snickering started among the students, particularly those in Nick's class.

"This magazine story does exactly that: It compromises Chadwick's name. In addition to the implication that students are drinking, this kind of thing is terribly embarrassing for the school. This is a college preparatory school, not just the place you go when you're not partying."

The students laughed.

"There's nothing humorous about it!" Dr. Wilkins said. "Any student suspected in the future of drinking, either on or off campus, will be suspended. I want the individual responsible for this article to see me in my office right after this assembly."

Nick sank down in his seat. This was worse than he thought. He wondered if this would get back to his parents; he had wanted them to be proud of him for the party, for how successful it had been, even though he had very little to do with that success. Now all he could feel was shame.

He didn't talk to anyone on his way out of the assembly, though he saw Phoebe, Lauren, and a few other friends giving him sympathetic looks. There was nothing for him to do but take his punishment, whatever it might be.

Nick showed up at Dr. Wilkins's office, but was asked by his secretary to wait. It was at least twenty minutes before the headmaster ushered him in.

"Nicholas," he said. "Please sit down." He motioned to a burgundy leather wingback in the corner of his book-lined office. Dr. Wilkins sat across from him. "I was just on the phone with your father."

"Sir, I can explain. I had no idea that the magazine—"

"Listen up. I had a good conversation with your dad. He told me about some of your ambitions, and he explained that this was all a misunderstanding. That is the power of the press, and you need to learn to be wary of it. He said you didn't even know there were reporters at your little event."

"Well, I—"

"What's important is that it doesn't happen again. Now, I'm going to have a discussion with the head at Whitford to make sure that Mr. Willson's exploits don't harm you further."

"I'm not too worried about that," Nick said. "Outside of the party, we're not even that close."

"That's good." Dr. Wilkins sighed. "I just want you to stay out of trouble. And do me a favor, don't get too caught up in, shall we say, your *social* activities, okay?"

Lauren was glad that she hadn't been dragged into any of the fracas about Nick's party, although she felt awful that Nick had to take the blame for all of them. Mostly, though, she had been thinking about her time with Alejandro. The night of Phoebe's gallery opening, he had been her date for the evening. He had insisted on holding her hand as they looked at the show. When they went to dinner at Bottino, an Italian restaurant nearby, he had pulled out her chair, asked her what she wanted, and then ordered for both of them, the way people did in old movies. There was this sweet side to him that was antithetical to the party-boy image he had cultivated. She wondered how much of that had been created by the gossip columns and blogs, by people who wanted him to be a certain way.

He lived with his parents in a suite at the St. Regis, which would have been the first drop-off for their cab, but he had insisted on escorting her home. They kissed the entire way uptown; it was one of those silly things that she now remembered fondly several days later, them trying to navigate a kiss as their cab bumped over potholes.

Even if her jewelry wasn't a smashing success, she thought, at least she had this—finally, someone who made her feel like everything else was worth it.

That all changed, though, when she got a call a few days later from Sebastian Giroux. It was early, before school started. Sebastian was always in a bit of a panic whenever he called, and this time was no exception.

"Lauren! Darling! You won't believe this!"

"What? Tell me!"

"According to Sabrina, we are completely sold out of your jewelry. We need more! We've ordered more stock from the manufacturer. But can you come up with other designs? Different designs? That's what people want. Things that are new. And—I must tell you. A boutique in Paris, one of the best, Colette, wants to carry your pieces! I have to go. Big kiss!"

She put down the phone in amazement. Maybe she had been too hasty in judging her own line. Maybe it just needed a little while to catch on. She knew she had more work to do.

On Friday afternoon, Patch was shopping at the Food Emporium on Third Avenue. Every week, it was his responsibility to get the groceries; his grandmother, who refused to learn how to use an ATM machine, would write a check out to "cash," and he would use it to buy the household provisions, enduring embarrassing stares from everyone in the checkout line as Genie's check was approved. This time, he was in the frozen foods section when he got an annoying text from a friend who raved about how amazing Nick's party at Twilight had been the night before. The reinstated ban on drinking had only made Jared and Nick's party more popular; everyone wanted to be part of the action, although they had to make sure they were never photographed. The club started enforcing specific rules on paparazzi being admitted, and Chadwick students were careful not to talk to anyone with a notebook.

Over the course of two months, Nick had become a person he didn't know anymore. Admittedly, Patch had ignored Nick at school, as well as at Lauren's birthday party and Phoebe's gallery opening. It wasn't only that he had been turned away at Twilight, a club Nick knew Patch had been dying to get into. Most of all, it was that everything Nick was involved in was now more important than their friendship.

It didn't matter that Nick had tried to apologize. It would take a lot more than an apology to fix this.

CHAPTER TWENTY-SEVEN

A few days later, during the week leading up to Thanksgiving break, Phoebe got a call from Michelle while she was walking home from school.

"There's a problem, sweetie," she said. "The works I told you about that were sold? They were picked up from the gallery, but not actually paid for."

"What do you mean?" Phoebe said. "Where are they?"

"That's the awful thing—we don't actually know. The client came recommended through a reputable art consultant, but we had never dealt with him before. He took the pieces on approval with the intention of buying them, which means he had the option of bringing them back if they didn't work out. We do this all the time; people like to test things out in their own homes, to live with a piece for a few days. But now we haven't heard from him."

"Did you get a credit card number or something?" This was so crazy. The money she was making was supposed to be saved for college. Now what she thought were some of her best works, the works that had contained Patch's imagery, were gone.

"We did," Michelle said. "But it turned out to be fraudulent. The authorization went through a few days ago, but then we were informed today that the card was a stolen one. I'm so sorry, Phoebe."

"This is absurd," Phoebe said. "So I don't get paid?"

"If you recall your contract, client damages are not the gallery's responsibility. It's rare that it happens, but it does. Phoebe, you have to remember that the rest of the show is terrific. You've been getting great notices. You'll be fine. Listen, I have to go. Talk later?"

"Sure," Phoebe said, snapping her phone closed and throwing it into her book bag. How could Michelle be so nonchalant about her works being stolen?

She looked at the caller ID. Michelle had called from the gallery, so she was sure to be there. Phoebe wondered if there would be any point to confronting her in person, but she decided against it. To push the issue with Michelle could get ugly, and it might put her mom's career at risk.

As she headed home on the subway, she blinked back tears, amazed that no one on the train noticed she was crying.

Maybe this was nothing more than the disappointment of life, the disappointment most people had learned to accept.

When she arrived at the townhouse, she collapsed onto her bed, exhausted, falling into a restless sleep.

A few hours later, Phoebe was woken by her cell, which she answered groggily.

"Phoebe, this is Parker Bell, Nick's father. There's a matter I need to speak with you about."

"Okay . . ." Phoebe said hesitantly, still dazed.

"I saw a preview of your show at the gallery, before your paintings were sold."

"They weren't sold," she said quietly. "Supposedly, they disappeared."

He ignored her comment. "I need to know where you got those photographs. You didn't take them yourself, I presume?"

"I had never seen them before in my life." She didn't know what to say. "I got them from someone in my class. I think you know him, he's a friend of Nick's?" She immediately realized what she had done and felt like an idiot for saying too much. Patch had specifically asked her not to reveal her source. "Mr. Bell, I'm not even sure they were really from him. I mean, I got images from all over: newspaper clippings, the Internet, old movies. It's hard for me to know which ones you're talking about."

"I think you know exactly which ones I mean. Did you ask him for the images, or did he give them to you?"

She thought back to that evening. She had asked Patch for the images, but the question of which images had been up to him.

"I don't know," she said. "I can't remember."

"As you know, the gallery can't sell those works. They have to be destroyed."

"What?" she asked, shocked. "Were *you* the mysterious buyer?"

Mr. Bell paused. "No, I wasn't. But some very concerned Society members arranged for them to be removed from the show. They found them quite disturbing."

Her works were *disturbing*? What were they talking about?

"Mr. Bell, they can't destroy my work! I mean, you must see how wrong that is."

"You have to understand that this is all for the best. They're only looking out for your interests."

As she had suspected, it had all been too good to be true. The dream always ended at some point. What was next? Would Michelle take down the rest of her show?

"Phoebe, this is important. We need to know the exact nature of the transaction between you and the individual who gave you the images."

Phoebe looked out the window, unsure of what to say. In a

moment of panic, she disconnected the call, hoping Mr. Bell would think her signal had dropped. She stood in her bed-room, out of breath. Who could she tell about this, besides Lauren? She couldn't mention it to Nick; he would find it too upsetting. She had no idea his dad could be so unpleasant.

She crumpled down onto the floor, barely able to breathe, and didn't move for several hours.

CHAPTER TWENTY-EIGHT

Late that night, unable to sleep, Phoebe knocked on her mother's door. There had been multiple voice mails on her phone, but she had ignored them all. Parker Bell had left her three messages, and there were two from the Administrator requesting a meeting to discuss the "gallery incident." Nick had sent her multiple text messages, but she didn't know how she could talk to him without telling him about his father. She wanted to call Anastasia, or even Lauren, for advice, but she was too ashamed.

"Mom, I need to talk to you."

"What is it?" Maia turned on the light and pulled out a pillow, motioning to Phoebe to sit on the bed with her.

Phoebe started sobbing. It felt as if the room were spinning. "I don't know where to start. There are these people, there's this group that I joined. It's so stupid. They're like this secret group, and they seem to know everything about me, and it's like I don't have any freedom anymore, and everything's messed up."

Maia looked at her strangely. "I'm not sure I understand. I mean, Phoebe, sweetheart, you're not making any sense. I know there was some confusion about one of Michelle's clients, but I thought all that had been resolved."

"Mom, there are these people. And they're really connected. They can do anything." Phoebe kept trying to explain her involvement with the Society to her mother, but she only managed to sound loonier each time.

"I think we'd better get you to a doctor," Maia said. "It sounds like your imagination is running away from you."

"No!" Phoebe screamed. "It's not my imagination. It's all real. Look at this!" She pulled away her hair and showed her mom the tattoo.

Her mother looked at it carefully. "Okay, so you got a tattoo. I can't say I'm thrilled, but it's nothing to get hysterical about."

"You're not understanding! We all have them. Everyone in this group. We're not supposed to tell anyone that we're in it."

"Why's that?"

"I don't know. They told us not to."

"Phoebe, honey, get some rest. I'm pulling you out of

school tomorrow. It's the last day before break anyway. I'll get you an appointment with a therapist. I think all the anxiety from the show has been getting to you."

Phoebe nodded, temporarily mollified. Maybe it would help to talk to someone about this, someone who could be objective. She used to have a therapist in Los Angeles, right after the divorce, but she hadn't seen anyone since moving to New York. She walked back to her bedroom, and even though her phone was still blinking with messages, she went right to sleep.

The next day, Phoebe and her mother took a cab up to Mount Sinai Hospital, where they were to see a well-respected psychiatrist, Dr. Alexander Meckling. Maia insisted on sitting in on the session. Phoebe explained what was going on with her, everything she was so upset about: the secret society, the gallery exhibit, the missing artwork.

Dr. Meckling gave her a saccharine smile. He was in his fifties, balding, and had a large red birthmark across the top of his head. "Phoebe, it sounds like you're suffering from what people call paranoid delusions. Are you really sure you saw all these things?"

"I know I saw these things. We all did. We were all there."

"Of course you were. Do you have any actual proof of all this? Besides what your friends say?"

Phoebe shook her head, thinking back to the printed scroll that she had dutifully destroyed back in September. "I have the tattoo. I told you about that."

Dr. Meckling nodded. "Yes, it's common for teenagers to get tattoos. You got it illegally, I suppose?"

"No, you don't understand—they gave it to me! I didn't have any control over it."

"Phoebe, that's a highly unlikely story. Why don't you tell us what really happened?"

"I already told you: There was a party, and they gave us this drink, and I don't remember much after that, but I know we walked out of there, and we all had these tattoos on the backs of our necks."

"Phoebe, this is all ridiculous," her mother said. "Just tell the doctor what really happened."

"Mom, you don't understand. Why won't either of you believe me? Where did you find this guy?"

"Who, Dr. Meckling? He's a friend of Daniel's."

A shiver ran to Phoebe's stomach. Daniel, who was also in the Society. She glared at Dr. Meckling.

"I'm out of here," Phoebe said, getting up.

"Phoebe! Sit down!" her mother said.

"Mom, you don't get it."

Dr. Meckling sat in his chair with a self-satisfied smile. His right hand went up to scratch something on the back of his neck.

Phoebe could guess what it was.

She couldn't believe any of this. Was her mother part of it, too? She was probably oblivious, but clearly she wasn't going to believe anything Phoebe said.

She took the elevator down alone, leaving her mother in Dr. Meckling's office. When she reached the street, Phoebe felt short of breath. She knew she should be in school, but she couldn't face it. She didn't even know if she felt safe going home. As she walked to the corner, she started seeing signs of the ankh everywhere: on buildings, in graffiti, carved into concrete. Maybe her mind was playing tricks on her. She hailed a cab and took it all the way downtown. Once home, she locked herself into her room, the only place she felt safe. She wished she could call Nick, but she felt too embarrassed about everything that had happened.

Her mother returned home an hour later. "Phoebe? Are you in there?"

"I'm not coming out. Not until you apologize. I don't know why you wouldn't believe me."

"The doctor gave me some prescriptions that I had filled. I'm going to leave them next to your door. You can come out when you're ready. Tomorrow is Thanksgiving Day. You can rest until you feel better."

Phoebe said nothing.

Later that day, after she had spent nearly five hours alone, she opened the door a crack. There were two vials sitting in the hallway. She snatched them up and read the labels: Xanax and Klonopin. She knew kids at school who would kill to get this stuff. She put the medications by her bedside table, not willing to take them, not yet.

CHAPTER TWENTY-NINE

Nick drove his Jeep out to the beach house late on Wednesday evening. He was meeting up with his family, including his grandfather and Nick's two brothers, Benjamin and Henry, who were coming home from Yale. It would be good to be out at the house, but he was nervous about Phoebe. He hadn't heard from her in two days, despite multiple texts and voice mails. He had done everything short of showing up at her house; he was worried that might seem like he was stalking her. He darted in and out of traffic on the Montauk Highway, passing luxury cars and minivans full of families, aware that he was driving too fast.

Things were not right. Phoebe had never not responded to him.

Everyone else had arrived earlier in the day, but Nick had

wanted to have his own car there. His Jeep was a broken-down old Cherokee, with a slight rattle whenever it started up and seating with a baked-in leather smell. It had been passed down from his two brothers, and it was a Bell family point of pride to be driving it. It was constantly going in to the shop, and Nick estimated that they had probably spent more on repairs than a new car would have cost, but it had become a family institution.

The gravel crunched under his tires as he pulled into the front drive. The Bells' main house was a classic 1920s shingle-style built on twelve acres in Southampton, two of which directly faced the beach. There were two tennis courts, a swimming pool, a formal garden, the cook's vegetable garden, a pool house, and assorted outbuildings, including a caretaker's cottage.

When Nick arrived at the house, he saw that Gertie had left a plate of meatloaf and string beans for him in the warming drawer of the white wainscoted kitchen. After he finished the meal, he padded back to his room to unpack. He had a whole wardrobe at the beach house, so he never needed to bring much. It was always comforting: tattered old jeans, ratty sweaters, the kind of clothes that fit perfectly and made you feel at home.

Before he got to his room, he heard a voice from the living room. The two double doors were closed.

"Nicholas, is that you?" It was his father's voice.

"Yes," Nick said, opening one door.

There was a roaring fire in the fireplace, above which was one of his family's most valuable pieces of art: an original Jackson Pollock painting. When it was up for auction at Sotheby's, his father had deemed it too modern, but his mother had prevailed, arguing it was appropriate that they show a local work, given that the painter had created it only a few towns away.

Nick's father sat with Nick's grandfather, Palmer Bell. His grandfather was an austere-looking man, lean and fit with a shock of white hair. He rose to greet Nick.

"Don't get up." Nick rushed over to him, but it was too late. Palmer Bell stood up to his full six feet four inches. Even though Nick was six-feet-two himself, it always seemed that his grandfather towered over him. "Give your granddad a hug," he said.

"When did you get back from Palm Beach?" Nick asked.

"Just this afternoon. Got in a round of golf this morning and then flew directly here. Can't believe the traffic at East Hampton Airport! Every jerk with a credit card flies private these days."

Nick nodded, not sure what to say.

His father broke in. "Nick, I'm afraid we have a bit of a situation."

Nick sat down. "What's that?"

Nick's father looked at Palmer. "We are among friends here," he said. "We can speak freely."

"Okay," Nick said.

"There is something we haven't been telling you. Your grandfather and I are very intimately involved with the Society. We didn't feel it was right until now for you to know."

"Involved how?" Nick and the other Initiates were so separate from the Society's leadership that he had never asked his dad more about the group. But now he remembered all the clues he had stumbled upon: the checkbook in his father's desk, the various comments Society members had made over the past few months.

The truth, he thought, was that his father hadn't exactly been forthcoming, and Nick hadn't really wanted to know.

"Were you there during the initiation?" Nick asked.

His father chuckled. "I was not. The Society leadership doesn't attend such functions of the junior membership."

"The Society leadership?" Nick was confused.

"Let me put it bluntly," his father said. "I am the current Chairman of the Society. That means I am in charge of all the Elders and of the Council of Regents."

A chill ran through Nick. "What are the Regents?"

"The Regents are the ruling body of the Society. None of your fellow Initiates know any of this, and they are not permitted to know until the annual retreat."

"The annual retreat?"

"Son, you must have noticed how your grandfather and I are away each year between Christmas and New Year's?"

"For your hunting trip, right?"

"We don't go hunting," Parker said.

Palmer snickered. "Haven't gone in twenty years. Almost wish I had."

Parker continued in a serious tone, "The annual retreat for the Society is on Isis Island. A private island off the coast of Maine. Not even on some maps. We welcome the Initiates; all the Regents, the Conscripts, and many of the Elders will be there." He paused for a moment.

"Nick, your grandfather, you should be proud to know, is the Chairman Emeritus of the Society. He was head of the Society for twenty-two years. Led it through some of its best times. Before things got, well, distasteful. The world has changed so much. With the way things are headed now, there are economic realities we must face. We can't afford to let our way of life be compromised over petty matters."

"What does all this have to do with me?" Nick asked.

"These are desperate times, Nick," Parker continued. "We must do what we need to do. And we have a problem."

"What's the problem?" Nick asked.

"The problem," his grandfather said, "is your friend Patch."

CHAPTER THIRTY

The night before Thanksgiving, Patch was working late in the editing suite. He was squeezing in every minute of free time he could in order to work on the show. The next day, he and Genie would have dinner together in the apartment, just a small turkey for the two of them. There were times when the Bells had invited them for Thanksgiving, but those invitations had dried up in recent years. Simone, who was also working late, came in from her makeshift office next door.

"We need to talk," she said.

"What about?" Patch said, turning away from the screen.

"I found some of your handiwork from the AVID."

"Yeah?"

She took a DVD from the stack she was carrying and popped it into a player. Images came up on the screen from the Society initiation. Patch swore he had stored it in a private file, password protected it, the works.

"Where did you get this?"

"One of the interns found it on the backup tape. Is there a problem?"

Patch groaned. That's right—he had password protected the material, but every night the server made a backup tape of the day's work. He had tested out some material from the Night of Rebirth, creating a rough edit, although he hadn't thought anyone would ever see it. But he had left it in his folder overnight, so the server had made a copy.

"I think we've got our story here. You've got everyone—the Bell kid and the two girls."

"No, Simone, you don't understand—we can't use this stuff. This was private. It was sort of a ritual thing that I taped. I wasn't supposed to be there. We don't have releases."

"Are these Chadwick students?" she asked.

Patch nodded. "The three of them are."

"Then we're sure as hell going to have releases for them."

"Simone, we can't do this—it's a very serious group. It's like a cult or something. You don't know what you're dealing with."

"Kiddo, I've dealt with much worse than a bunch of sixteen-year-olds partying and getting tattoos. Try chasing insane meth dealers all over Jersey and then tell me about danger."

Patch sank back in his chair. "I'm not sure you understand. I will get my ass kicked if this goes public."

"Look, we'll see about that. But in the meantime, we need more stuff like this."

Patch shook his head. "No can do."

"If you want to get this show made, you're going to have to get in there. You have no idea the kind of competition we're up against."

"Let me think about it," he said, hoping it would stall her. Maybe the show wouldn't get made. He would miss out on the chance to distinguish himself through his work. After all, he wasn't part of any secret society. He didn't have rich parents; he barely had parents at all. He was tired of getting everyone's sympathy. He wanted to stand apart from his classmates, and *Chadwick Prep* was the way he could do that.

"Patch, you signed over the rights to all footage involving Chadwick students," she said. "Whether or not we get releases, we own this."

He nodded. The check he had gotten, a ten-thousand-dollar option that was good for one year and gave the producers the right to use his material and sell the show to a network or cable channel, had authorized them to use any and all video that he had taken.

And that would include the Society initiation.

He had never intended for Simone to find it, but he had also never thought she would go poking around in some archived files on the backup tape.

"Take the DVD home and think about it," Simone said. "And don't you worry—I have a copy."

Patch signed out for the day, saying good night to Simone and cursing the fact that he had ever left the material on the server. He headed out to West Thirty-sixth Street, a dimly lit industrial block, full of warehouses, parking garages, and storage facilities—not the type of place where it felt safe to go walking at night.

There was a black town car idling by the curb. Its window slid down, revealing a brutish man with a prominent white scar on his neck.

"Car for Patchfield Evans?" said the man.

"I don't think so," Patch said, as he turned to go down the block.

The man in the passenger seat and the driver stepped out, both in dark suits.

"Let us give you a ride home," the first man said.

"Why?"

The men stepped forward, one on each side of Patch, gripping his shoulders. "Just get in the car, kid."

Patch struggled, but they had a stronghold on him. They pushed him into the backseat of the car and got back in. The driver started up the engine and began driving east.

"What do you want?" Patch said. He frantically examined his surroundings. Standard black town car. Doors locked.

Shiny chrome and wood trim.

"You have some footage that's been causing a lot of trouble," said the man with the scar.

"I don't know what you're talking about," Patch said. They were crossing Ninth Avenue, heading toward Eighth. He wondered if they got stuck in a more populated area, they might be stalled long enough for him to jump out. He tried the lock on the door, but it wouldn't move.

"You know exactly what we're talking about."

"No, seriously, I don't," Patch said.

"Maybe your grandmother can convince you. Why don't you give her a call?" They had turned and were now on Eighth Avenue.

Patch nervously dialed home, and a man picked up on the second ring. "Yeah?"

"Let me talk to Genie," Patch said angrily. "If you have done anything to her—"

There was a rustling on the line, and then Patch heard Genie's voice. "Hello?"

"Genie, are you okay?"

"I'm fine, dear. I think you should know there are some men here who came to see me."

"How many men?"

"Two."

Goddammit. He had always worried about this day when someone would trick their way into the building. It was far too easy to fool Genie, even as sharp as she could be. She probably thought it was a food delivery or something.

"What do they want?"

The tone in her voice changed, just enough so Patch could recognize it. "I think you'd better speak to whomever you're with and do what they say. You understand?"

Patch nodded. "I understand. Genie, be careful."

"Don't you worry about me." Her voice suddenly became steely, clearly addressing the men in the room. "These men are just leaving, aren't you two?"

She hung up.

Patch addressed the men. "What do you want?" he said, shaking a bit. They had passed Columbus Circle and were heading up Central Park West.

"Give us whatever footage you have, and consider this a warning that you'd better not do anything with the rest. The smartest thing for you to do would be to destroy it. You got that?"

Patch couldn't stop shaking. He rustled around in his messenger bag and held up the DVD. "Here's all I have. Just don't, don't hurt my grandmother. I'm calling the cops if those guys aren't gone when I call her back."

"You're not calling anyone. Get out of the car. And kid?"

"What?" Patch said.

"Watch yourself. We're not the only surprises they've got in store for you. I think your grandmother would be really upset if something happened to you."

The car pulled to a stop on Central Park West, near Tavern on the Green. They unlocked the door, and Patch scrambled out, still shocked. He needed to walk this off. They seemed to be satisfied to have the disc, as the car merged into the traffic heading uptown.

He decided that the best thing to clear his head would be to walk home, across the park.

III

CLEOPATRA'S NEEDLE

CHAPTER THIRTY-ONE

The news reached everyone on Thanksgiving Day.

Murders and suicides happened all the time in New York, but it was rare that they were so dramatic: a body found at the base of Cleopatra's Needle in Central Park on Thanksgiving, nearly naked but apparently untouched. When Nick saw the crime scene footage on the local news channel, he gasped. The victim, still unidentified, was around his own age.

"This is absolutely horrible," said Nick's mother, as they were sitting in the breakfast area with the late edition of the *Post*. "I don't know how things like this happen." She poured fresh-squeezed orange juice from a glass pitcher for everyone.

"Fast living," said Henry, who was by far, among the three brothers, the most uptight.

The whole thing gave Nick a queasy feeling. During his conversation with his father and grandfather the previous evening, he had let it slip that he knew Patch had taken the video. They were already aware of its existence, but it was particularly awkward to have to admit to them that Patch had told him about it two days after the Night of Rebirth. His father was angry that Nick hadn't gone directly to him, but Nick wasn't buying it. After all, his dad had given him no directives on how to deal with a situation like this.

And besides, did they expect him to rat out his friend?

He had gone over the issue with them, trying to convince them that Patch was not going to be a problem, that Patch understood the potency of the material and would keep it under lock and key.

Neither of them had seemed convinced.

The following morning, Phoebe was making some tea in the kitchen, the first time she had been out of her room in nearly twenty-four hours. She opened her phone to find a text message:

BE READY FOR THE BEACH IN AN HOUR.

She groaned. The beach? At this time of year? She was so confused. She had been sleeping almost constantly since her breakdown; she had even begged off Thanksgiving dinner, which her mother had had with Daniel at a restaurant in Tribeca. There were tons of voice mails on her cell, but she hadn't found the courage to listen to them yet. She finally decided she would call Nick to ask his advice on what to do.

He picked up on the first ring, and she felt an instant sense of relief. "Hey," he said. "I was worried about you. I think somewhere between messages nine and ten, I got the idea that maybe you were ignoring me."

"I'm sorry," Phoebe said. "I had—what's the best way to put this—let's just say I had a bit of a meltdown."

"It's vacation, you should be relaxing."

"I guess that's what I've been doing, if you can call napping in a Xanax-induced stupor relaxing."

"I'm so sorry, Phoebe." His voice was so quiet, so serious, that it made her want to be with him.

"Don't stress, I'll be fine," she said, attempting to brush off his concerns.

"So what's up?"

"I need to know—did you get this message about the beach?"

"There's a meeting at a house in Southampton. That's all I know. There's some kind of special situation. I think it has to do with the body that was found in the park."

Phoebe paused. She had read about it yesterday online; the

news was so appalling. "Nick, I can't do this anymore. This is all too messed up. I mean, you heard what happened to my paintings, right?"

"I did," he said. "No one blames you, Phoebe. It was just a weird thing. You didn't know Patch was going to send you those images of the initiation."

"I'm sorry—what did you say the images were of? And how did you know they were from Patch?"

"Phoebe, they were from the initiation—Patch filmed it. You were there. You don't remember?"

"Not those parts of it." Phoebe shook her head. "I blacked out that night. Oh, my God. No wonder they've been furious with me." She thought for a moment. "I, um, feel weird talking about this, but your dad called me."

"Oh, man, you can't take him that seriously. Look, just pack up and come out here. You can stay with me."

"Nick, I'm not sure your family wants me around."

"I'll explain it to them. It'll be fine. I'll tell them it was a misunderstanding. That you didn't know what the images were of."

"Okay," she said, resigned.

"Phoebe?" Nick paused for a moment. "I can't wait to see you."

CHAPTER THIRTY-TWO

By Friday, word had gotten around the Chadwick community that a young man, possibly a prep school student, had been found dead in the park. For Patch, as he read the horrible news in the papers, it hit far too close to home. The evening of the murder—if, in fact, it was a murder—Patch had walked across the park, right past the needle, had seen it glimmering in the moonlight.

It could have been him.

He sat in the kitchen with Genie, the Friday papers surrounding them. "Genie, you have to promise me: no more letting strange men up into the apartment anymore." He hadn't wanted to be too hard on her on Thanksgiving, but now that it was Friday, Patch felt like he had to drum it into her.

"Patchfield, I'm sorry. They said they had a food delivery.

I thought maybe you'd ordered something ahead of time so that it would be here for you when you got home. Remember how upset you were with me a few weeks ago when I didn't let up that Chinese delivery boy?"

"I know. I'm sorry. I'll always let you know if I'm going to do that in the future."

Patch thought about everything that had happened. The game was up. There was no way he could use the material: Being threatened over it made it impossible even to think of involving the Society in his show.

Chadwick Prep wasn't going to happen. Which totally, completely blew.

Patch sighed. Why was it always this way? Why did there always seem to be some bigger, richer, more powerful group or person who was getting in the way of his dreams? Throughout their childhood, it had always been Nick who was the popular one, and now it was the Society that was messing with his aspirations of having his own television show. Maybe he would have to wait, he thought. Maybe having his vlog would be enough for now.

Adding to everything, Simone had called him on Thursday morning, when he had barely had time to process the events of the previous night. She wished him a happy Thanksgiving before getting to the point. "You've heard the news by now, right?" she had said. "I'm sending a cameraman over to the scene. I think we've got a major story here. This could be one of our arcs that would really get a network hooked."

"Wait, what are you talking about?" Patch asked.

"You don't know? The kid in the park. It's someone from your social set. They're saying it's an Upper East Side kid."

This was too much—it was gruesome. The onlookers, the media, the images of the body being taken away. The press was lapping it up, and Patch didn't want any part of it. He imagined how the guy's parents must have felt, how his friends were feeling, whoever he was.

Detectives had been saying how bizarre the death was, how the body was presented as if it were some kind of ritual offering. The cause of death had been hypothermia, but it was unclear why he was nearly naked at the end of November, and why he had been placed at the foot of Cleopatra's Needle, below seven stories of Egyptian hieroglyphics. Was it a drug thing? A cult? It didn't make sense.

Even with the scantest amount of information, Patch suspected the Society may have had something to do with it.

"Patch, are you there?" Simone had said. "I want you to go over to the needle. Check out the scene. Get some more material."

"You're joking."

"You say you want to be in television. That means doing difficult things sometimes."

"Simone, I can't." He took the phone into the hallway. "It's too . . . too exploitative. This guy died and it's really sad, but we should let the real news cover this stuff."

"Patch, you don't seem to get it. I'm not *asking* you to do it. I'm *telling* you to do it."

Patch took a deep breath. "And I'm telling you that I'm not doing it, Simone. I'll see you on Monday. Enjoy your Thanksgiving."

CHAPTER THIRTY-THREE

Phoebe arrived midday on Friday at the Southampton house in the car that had been sent for her. So many different scenarios about the Society had gone through her head during the two-and-a–half-hour ride, she didn't know what was the truth. She knew she trusted Nick, but she was unsure about everything else. How was his family involved? Why was his father such a jerk? And what about her mother? How had she allowed herself to be romanced by this guy Daniel? To send her to a doctor who was clearly part of the Society? And now these pills: She had been taking them, although she knew she needed to stop. She hadn't wanted to at first, but they did relax her to the point that she no longer worried so much about things, that she could at least function, sleep through the night. They made her feel like everything was going to be fine.

The house was a 1904 Tudor revival on eight acres of land, surrounded by an English parterre, a croquet court, tennis courts, a reflecting pool, and beyond that, potato fields to shield the property from onlookers.

Phoebe ran into Lauren in the entryway of the large home, and the two hugged. "Where have you been?" Lauren asked. "I left you, like, five messages."

"I'm sorry," Phoebe said. "I'll explain later."

Nick came up behind her and gave her a hug. She inhaled the comforting smell of his freshly washed hair.

"Everything's going to be okay," he whispered. "I promise." She wanted to hold on to him, to stay in his arms, grab onto his green wool sweater, and make everything else disappear.

The Administrator rang a bell for all of them to convene in the living room; Miss Stapleton seemed particularly anxious to get the meeting underway. It was the entire class of Initiates who had gathered, as well as all the Conscripts; apparently most had already been on the East End, and those who hadn't had cars sent for them.

The Administrator spoke, and Phoebe saw that her comments were directed at Nick's father, who was sitting in a leather wingback in the corner. "The doors are secured, sir."

"Thank you, Miss Stapleton." Nick's father stood up. "Good afternoon, everyone. My name is Parker Bell, and I am representing all the Elders today. We are extremely distressed by what happened to one of our current class of Conscripts. As you may know, the police announced an hour ago that the body found in the park was that of Jared Willson."

The group gasped as Mr. Bell continued.

"The authorities are searching for the precise reasons behind Jared's death. I think we can firmly say that his passing can serve as a cautionary tale about the dangers of alcohol abuse. Jared, as some of you know, had issues with chemical dependency. One fact that young people don't realize is that copious amounts of liquor, combined with near-freezing temperatures, can be fatal. The sense we've gotten from the police is that that is what happened to Jared."

A wave of whispers rippled through the crowd. Was Mr. Bell saying Jared had *frozen to death*?

"Meanwhile, we are extremely concerned about all of your well-being. We have a world-renowned psychiatrist here to help any of you with your particular grief issues. You can see him if you have any problems or even if you just want to talk. Dr. Meckling, will you stand up?"

Phoebe felt her neck grow white-hot, as Dr. Meckling stood. She shot Nick a look, although she was sure he wouldn't know what it meant.

Dr. Meckling gave a friendly wave to the crowd. Phoebe doubted that anyone would want to speak to him.

"We will take questions individually after the meeting," Mr. Bell said.

"I have a question right now, actually," Thaddeus Johnson said, standing up. "Who is the leader of the Society? Will we ever find out who's running the show here?"

The crowd started whispering again. Phoebe admired him for speaking up.

"As the current class of Conscripts knows, much more will become apparent during the retreat at Isis Island. Now, why don't you all enjoy the buffet lunch that's waiting for you out on the sunporch?"

After the group broke up and started eating, Phoebe went to the powder room, which was halfway down a long hallway in the east wing of the house. When she came back, she saw someone sitting in the library, past an arched corridor at the end of the hall. It was a girl muttering something to herself. Phoebe walked closer to see that it was Anastasia, scribbling furiously in her notebook.

Phoebe didn't want to interrupt her, so she crept quietly into the room.

Anastasia was murmuring to herself, *"You join and they own you. They always try to phone you. Say something and then you're dead. Get a drug right in your head . . ."*

It was like a childhood nursery rhyme, and it freaked Phoebe out. She turned away, hoping they wouldn't need to talk, when Anastasia called out her name.

She turned around slowly. "Hi," she said. "Um, are you okay?"

"I'm fine," Anastasia said. "I'm just upset. Jared and I were sort of . . ."

"Together?" Phoebe asked.

"Yes. And I—to have him gone like this. It's such a shock."

"What was that that you were saying a second ago? I'm sorry, I overheard."

"Oh, I was just writing something. Like a poem."

"Sounded sort of strange."

Anastasia smirked. "Well, I guess I have permission now to be a little strange, don't I?"

Phoebe gave her a hug, because she didn't know what else to do. The whole goth artist act had never really appealed to Phoebe. She hated herself for thinking it, but it was almost as if now Anastasia really had something that would make her the center of attention, more so than reading her diary on the train or making films of herself sitting on the toilet.

"Anastasia, can I ask you something?"

"Of course." She smoothed away her black bob.

Phoebe lowered her voice. "Can you tell me what's going on here? I mean, who is running this whole operation? Thad asked the question, but no one wanted to say anything. Clearly, Nick's dad is a big part of it. But whose house is this? Where does all the money come from? Like, who pays for the lunch that everyone's eating right now?"

"Phoebe, I can't talk about stuff like that. You know I can't."

Phoebe groaned quietly. "This is so frustrating, though! Why are they keeping so many secrets from us?"

Anastasia put her hand on Phoebe's, as Phoebe noticed her bloodred nails. "You have to trust me on this. A lot will become clear during the retreat. The whole class of Conscripts and all the Initiates are together, along with a lot of the Elders. It comes out to something like two hundred people. They explain to you more of what's going on."

"Why can't they make it clear now?"

"They're testing you," Anastasia said. "They want to make sure you can be loyal, to make sure you can survive in a group. Of course, with what happened to Jared, I don't think they'll have any problem with our class."

"What do you mean?"

Anastasia looked down the hallway, toward the sound of the voices in the other rooms that were chattering on. She spoke slowly. "Jared was with all of us on the night that he died. We all saw him."

"How is that possible?"

"There was a dinner for our class, followed by a ritual in the park. It's something the Conscripts do every year, or so we were told. It was a freak accident—we didn't know what to do when we found Jared collapsed like that. It was Charles who found him, and he tried to revive him, but it was hopeless. It's not normally that cold at this time of year, and most people don't drink like Jared does. It was a horrible combination of circumstances."

"Why was he almost naked?"

"That was part of it. One member was to be nominated to say a purification ritual in front of the needle, to atone for the sins of the group, while the rest of us waited nearby, under Greywacke Arch. Charles and the other guys nominated Jared to do it."

"So Jared was your martyr."

Anastasia looked at Phoebe as if she had insulted her. "Yes, but in a symbolic way—nothing was supposed to happen to him!"

Phoebe was silent.

"We were all drinking," Anastasia continued. "We were all drunk. I mean, how would he have known?"

Phoebe nodded, although she was hardly satisfied by the answer. "So will you all be questioned by the police?"

"We can't. The publicity is too much. We all want to get into college. Imagine what the media would say—they would want a list of everyone who was there."

Phoebe was already picturing the headlines about cultish rituals and last suppers.

"So you all have to stay silent," Phoebe said.

"That's what they're saying. Charles called us all individually. The case will be closed in a few days. They're very connected, you know. All it takes is one call to the right person and the case gets shut down."

"But that's impossible!"

"Think about it, Phoebe. You know how there are certain deaths where no one ever really knows what happened?" She named an actor who had died the previous year of mysterious causes in his hotel room. "Remember how there was a big scandal for a week and talk of an investigation, the cover of *US Weekly*, the whole works? And then everyone just forgets about it? The same thing will happen. People will forget about Jared." She started crying.

"You have to stop that from happening!" Phoebe said. "You have to fight for what you believe."

"I can't do that, Phoebe," Anastasia said. "I know from past experience that it doesn't pay. The only person who gets hurt in the end is the one who speaks out."

CHAPTER THIRTY-FOUR

On Friday afternoon, Patch and Genie took the train up to Westchester to visit his mother, Esmé, at the Stoney River Psychiatric Hospital. Patch had dreaded the visits ever since his mother had been institutionalized. The facility had steel doors with double-glazed panes, bars on the windows, and no locks on the restrooms, in case someone tried to kill herself. Adding to the fact that the hospital was depressing in and of itself—and it was known to be one of the nicer ones in the area—it was awful to see his mother in such a state.

Esmé had her own room, and she spent her days reading newspapers and magazines; she had ten different subscriptions. She refused to go outside, which Patch always thought was odd. The facility in Ossining had landscaped grounds (albeit grounds that were surrounded by a chain-link fence), but she wanted to stay inside, content to look out her window.

The first visit was to her doctor, whom they always consulted. "She's doing better," he said. "Your mother, as you know, has borderline personality disorder, which takes form in obsessive ruminating over one particular topic. Is she ready to come out anytime soon? I don't think so. The topics change, from month to month. But we can't have her out among the other residents for too long at a time, because she scares people. And if she can't handle that, she certainly can't handle the outside world."

Patch and his grandmother nodded. He knew it was awful for Genie, seeing how her daughter had deteriorated over the years; although she was no longer immobile, as she had been when she was admitted ten years ago, she still lacked many of the basic skills needed to function in the world. Genie visited once a week, but she felt Patch should visit only every few months, as she said she knew how difficult it was for him to see his mother in this condition. Besides, the facility's visiting hours often conflicted with his class schedule.

When they entered her room, Esmé was surrounded by reading material. Apparently, she read everything cover to cover, but when the attendants asked her what her name was, she could answer them only half the time.

"Hi, Mom," Patch said, sitting on the edge of her bed, where she was perched cross-legged like a child.

She pointed to the *Post*, to the story about Jared Willson. "They got him," she said.

"What do you mean, 'They got him'?"

"That poor boy. Didn't know what was happening. Got lost in the night. Dead in the morning."

"Mom, you're not making sense. Maybe you shouldn't be reading this kind of stuff. It's too sad."

"Don't tell me that!" she screamed. "Everyone tells me that. I don't even know why I'm here."

Genie spoke firmly. "You're here because you hit your doctor in the face five years ago. Remember that? You're here because you ran away from home constantly. Because you lost Patch in the park one day."

It was true: When Patch was six years old, shortly after his father's death, Esmé had forgotten to bring him home. Patch had spent three hours at the playground in Central Park, with no idea where his mother was.

"I am not fit to be a mother," Esmé said.

"Oh, come on, Mom, nobody's saying that," Patch said. "I think you're great. You just need to take your meds and get rest and be good to yourself. Are you going outside at all? Did you see the fall leaves?"

"No! No going outside! People get killed going outside. People get killed by groups. Groups of people killing."

"Oh, dear," Genie said. "Let's try not to rile her up."

"We're going to go for a walk now," Patch said. "We'll be

back in a little bit."

He gave her a hug and then turned away. He felt tears welling up inside him, but he willed them to go away.

Genie reached the hallway, grabbing his hand. "You need to be strong," she said. "You have to know that it's not her. She has no control over what she's saying. Let's go outside. If your mother isn't going to enjoy the grounds here, at the very least we can."

They went downstairs and out the front door. The leaves had turned, and while many were on the ground, there were still a few sparse survivors hanging from the trees. Patch wrapped his wool scarf tightly around his neck.

"What do you think she meant, Genie, when she said, 'They got him'?"

She shook her head. "I don't know. Esmé supposedly suffers from paranoid distortions. She says some variation of 'They got him' or 'They got her' every time she reads about a death or a murder. Doesn't matter who it is, where it happened. There's always a mysterious 'they.'"

"I want to take her out. Being out in the world, getting some fresh air, might make her feel better."

The leaves crunched under their feet. "We've tried," she said. "You remember, two years ago."

"I know, it was a disaster." The first night she had stayed in the apartment, his mother had wound up naked and running down Fifth Avenue. When the police picked her up and brought her back home (thankfully, the doormen recognized her), she claimed she was just going out to get the mail.

"She can't be outside," Genie said firmly. "Not when she's behaving like this."

"Do you think . . ." Patch paused, not knowing how to say it. "Do you think the Society has anything to do with this?"

Genie didn't reply as they headed back to the hospital's entrance. Before he could press her, something caught his eye. Carved into a wood panel on the lobby wall were the names of individuals and corporations who had donated to the hospital's renovation. Near the top of the list, one name stood out: THE BELL FOUNDATION. He wondered why they had made such a prominent donation. Patch knew that his parents and the Bells had all been friends once, long ago, but those days were gone. The Bells didn't like to associate themselves with anyone sick or infirm, and his mother most definitely fell under both categories.

When they got back up to her room, his mother was more subdued; Patch imagined that a nurse had given her a sedative. She sat at a makeshift dressing table in the corner of the room and was pinning up her hair.

Genie put her hand to her mouth, as if she were seeing a ghost of someone she had once known.

Patch saw what he had never noticed before.

Branded into the back of his mother's neck was a half-inch-tall scar in the shape of an ankh.

CHAPTER THIRTY-FIVE

After lunch, Lauren met up with Alejandro in the back gardens of the Southampton house, near the croquet court. "Can we get out of here?" she said. "This place scares me. I already said good-bye to Phoebe and Nick."

Alejandro's parents were renting a place nearby for the season, and he asked Lauren to follow him there. She was borrowing an extra car, an older Volvo that belonged to her mother's friend Madeline, so she followed Alejandro, who was driving his father's Jaguar. They arrived at the house, pulling into the gravel driveway. "My parents are away for the rest of the day," he said. "The place is ours."

The house the Callejas were renting was a boxy white palace—more like something out of South Beach than Southampton—that was filled with mid-century modern furniture.

Out back, there was a heated swimming pool and a hot tub that emptied into it from a height of five feet, creating a bubbling, churning pool. Steam rose up from it, as Alejandro said it was kept at eighty degrees, year-round.

"Want to go swimming?" he said.

Lauren blushed. "I don't have a suit."

He dragged her outside, grinning. "Neither do I." He started throwing off his clothes, and for a moment she thought he was going to go in naked. But he stopped at his briefs—they were, it seemed, the skinniest micro-briefs Lauren had ever seen—and jumped in, executing a perfect dive into the frothy bubbles, his legs leaving barely a splash before they disappeared underwater.

Lauren shrugged and stripped down to her underwear. Maybe this was what they needed: something fun to balance out all the insanity. She jumped into the water, bobbing up next to him. Alejandro pressed a button on the floating remote in the pool, and music came out of the underwater speakers. The water enveloped them, hugging them, saving them from the madness that they had left behind at the house.

"Sorry, it's not my music," he said. "The people we're renting from left their iPod here."

Lauren shrugged. "I love it. Like an underwater concert." It was playing a remix of the Rolling Stones' "Sympathy for the Devil."

They splashed around for a bit, and he embraced her in

his strong arms, kissing her. She wished they could stay in the warm pool forever. Lauren wrapped herself around his muscular body and let him lift her up on his shoulders, laughing as they both fell, crashing into the water again. Alejandro kissed her while she was holding her breath underwater, which made Lauren laugh so much, she had to come up for air.

When they were tired, they swam over to the steaming hot tub. Alejandro flipped a switch, and the spa stopped flowing into the pool. It was nearly silent, save for the sound of birds in the distance and the rustling of nearby trees.

"It's gorgeous here," Lauren said, as she gazed at the overcast sky, framed by evergreens. "Almost makes me forget everything else."

"I think that's what we need," Alejandro said.

"Do you ever feel," Lauren asked, after a pause, "like maybe they're trying to make us into something we're really not?"

"Sure," he said. "But they can't make you into anyone you don't want to be." He stroked her wet hair.

"Do you believe that?"

"I don't know," he said. "I do know that I can't live like this. Too many expectations. I want to break free and not have to worry about what any of this means to the Society or to my parents or whatever."

"What do you think happened to Jared?" she asked. "Do you think he really died of exposure? It seems like such a messed-up thing to happen."

"I can't say. I never knew him. I guess maybe Nick would know? But it sounds like they didn't know each other all that well."

"Can I ask you something?" Lauren said.

"Of course."

"Are your parents Society members?"

He shook his head. "I don't think so. I think I would have known by now."

"I don't think mine are either."

There were so many questions unanswered, but for the first time in ages, Lauren felt relaxed, as if she could let go. They enjoyed the warmth of the hot tub, kissing again, her body against his, as he sat on the spa's underwater steps. After a few more minutes, Alejandro gently motioned to her that they should get up. He grabbed two towels for them from a nearby cabana, and they rushed inside to warm up again.

She followed him upstairs, a pile of clothes in her arms, not quite knowing what to expect. At his room, he handed her a pair of pajamas and showed her the bathroom, so she could change.

He put on a pair as well, although he kept the top open, which she didn't mind at all—Alejandro had one of the best bodies she had ever seen on a seventeen-year-old, much more impressive than her ex-boyfriend's scrawny physique. On the couch in his bedroom, she started kissing Alejandro again, inhaling the scent of chlorine and fresh laundry, and instead of feeling fun and silly like it had in the pool, this time it felt electric, as if his body's energy were coursing through her. She decided to let whatever was to happen, happen. The Society couldn't touch them here.

As he tried to enjoy the last few days of Thanksgiving break, Patch couldn't stop thinking about something Genie had said to him when they were in the train headed back to the city. His grandmother always acted a bit stoic after visits to her daughter. He didn't want her to be sad, but it was hard not to be, especially after his mother's nutty behavior.

"Genie, I need to ask you something," he had finally said.

She had looked at him warily. Behind her, he could see the Hudson River through the window, its waters moving slowly with the current. They passed the different stops: Philipse Manor, Sleepy Hollow, the land of Ichabod Crane and the Headless Horseman. Greystone, Riverdale, and Spuyten Duyvil, a name he had always thought was so strange when he took this route as a child.

They would be heading into the city soon.

"The Bells—why are they on that wall at the entrance to the hospital?"

"They gave a donation," she said simply.

"I know that. But I mean, why there? Why not somewhere nicer, somewhere closer to the city? Is it because of Mom?"

Genie moved so she was sitting right next to Patch. "The

Bells and your parents used to be very close. A long time ago, before her breakdown."

"Why won't you ever talk about what happened? It was before Dad died, right?"

She nodded. "Patch, I can't talk about it. You know that."

"Does it have anything to do with the Society? The ankh on her neck—was my mother . . . a member?"

"It was so long ago, Patch. I think it's better if we don't speak about it."

A look passed between them. Genie knew him too well to think an admonition like that would keep him away.

Phoebe's expectations of the Bell household were completely confounded by its reality. It was a large estate with a full household staff, which she had expected, but other than that, everything seemed so normal. She met Nick's mother, Gigi, for the first time, and the woman treated her as if they had known each other for ages and were going to be best girl-friends. Mr. Bell was in his study, but when he came down later, he seemed truly pleased to meet her. Although Phoebe couldn't stop thinking about it, he acted as if their conversation on the phone earlier that week had never happened. Everyone treated her like Nick's new girlfriend, which secretly excited her.

Nick seemed embarrassed by it all, and his older brothers, Henry and Benjamin, even ribbed him a bit, giving Nick winks and nudges. For the first time, Phoebe saw Nick actually blush, something she hadn't even thought him capable of. Instead of the household of a captain of industry that she had expected, the Bells seemed so welcoming that Phoebe tried to forget about Parker Bell and his ties to the Society. She got settled in an upstairs bedroom, right down the hall from Nick's, a bedroom that was usually, according to Nick, occupied by Patch. It made Phoebe wonder if she would ever be more than Nick's friend.

They installed themselves on the sunporch and watched stupid action movies and ate Thanksgiving leftovers. Nick seemed to want to numb himself from the horrible news about Jared, to pretend it hadn't happened. Phoebe looked at the flickering light from the television on Nick's handsome features. He was beautiful all the time, but particularly when he was concentrating.

Only she would think that was cute. She could be so dumb sometimes. If he liked her as more than a friend, he would have made the moves on her by now, wouldn't he?

She sank back into the chintz sofa, dejected, taking a long, last swig of her beer as the movie ended. Back to reality. Back to the Society and everything they couldn't figure out.

Nick looked at her, giving her a friendly poke on the arm. "You doing okay?"

"Um—actually, I'm not really sure. I'm kind of freaked out. All this—the Society, the doctor my mom made me see,

Jared dying—I'm sorry, I know I shouldn't be talking about it." She felt tears coming. No, she wouldn't do that. But she couldn't stop them. First one, then another. Why couldn't she be cool about all this stuff, more like Lauren?

"I'm so sorry, Nick," she said, as she tried to stop her tears. "I must be such a drag to be around."

Nick moved closer on the sofa and started gently rubbing her back. She felt a slight quivering in his hand, as if he were nervous, and she turned toward him.

"It's okay," he said, in the same assured way that he had that day at the coffee shop, when he had promised he would be there for her.

She smiled through her damp eyes. "I'm so ridiculous. I shouldn't be breaking down. This is so embarrassing." She rubbed the back of her hand across her face in an attempt to wipe her tears and the snot in her nose. She couldn't look at him, not in this state.

"You're not ridiculous," he said, as he parted her hair with one finger and tucked it behind her ear. "You're beautiful."

She looked up, and before she could do anything, he kissed her.

It was everything she had been waiting for, the smells she had grown used to, being around him, but had never experienced up close. So silly, she thought, what she was noticing in this moment: the feel of his arms under his sweater, the smell of his body, a hint of sweat, shampoo, the taste of his mouth, the feel of his teeth on her tongue. He was pushing against her, as if he had waited forever for this, and she realized how wrong she had been about Nick Bell.

Lauren was mortified when she woke up on Saturday morning, asleep on the couch in the Callejas' media room. She and Alejandro had started watching a movie together the night before, but she had fallen asleep, exhausted. He had put a blanket over her and had left a note to wake him if she were up first in the morning. She didn't want to—it would be breaking all the rules of dating she believed in: Don't let the date last too long, don't stick around for breakfast the first time you sleep over, don't hang out with him as if the two of you are only friends. And what would the Callejas think about this strange girl who was asleep on the sofa?

She didn't want to know.

She threw on her clothes and crept out quietly, hoping she could get back home before her mother and her friend Madeline were up and about. Madeline, however, liked to take her dogs out walking early in the morning, and so Lauren was forced to walk up the driveway and exchange an awkward hello as Madeline left the house with her two English bulldogs and headed to the local farm stand. On her way upstairs, Lauren ran into her little sister, Allison, who was home for the holiday.

Allison rolled her eyes and made a lewd gesture.

"Not a word from you," Lauren said. "If you tell Mom, no more rides into town."

Allison nodded. "Okay, but we're going to Scoop, and you have to buy me something—and not from the sale rack."

Lauren laughed. "You drive a hard bargain. Now go mention to Mom that I'm just getting up."

After spending the day with her little sister—who, despite her freckles and penchant for magenta, seemed far more sophisticated than Lauren had remembered being as a freshman—Lauren decided to have a quiet Saturday night. After everything that had happened with Alejandro and the Society meeting the day before, she didn't want to go out to a club or a party. She even decided to turn her phone off. On Sunday morning, when she turned it back on, the messages came spilling out, all from Alejandro:

10:18 P.M.: WHERE R U . . . COME OUT
& PARTY W ME
12:32 A.M.: ITLL B FUN
1:19 A.M.: NEED TO TALK TO U
2:35 A.M.: IM SORRY

Lauren called Alejandro, but only got his voice mail. Typical boy behavior. Wants to talk, but then isn't available. She turned her phone on silent; she needed time to think. She was confused and angry and frustrated that he could be such a flake.

Adding to her troubles, her mother kept asking her to bring him over, and she had no plausible excuse why she couldn't reach him.

Later in the day, a friend emailed her a link to a Hamptons gossip website. She clicked on it and saw pictures of Alejandro being pushed into a squad car. The story said that he had gone out clubbing the previous night with some friends at the Purple Elephant, got really drunk, and picked a fight with a bouncer over a coat he had left inside. When they wouldn't let him back in to retrieve it, he had screamed at them, "I know people who can get you. You'll all be screwed!" He had then attacked the bouncer, the police had been called, and he was taken away. His parents had needed to bail him out that morning.

Lauren sighed. Maybe she and Alejandro had one of those fantasy relationships that was never really meant to work out. Skinny dipping in November? Bossa nova singers? A house all to themselves? There had to be a downside, didn't there? It had all seemed too good to be true.

CHAPTER THIRTY-SIX

On Monday morning, Patch's producer called him in for a meeting. He had told Simone what had taken place on Wednesday night with the two thugs who had been sent by the Society, but she was undeterred.

"I want you to know that what happened on Thursday was unacceptable," she said, after taking a sip from her ever-present coffee mug. "I need to be able to trust that you're on board with me."

"Simone, it was Thanksgiving Day," Patch said. "And you expected me to cover a death in Central Park?"

"This is not always a fun business. Sometimes you have to do things that you don't want to do. You're supposed to be covering this scene: the good, the bad, the ugly."

"I understand that," Patch said.

"Good. I had a feeling you would. Which is why I know you'll understand the next thing I'd like you to do."

"What's that?"

"Figure out a way to get inside the Society."

For Phoebe, classes started up uneventfully after Thanksgiving break. Aside from the occasional passing reference, no one talked about what had happened to Jared nor about what happened to Alejandro, although many Chadwick students knew of the incidents. As Anastasia had predicted, these things had a way of drifting into the past. Jared's family held a memorial service, which Nick attended begrudgingly, mostly because it was the right thing to do. He told Phoebe that it had made him sick.

Aside from Nick, Phoebe didn't see much of anyone. She had filled Lauren in on what had happened between them, but mostly, she was trying to keep her head low, hoping no one had found out about her mini breakdown. Of course, no one had; she realized she was being silly for even thinking that anyone cared.

She recognized, too, through hanging out with Nick, doing simple things, like grabbing a grilled cheese or coffee together, how much she always overanalyzed everything. Phoebe wanted to be more like Nick, to live more in the moment, not to care if her hair looked perfect or if she were wearing the right outfit. She resolved to do that for the new year.

It was a distracting time, with exams and final papers and Christmas plans—possibly the worst time to start a new relationship. And yet Nick, in his dogged, stubborn way, seemed intent on making it work.

The two of them were hanging out together after school one afternoon, getting chai lattes at the Starbucks near Chadwick. Phoebe said they were being corporate whores by going there, but Nick insisted that their lattes were the best, so she had acquiesced.

They sat together at one of those round crowded café tables that give you the awkward illusion of privacy when you're in a room full of strangers. It was a chilly day, and Nick pulled off his brown wool cap, shaking out his messy, unkempt curls. He was wearing his German army jacket over his Chadwick blazer, which Phoebe thought was adorable.

He gulped his chai latte before looking at her. "So I guess we should, you know, um, define what we are?" he asked, as tentatively as she had ever seen him.

She shivered a bit, although it wasn't only from the cold. "What do you mean?" She wasn't going to be the one to define it—no, she had seen her girlfriends make that mistake too many times.

"Well, Phoebe Dowling." He leaned forward and looked

into her eyes, clutching a paper napkin in his hand. "I would like to ask you to be my girlfriend."

Phoebe grinned. "And what do I have to do to earn this honor?"

Nick paused. "Chai lattes once a week?"

Phoebe leaned forward and gave him a kiss on the lips. "Done."

The conversation with Simone had occurred nearly a week earlier, and Patch had been mulling over her demands. Was it unreasonable what she was asking? It made him feel like a fraud, a sham. You were supposed to be asked to be part of a secret society. You weren't supposed to spy on them, to claw your way in. In some ways, though, it was exactly what he had always wanted to do. Here was an incredible investigative story, as well as a medium for telling it.

And maybe, just maybe, he could learn more about his family's past.

He would be foolish not to take the chance.

On Saturday morning, he went down to St. Mark's Place, a street in the East Village that was known for its carnivalesque display of tattoo and piercing parlors, cheap pizza and falafel joints, college bars, and vintage clothing stores. He picked the store that was least likely to give him a hard time with his fake ID.

He didn't bother flipping through the book of tattoo

designs. He pulled out a photocopied piece of paper with a sketch on it. If he wanted to infiltrate the Society, he figured he should look like a member.

After lifting up his hair, he showed the woman where he wanted the ankh: on the back of his neck.

CHAPTER THIRTY-SEVEN

Exam week flew by, as most Chadwick students were consumed with doing well on their tests. The last exam was scheduled for Friday, the day school let out for holiday break. That afternoon, Phoebe was packing up her book bag when she received a text message about the evening, from the cryptic number she now recognized as the Society's.

The address that had been given was down on the Lower East Side, but when they arrived, there was nothing that looked like a nightclub or party space, only a little bodega. Could they have gotten the address wrong? About ten of the Initiates were standing around outside, clueless and confused.

It felt like another test.

"Wait," Lauren said. "I have an idea. I read about this in a magazine."

There was, curiously, a pay phone booth (which no one ever seemed to use in the city anymore) next to the deli, against the wall of the building. Nick peered inside the grocery store and pointed out to everyone that the lines of the wall didn't match up; it was as if the bodega had a false wall, or a secret passageway. Lauren went inside, picked up the phone, and said a few words. The wall behind the pay phone opened up to reveal a door. She looked back, grinned, and motioned for the others to follow.

Phoebe was right behind her. "How on earth did you know to do that?" Phoebe asked her.

"I read about a place like that in the East Village," Lauren said. "Like a secret after-hours club. It was a lucky guess."

"Lucky indeed." Phoebe shook her head in amazement. Was any of this more than a giant twisted treasure hunt? And if so, what was the treasure? They had been through so much in the past several weeks that Phoebe felt like they didn't need any more nonsense.

Nick held her hand as they followed Lauren and the others down a dark alleyway that clattered with steam pipes. Graffiti covered the walls, and fire escapes dangled from the windows above. They walked through another tunnel and then to a large black door, behind which they could hear the faint sounds of thumping music.

"Do we just go in?" someone asked. Nick pulled on the wrought iron door handle, and it opened.

The club was called Prohibition, and it had been open for only two weeks. A DJ was in a booth that looked over the wood-paneled room, playing MGMT, Mark Ronson, and Vampire Weekend. Apart from the music, it was as if a Victorian bordello had been re-created on the Lower East Side. There were red velvet drapes, large plush banquettes, and little mirrored tables. In a nod, Lauren thought, to *Alice in Wonderland*, people drank cocktails out of old teacups; beer was served in paper bags. It all had the feel of an outlaw party. After the tunnel they had gone through, Lauren didn't even know which direction they were facing, which was an unusual sensation.

That was the thing about Manhattan: No matter where you were, you almost always knew which way was uptown.

Unless, of course, you were thrillingly, hopelessly drunk, which was exactly what was happening to everyone, as waiters in white gloves continued to pour drink after drink. The word was that the party was to celebrate the Initiates and their bonding over the last semester.

Lauren wondered how much they actually had to celebrate.

In a room with green tartan wallpaper across from the DJ booth, a group of seven Initiates was sitting around a table. Waiters brought out tray after tray of large silver cups, which were filled with drinks of varying colors. One was blue, another was green, another was purple. Everyone had to drink from the cups, like a ritual sacrament being taken.

"Come on, Lauren." Claire Chilton motioned to her. "Isn't this a hoot? Just like my dad always talks about at Yale."

Lauren nodded. She had heard about Mory's, the Yale eating club where they did this. But what did this club on the Lower East Side have to do with that? It all seemed like an elaborate imitation of Ivy League life, as if by copying the manners and mores of a Yale eating club, the fifteen of them might feel like they were destined to be part of the real thing.

She went over to sit next to Alejandro. Lauren had been disappointed after what had happened the previous weekend, but she knew he felt bad about it. His parents had been on his case as well, not letting him go out at all during the week, which was probably for the best. Despite all the awkwardness between them—the text messages, his drunken shenanigans, his flakiness—Lauren couldn't ignore her feelings for him.

When she sat down at his booth, Alejandro scooted next to her—they were sitting so close, she could feel the warmth of his body. Bradley Winston, Thad Johnson, and a few other Initiates were all downing glasses of champagne. Thad, who Lauren knew was much smarter than the other boys, looked slightly out of place, but appeared to be trying to keep up.

"We need more drinks!" said Bradley. His bowtie was askew, as if he were headed for a rough night.

At that moment, Charles Lawrence, one of the Conscripts

who seemed to be a sort of chaperone for the party, came over. "You guys having fun?"

Everyone nodded.

A waiter arrived with a fresh bottle of champagne. It was poured, and Alejandro and Lauren sipped from their glasses. Then a favorite CSS song of his came on, and both of them headed to the dance floor.

When they came back, Charles handed them fresh glasses. Lauren noticed that he was wearing gloves.

"What's with the gloves?" Lauren asked.

"I guess I'm your waiter for the evening." Charles grinned and then went off to join the other group.

Alejandro gulped his champagne as if it were water.

A few moments later, he started to slur his words.

"Oh my God," Lauren said. "How drunk are you?"

"I just had a little bit of—" His eyelids started fluttering, before he shut his eyes. He slumped down in the banquette, his whole body gone limp like a rag doll.

"Alejandro—what the hell? What's going on?" The music was blasting, and nobody could hear her. Drinking, smoking, dancing, the business of partying all around her. She started shaking him as her heart pounded. "I can't—oh my God!" People at the table had started to notice. They prodded Alejandro, but he didn't move. Thad took some ice and put it to his forehead, hoping it would rouse him.

Lauren picked up her phone and started dialing 911. A

hand grabbed hers, and she saw it was attached to a burly security guard who looked vaguely familiar. "Put down the phone, miss," he said. "There's no need to call. We're going to take him to a hospital."

"A hospital? But how do you know what's wrong with him?"

"He needs medical attention. That's clear." His partner grabbed Alejandro's body and hoisted it over his shoulders. In comparison to the 250-pound security guard, Alejandro looked tiny.

"Can I come along with you?"

"I'm sorry, miss, we can't let you do that."

"What hospital are you taking him to?" The music kept pounding; she wished she could have a moment of silence to think.

The guard gave no answer. Everyone was staring, as if the party had stopped in mid-song. Lauren saw Nick and grabbed him.

"What should we do? They're taking him—but they won't say where!"

Nick followed the security guards, and Lauren chased after him, knowing Phoebe would understand. They ran out the entrance of the club, along the dark alleyways and into the street. The guards were loading Alejandro into a black town car.

Lauren started screaming. "Where are you taking him?"

"Come on, just tell us which hospital!" Nick shouted. "We'll meet you there."

The guards said nothing. As the car drove away, Lauren pounded angrily on its hood.

A few people on the sidewalk stared at the spectacle, and Lauren realized they must have looked like two drunk kids causing trouble. She was out of breath. She crumpled down on a front stoop.

"Should we try to follow them?" she asked.

"There's not a cab in sight," Nick said.

"What the hell just happened?"

He shook his head. "I don't know."

She looked at her phone. Was there anyone she could call? What would she say? *My friend passed out and was kidnapped?* No one would believe her. And it would mean the cops would show up at the party—which would get back to Chadwick and their parents. There was nothing to do.

"I don't want to go back in," Lauren said. "My purse is still in there. Can you get it when you come back with Phoebe?"

The door they had come out of was locked from the street, so Nick walked back through the phone booth and into the tunnel, nodding to the guard who was manning the door. When he returned to the party, the mood was decidedly different. The DJ had switched over to lounge music, and people were standing around uncomfortably, not really sure what they should be doing. The waiters in white gloves were rapidly collecting glasses and carrying them away on trays. It didn't seem appropriate to continue, but no one really wanted to go home, either.

Nick ran into Phoebe. "I think we should go," he said. "Do you know where Lauren's purse is?"

Phoebe pointed to the banquette; Nick recognized the bag as the one that had been given to her by Sebastian Giroux. He grabbed the bag, took Phoebe's hand, and led her outside.

Out on the sidewalk, there were cars waiting for them. "Should we take one of those?" Lauren asked.

Nick shook his head. "Come on. We'll get our own rides tonight."

"What happened to him?" Phoebe asked. "One minute he was fine, and then, suddenly, they were carrying him out."

"I don't know," Lauren said. "I mean, I'm not going to lie—I know he likes to party. But I don't think he'd done anything that serious tonight."

"Maybe someone slipped something in his drink," Nick said. He looked up the street and saw the stream of black town cars taking the other Initiates home. "I think we need to watch our backs."

CHAPTER THIRTY-EIGHT

Phoebe was woken the next morning by her mother knocking on her door. "Honey?"

"Mmmph?" Phoebe said, through a yawn. Her head still pounded with the beats from last night's music.

"Lauren is on the phone. She said she couldn't reach you on your cell."

Maia handed Phoebe the phone. "Hey—what's up?" Phoebe mumbled.

"I can't get in touch with him."

"What? With who?"

"Alejandro. I don't know where he is. There's no answer at his hotel. I can't reach his parents. This is such a mess!"

"Calm down, he's probably fine," Phoebe said. "Maybe

he lost his phone or something? Didn't they take him to the hospital?"

"I think, but which hospital? No one would tell us."

Phoebe sat up in bed. "Nick and I could call all the ones in the area. I mean, it's not like there are that many that he would possibly be at."

"Would you guys do that?"

"Of course," Phoebe said. "It's not a problem."

"And Phoebe?"

"Yeah?"

"Can I come over? I really don't want to be alone."

Within a few hours, Nick and Phoebe had called dozens of hospitals in Manhattan, focusing on ones that were downtown and close to the club. It wasn't an easy task, but they worked quickly, each updating the other on their progress every half hour.

When Nick was done, he took a cab down to Phoebe's house. It was the first time he had been over, and he wondered if he would have to meet her mom. He had put on a navy Brooks Brothers sweater in an attempt to look nice for the occasion, and he hoped that his frayed jeans didn't look too sloppy.

Lauren sat in the corner of Phoebe's bedroom in a bean-bag chair, nervously drinking a cup of coffee. Nick arrived and gave Phoebe a quick peck on the lips.

"I'm done with my list," he said. "No one of that name or description was admitted in the last twenty-four hours."

"I don't understand what's going on," Phoebe said. "Where on earth would he be? A private facility? A family doctor? I can't imagine that his parents wouldn't know about this—do you think we should call them?"

"We can't," Lauren said. "He told me last night that his parents are already in Argentina for the holiday. I tried their suite at the hotel this morning—they wouldn't give out a for-warding number, and they said they couldn't guarantee that they could get them the message. They have like four differ-ent places in Argentina, so who knows where they are?"

"I don't know," Nick said. "The Callejas are extremely prominent. Maybe he was admitted under a fake name or something. Or maybe he went home and was treated pri-vately."

"Oh, what, like they loaded him on a plane last night?" Lauren said. "That makes no sense."

Nick frowned. "I have heard of people being carried away—" He suddenly stopped.

"What do you mean 'carried away'?" Lauren asked.

"No, I'm sorry, it's a bad example." He realized he shouldn't have said anything.

"Just tell us what you're talking about," Phoebe said.

"Okay, look, I'm not saying this is what happened. But

254

nightclubs that are really druggy are sometimes known to take patrons who are ODing and, instead of calling an ambulance, just grab them and dump them on the street."

"You mean, leaving them to die? That's ridiculous." Phoebe clearly didn't want to worry Lauren any more than necessary. "There's no way that could have happened."

"I know it sounds crazy, but they don't want the liability. If the person is recorded as ODing on the street, then it's not the club's fault. It's crappy, but it happens."

"But this was a private party last night," Phoebe said.

"Exactly," Nick said. "And who do you think was in charge of security?"

"I knew I recognized those guys from somewhere," Lauren said. "It was the same guys who manned the door at the Society luncheon back in September. One of them was so beefy, he was sort of hard to forget."

"So what do we do?" Phoebe said. "Should we file a missing persons report?"

"I think we should," Lauren said. "I'm going to call the police."

"But what if they want to question us?" Nick asked. He hated to be selfish, but he couldn't afford for the school to learn about his being at the party.

Lauren's phone buzzed. She answered and took the call into the hallway. Phoebe put her head in her hands, groaning. "This is so awful."

"Just stay calm," Nick said. "We'll work it out."

Lauren came back into the room. "You're not going to believe this. That was Alejandro's father. The hotel reported that he hadn't returned home last night, so Mr. Calleja called the police. He and his wife are flying back from Argentina."

"How did he have your number?" Phoebe asked.

"They got it from the St. Regis. I guess they reached them with my message."

"So we really don't need to report this," Nick said.

"Shouldn't we tell them what we know?" Phoebe asked.

"I told Mr. Calleja that he was down on the Lower East Side last night. I didn't mention any names. I sort of—"

"What?" Nick said.

"Well, I sort of lied," Lauren said. "I got freaked out when I was talking to him and I said I had heard that Alejandro was down on the Lower East Side. I said I didn't know who he was with. I mean, this whole thing with Chadwick and the drinking—I don't want anyone to get kicked out over this. Should I have told him more?"

They were all silent for a moment.

"It's somewhere for them to start," Nick finally said. "We need to let them do their jobs. Besides, maybe we're overreacting. Maybe it'll all be sorted out by Monday." He looked at Lauren and then back at Phoebe, but he knew neither of them believed that would be the case.

CHAPTER THIRTY-NINE

Patch couldn't stop thinking about Genie's comments regarding the Bells and about what Simone had wanted him to do. Maybe his plan of getting the tattoo had been ill-advised, although his intuition told him that if he could convince one of the Society members that he was an insider, he might be able to get some information—information he hoped could help him understand what had happened to his mother.

How he was going to meet a member who didn't know him already, he had no idea.

Finally, as school was about to let out, Patch had realized what he should do. One afternoon, he crept downstairs to the utility room of his and Nick's apartment building. From growing up there, he knew exactly where everything was. He brought with him a small transmitter he had bought at a spy shop that he could connect to the Bells' phone. He decided he would tap the main line as well as the second line, which he knew from childhood experience was Parker Bell's private phone line. Every time a call was made or received, Patch's computer would record a digital file.

During each day that followed, he listened to all the files. It was easy to determine which ones would be of interest: He ignored the housekeeper ordering groceries, Nick's mother on the phone with her friends, the doorman buzzing people up. On Saturday afternoon, he heard dozens of calls during which Nick spoke to hospitals about Alejandro Calleja's whereabouts, which Patch thought was strange. And then on Sunday afternoon, he finally heard something of interest. Parker Bell was on the phone with Nick's grandfather Palmer. They were talking about some kind of retreat between Christmas and New Year's, clearly a Society event. They were arguing about how information about the retreat would be disseminated. Parker wanted it sent to private email accounts, but Palmer argued that once something was digital, it was far too easy to forward to others, and that with everything that had happened, they couldn't afford to take the risk.

The two finally agreed that the information packets would be delivered by private messenger, the following night at ten P.M., to each Society member's door. Each member would have to sign for his or her package.

It would give Patch just enough time to make preparations. In order to intercept Nick's package, there was only one thing he could do.

Patch would have to *become* Nick Bell.

The next morning, only two days before Christmas, Patch woke up, shivering after a nightmare. After listening to the phone call yesterday, Patch had gone to Anthony's Barbershop, bringing with him a picture from *Hamptons* magazine of Nick at a party last summer. "I want this guy's haircut," he had told the haircutter, a large Russian woman wielding a pair of clippers.

"Who is he?" the woman asked. "He look like model."

"Sure," Patch said. "He's a model."

Patch had been letting his hair grow long that semester. It was so shaggy and wavy at the back, you couldn't even see his neck. Now the woman trimmed and shaped his hair so that it was a pretty good approximation of Nick's cut.

In the middle of the day, during an hour when he knew everyone would be out of the Bell apartment, Patch jimmied the lock from the service entrance and snuck over to Nick's room. He knew where Nick kept all his clothes, so it wasn't a problem putting together an outfit; the trick was stealing a set of clothes that Nick wouldn't miss. Patch finally settled on a sweater from the bottom of his bureau and a pair of ripped jeans that Nick had often worn the previous summer. He took a scarf and then paused for a moment to figure out the issue of a coat. Nick would miss a coat; Patch was almost sure of that. Then again, Nick was never one for conformity. Maybe it would be believable that Nick was going out without wearing a coat.

Patch quickly put on Nick's clothes and examined himself in front of the mirror. He had already switched out his glasses for contacts.

Not a bad facsimile, he thought, especially when he added a baseball cap of Nick's.

He heard a noise in the kitchen. He stepped out into the hall, but saw that it was only the housekeeper. He would wait until she left.

Later, in his bedroom, he looked at himself again in the mirror. He had been working out at Chadwick's fitness center, which made him look even more like Nick. He pushed back his hair the way Nick did, and postured in his typical swagger.

He could pass, at least from afar.

It made him feel like a terrible fraud.

Sometimes, when he and Nick were in elementary school, people had accused him of wanting to be a Bell, with the way he and Nick were so close. Now here he was trying to imitate a scion of the Bell family.

That night, Patch made his way down to the lobby, timing it so that he would step out of the elevator when the clock struck ten. If he was lucky, it would be the night doorman, Roger, who was never quite as attentive as the ones during the day.

As Patch entered the lobby, Roger was talking to a messenger. "I can't ring the Bell apartment at this hour," he said. "You can leave it here, and Master Bell will get it in the morning."

"I need to deliver it to him personally," the messenger said. "I was given specific instructions."

Patch spoke up. "I'm right here, Rog," he said.

"You're Nick Bell?" the messenger asked.

"That's right," Patch said.

"Thank the Lord, Nick. I thought I was going to have to toss this guy out," Roger said.

"No worries, Rog." Patch signed an approximation of Nick's handwriting. "I'm headed out. I'll take it with me." He breezed past the doorman, and the messenger with the sealed manila envelope in his hands.

"I'm going to need to see some ID," the messenger said.

"No need for that. I can vouch for him," Roger said.

"Thanks, Rog!" Patch said. As soon as he was out of view of the front doors, he broke into a run all the way up Fifth, around a corner, and toward a diner on Second Avenue, where he planned on settling in with a soda to read the envelope's contents.

His body was quaking, though it wasn't because of his deception.

As he slowed to a trot, he recalled the nightmare he had woken from that morning. In it, he was lying at the base of Cleopatra's Needle, staring at a brisk November sky.

CHAPTER FORTY

The next day, Phoebe waited for Lauren and Nick outside the Society townhouse on East Sixty-sixth Street. They had requested a meeting with Nick's father. Phoebe didn't understand why they couldn't do this at Nick's apartment, but she had agreed on meeting up at the Society's headquarters— or at least what she and the other Initiates had assumed were its headquarters.

Nick and Lauren arrived, and Nick rapped on the big brass lion's head knocker, worn from years of use.

Charles Lawrence answered the door, casually dressed in a cashmere sweater, as if the three of them would be joining him for drinks. "Hey, guys," he said. "Mr. Bell got pulled away to a last-minute meeting. He wanted me to handle this for him."

"Charles?" Phoebe said. "What are you, like, his little errand boy or something?" She couldn't believe her audacity, but somehow it seemed rude of Nick's dad not to show up, particularly considering her new status as Nick's girlfriend—though, admittedly, she realized that Nick may not have told his parents about them.

Charles smirked at her and motioned for them to step into the front parlor. "What can I help you with?"

"Where is my dad?" Nick asked.

"He had to deal with something that couldn't wait. He sends his regrets."

Nick slumped down in an armchair in the drawing room on the first floor of the townhouse.

"We know about Alejandro," Lauren said.

Charles paused. "What about him?"

"He wasn't admitted to any hospitals in the area. We called them all."

"Okay, and this worries you because . . ." Charles was looking at them like they were stupid.

"Tell us where he is," Lauren said.

Charles laughed. "I have no idea where he is. If I did, I would certainly tell you. Have you tried his parents?"

"Yes—and they've called the police," Lauren said.

Charles looked unconcerned. "That's good. I'm sure they'll find him."

"What is this all about?" Phoebe asked.

264

"What is what about?" Charles asked, twirling a pen in his hand.

Phoebe continued, "This. The Society. Everything we've been doing over the past few months. It's like we've all been pupils in a class, but we're not sure what we're studying."

Charles sat down, apparently thinking carefully before answering. "What you three need to understand is that you are preserving a way of life."

"What way of life are we preserving?" Lauren asked. "That tells us absolutely nothing."

"These times are uncertain, economically, politically. You are preserving the life that your parents want you to live and that you will want your children to lead."

"How do you even know what our children would want?" Phoebe said. "Isn't that a little presumptuous? You don't even know if we want to have children!" She looked at Nick as she said this to see if he had any reaction, but he didn't.

"You'll understand soon," Charles said. "Just wait until the retreat at Isis Island. Everything will be made clear then. You should have gotten your packets last night."

"Right," Phoebe said, nodding as she recalled the bizarre messenger delivery she had signed for the night before. "The famous retreat."

"I never got a packet," Nick said.

"I'm sure your father has all the information," Charles said. "Don't you worry about a thing."

Soon the three of them were back on the sidewalk, shivering in the cold. They started walking east, where they could find a coffee shop. Nick realized he hadn't eaten lunch.

"I want out," Phoebe said after a few moments of silence. "This is not how my life is supposed to be. I want to be a normal teenager again."

Nick and Lauren nodded silently.

"Phoebe, you don't understand," Nick finally said. "We can't leave. It's not like a gym membership, something you can cancel and forget about."

"But what are we truly getting out of it? Nothing but trouble. Nick, you admitted that your club night didn't turn out how you wanted it to, and, Lauren, your jewelry's amazing, but you could do that stuff without their help. Besides, what's going to happen to us if we leave?"

"We don't know what happened to Alejandro," Lauren said firmly. "We have to stay in until we figure that out, don't you think?"

"This could all be a wild goose chase," Phoebe said. "We have no idea what happened. They're totally stonewalling us."

"What if he really is in rehab and his parents don't want anyone to know?" Lauren said. "There are all those rumors floating around. What if he's in one of those places where they take away your phone, don't let you call anyone? Like in,

I don't know, the Arizona desert or something."

"Did you get his parents' number? Maybe you could check on what's going on," Phoebe said.

"I told them to call me if they found out anything. I guess I could try them again at the hotel."

Phoebe put an arm around Lauren as they walked.

"Look," Nick said. "Let's at least stay in until we find out what's up with Alejandro, okay? Maybe more will become clear at this retreat thing."

"Do we even have any information about it?" Lauren asked. "I mean, we got this whole packet telling us what to bring, but we don't even know where we're going."

Nick decided he would tell them as much as he knew. "It's an island off the coast of Maine," Nick said. "I say we get through Christmas, and then we go."

CHAPTER FORTY-ONE

For Nick, the Christmas season passed in a haze. He escorted Phoebe to a few parties in the days leading up to the holiday, but it all felt phony. They had experienced so much together, real things, that to take her to a formal dance seemed fake. They would dance together, kiss at all the appropriate moments, do everything expected of a couple, but privately, they could only think of the upcoming retreat and whether attending it was the right thing to do. Nick wanted her to have a good time, but he couldn't tell if she was happy.

He told Phoebe about everything that had happened with Patch in greater detail, how he felt complicit in the breakup of their friendship. It was like the Society had the power to disband friendships and form new alliances.

Out at the beach house and missing Phoebe terribly, Nick

spent a strained Christmas with his family. Every time he saw his father, he kept his head low. How could he have trusted his parents for so long, only to find out they were tied up in all this?

On Christmas Eve, his father asked to speak with him in the library. His grandfather was already waiting there, and his mother came in with a glass of hot cider. The room was always warm and cozy, though at this time of year, it seemed even more so. The fireplace mantel had been festively decked out with garlands and poinsettias. Henry and Ben stood to one side of the library, ostensibly examining a portrait of their great-grandfather, though Nick knew that wasn't what the sheepish duo was doing there. A day earlier, Nick had asked Ben, who was a sophomore, if he knew anything about the Society. With his pot-smoking buddies from his singing group and a never-ending parade of girlfriends, he had always struck Nick as more of a free spirit, so Nick had thought his brother would be honest with him. Ben hadn't denied any knowledge, but he had said that all questions had to go through their father, which really wasn't helpful at all.

Nick's mother and father sat on the tweed settee that flanked the fireplace, and they motioned for Nick to sit across from them. Nick's grandfather, Palmer, stood on the other side of the library next to a Chippendale chair. He put the volume he was reading back in its place on the walnut bookshelf.

Nick felt like he was surrounded.

He feared that they all wanted him to deal with the Patch issue, which he had been ignoring. He had done enough to hurt Patch already.

"I think you know why you're here," Parker Bell said, as he put his martini on the glass and wrought-iron coffee table.

"No, Dad, actually I'm not sure," Nick said.

"What you need to comprehend, Nick, is that your entire family is part of this," Parker said. "Your mother is an Elder. Your grandfather, as you know, is Chairman Emeritus. Both of your brothers are Elders. We hope that your children will be members, too. Nick, this is part of our life, part of our heritage."

Nick started at the realization that his suspicions were now confirmed about his family. "Dad, I can't—I don't understand what it is you want me to do."

"You need to get in touch with Patch and tell him to destroy those videos. We have seen parts of them, and they have the potential to be very damaging. We know he has more. The disc the Guardians asked him for—it's very clear that they were cut from some master tapes."

"Wait—the Guardians? What are the Guardians?"

"The Guardians are a private security force that works only for the Society."

The words *private security* put Nick on alert—like the security guards who had dragged Alejandro off six nights ago.

"And they did what—you said they asked him for the footage?"

"Nick, it's easy for all this to escalate. And we don't want that to happen. There are some extremely important people and interests at risk here. All he would have to do is to leak that material onto the Internet or send it to a major news source. You can imagine the pandemonium that would take place."

Nick stared at the five of them. "I can't believe—how could all of you have been part of this for so long and not told me about it?"

Parker Bell spoke. "I had hoped that my hints were enough. I thought I made it clear that we were part of something very special."

"And you, Mom?"

"Darling." She reached forward as if to hug him, but he pulled away. "Your father is in charge of all this. It wasn't my place to say anything."

Nick looked at his two brothers, Henry and Ben. Nick guessed in their eyes he was the traitor. But maybe he had to play along.

"I'll get in touch with Patch when I'm back in the city," Nick said. "I'm sure I can talk some sense into him."

"This must happen before the retreat," Parker Bell said. "The Council of Regents is extremely concerned. We need to have those tapes, as well as Patchfield's sworn affidavit that there are no other copies."

"And what's in it for him?" Nick asked. "Why would he want to give you everything?"

"He will be compensated accordingly. We'll work something out with him," Parker said.

"Compensation! That little cretin should have been gotten rid of a long time ago," Palmer Bell said.

"Father!" Parker said.

"I'm sorry, Parker. I know the boy has been in your lives for some time now. And Nick, I know he's a friend of yours. But certain things must come before friendship."

"Can I ask something?" Nick said. "What is the point of all this? Everyone wants to know."

"That always happens in the Folly," Parker said. "It's normal for your fellow Initiates to have questions."

"What is the Folly?" Nick asked.

"The Folly is the period from the Night of Rebirth to Conscription. It's when you get to enjoy the fruits of Society membership, and you don't need to worry too much about your responsibilities."

"I'm not sure that's really been the case," Nick said.

"Are you referring to Ms. Dowling's little debacle at the art gallery?" Parker asked.

"Among other things."

Gigi spoke up. "What happened to Phoebe never should have taken place. She was tricked. She's a good girl. We know she would never betray the Society willingly. She wants too badly to succeed. I'm happy for you two, about, you know—"

"Gigi, I think Nick can manage his own affairs," Parker said.

"I know, I'm sorry, dear. I'm just saying I'm pleased. Isn't a mother allowed to do that?"

Nick wondered whether his mother, or any of his family, really knew Phoebe at all. And how did they know they were dating? Maybe it was obvious.

"Everything will become clear during the retreat," Parker said. "You are all bound together, in a bond that's tighter than blood. These bonds will follow you throughout your entire life. If you use them wisely, you will benefit beyond your wildest expectations."

Nick wanted badly to ask about Alejandro, but he didn't feel it was a good idea.

His family was in deeper than he had ever imagined.

The next afternoon, after an early Christmas dinner with Genie, Patch slipped out the door while she was napping. He took the subway downtown and then a PATH train to Jersey City. He found the nearest truck stop and started approaching drivers. Finally, one of them, a paunchy guy with a goatee driving a truck labeled Northeastern Lines, seemed receptive.

"Where you headed, kid?" he asked.

"Maine," Patch said. "I'm headed to Maine."

CHAPTER FORTY-TWO

The day after Christmas, Nick returned to the city. He wanted desperately to see Phoebe, to fill her in on everything he had been told. The revelations about his family were surprising, but what had he really expected? He knew his father and grandfather were involved, and he should have guessed that his brothers and mother were part of it, too. Why had they kept this from him for so long? It made him feel betrayed.

He shared what he knew with Phoebe over coffee at a brasserie on Lexington. She was incredulous at first, but soon understood what was going on.

"So basically you're saying your family is in tight with all this. But where does that leave you?"

"I don't know," Nick said. "It almost feels like I couldn't

leave if I wanted to."

"You have choices," Phoebe said. "You have to remember that."

"Yeah, but at the cost of what? Getting thrown out? Getting cut off financially? They essentially said that Society ties were even stronger than family."

"Until you screw up, right?"

"Exactly," Nick said. "It's, like, one wrong move and they show you who's in charge."

"We need to hang in there. We need to see what's going on, to go on this stupid retreat."

They went back to Nick's apartment, where no one would be home but the housekeeper. In the lobby, they ran into Genie, Patch's grandmother.

"Nicholas," she said. "It's been so long." She gave him a hug and a kiss. She smelled like tuberose perfume. "Who's your pretty friend?"

He introduced Phoebe.

"Do you know if Patch is home?" he asked.

A worried look crossed her face. "Oh dear, I thought you would have known. I think you'd better come upstairs."

Nick and Phoebe followed her into the elevator.

He hadn't been in Patch's apartment since the end of the summer; being back now made their rift seem even deeper. He had forgotten the smells of the two-bedroom co-op, and he had missed its coziness, the small entryway with its cracked marble transom, the living room in need of a paint job, the fact that Patch was allowed to put stickers on his door, something Nick's own mother had declared off limits, as the decorator had said it would ruin the "continuity" of the Bells' hallway.

"I've missed being here," Nick said, although he didn't pursue the topic.

"Patch left this note for me yesterday," Genie said.

> *Genie,*
>
> *I have to go on a short trip, maybe as long as a week. I will be fine, but I will send you a text message on your cell phone (it is in the charger in your bedroom) once or more every day to let you know I am okay.*
>
> *I'm sorry I didn't ask you about it first, but it's something I have to do, and I was afraid you'd say no.*
>
> *I love you.*
>
> *Patch*

Nick looked at the note, scrawled on a piece of binder paper. "Has he sent any messages yet?"

"I believe so. The thing keeps beeping." She went to the bedroom and came back with her cell phone. "Can you see what it means?"

Nick took the phone from her and went to the messages screen. There were three:

I'm fine.

Save me a piece of pumpkin pie.

I hope you'll all forgive me.

The phone beeped in Nick's hand. A fourth message came through. When he read it, he felt chills.

St. Nick should be reading this now.

"His timing is uncanny." Nick laughed grimly.

"Is he nearby?" Phoebe said, looking at the message. "Does he somehow know we're here?"

"No, I think it's exactly the opposite," Nick said. He realized he would have to explain that part later, when they weren't around Genie. "Look at how the messages themselves mostly don't make sense. Patch and I used to play this game in class, where we would pass notes. They're acrostics: The sentences aren't always logical, but the first letters taken together make a word."

I'm fine.

Save me a piece of pumpkin pie.

I hope you'll all forgive me.

St. Nick should be reading this now.

The three of them looked closely at the string of texts.

"I-S-I-S," Phoebe said.

"Exactly," Nick said, looking at Genie. "He knows."

Genie prepared a pot of tea as they sat in the living room. The old woman seemed relatively calm, considering that her grandson might currently be trying to infiltrate the bastion of the Society. Phoebe feared she would be sick.

"I assume you know what's going on," Nick said to Genie.

"Well, I suspected. I'm not really sure how much I should say about all this. I want to make sure Patch is okay. If you're part of it all, can I be assured of that?"

"Genie, Patch's safety is the most important thing to me. Especially after everything that's happened. But I need to know—you don't think we're horrible for staying in it, do you?"

"You know," she said, as she fiddled with a locket she was wearing around her neck, "sometimes the best way to rebel against something is from the inside."

"Are we safe to talk here?" Nick said.

"I don't know. Two very threatening gentlemen came to visit us last month, so that Patch could give them some kind of recording. He wasn't here, so I had to deal with them."

"They came to your *apartment*?" Nick said. He seemed truly shocked. Phoebe had no idea it had gone this far. Secret meetings were one thing, but threatening old women?

"Nick, you act so surprised. I would have thought you

278

would know a bit more about all this, given your . . ." Her voice trailed off.

"You mean my family?"

"That's right. I suppose there's no need to beat around the bush."

"You know about all that?"

Genie chuckled. "Oh, Nicholas, there's so little that you and Patch know about our families' early history together."

"What do you mean 'together'?"

"Your grandfather, Palmer Bell, and I were once engaged to be married."

"I had no idea."

Genie put down her teacup. "You see, Nick, in a sense, I could have been your grandmother."

Nick stood silently with Phoebe in the elevator as they made their way up to his apartment. "I can't believe this," he finally said. "I knew my grandparents traveled in the same social circle as Patch's, but I didn't know—"

"Do you think he's okay?" Phoebe interrupted him.

"Sometimes Patch does these things. Two summers ago, he met these fishermen in Sag Harbor and followed them all the way to Montauk. He was gone for three days. Slept on their boat. I guess you could say he has more of a sense of adventure than most people."

"So he can fend for himself?"

"I think so. Here's the thing, though—did you see when those messages were sent? Right on each hour."

"What does that mean?"

"He's not sending them himself. He's using a computer to send them."

"How would he do that?"

"He wrote them beforehand and uploaded them with a time delay. He could be anywhere."

"Why don't you just call him?"

When they reached the apartment's vestibule, Nick took out his phone and dialed. It went directly to voice mail. Patch was either out of range or his phone had died.

Or, even worse, he no longer had his phone with him.

"Great," Nick said. "As if this retreat wasn't already giving us enough to worry about."

The instructions for the retreat had said they would each be picked up at their homes at eight A.M. on December 28. There had been a packing list and some general guidelines: no cameras, no computers, no cell phones. Nick imagined everyone would be ignoring this last instruction. It was creepy, somehow, how solitary the Society wanted them to be. But maybe it was to prevent people from taking photographs.

They entered Nick's apartment. It was quiet as everyone was still at the beach house and the housekeeper was working upstairs.

Nick and Phoebe flopped down on the couches in the

living room, something they would never be able to do if his parents were around. Nick hadn't seen the apartment so still in recent memory.

"It's so freaky, somehow," he said. "To think I was raised for all this."

"At least you have an idea of what to expect," Phoebe said. "From your family, I mean." Phoebe looked worried as she sat back on the couch, biting her lower lip.

"It's so convoluted, though. Is this like my destiny or something?" He laughed. "Sorry, I know that sounds stupid."

"Maybe it is your destiny," Phoebe said. "Or maybe your destiny is to get away from it all."

IV

THE POWER OF FOURTEEN

CHAPTER FORTY-THREE

The ride in the semi took eight hours, including a meal at a truck stop off Interstate 95. The driver hadn't been terribly chatty, but had agreed to drop Patch off outside Portland.

After reviewing the materials he had intercepted, Patch decided he needed to find a way into the retreat. He kept listening in on the Bell household's phone calls and was finally able to get a location, something the packet didn't specify: a place called Isis Island, off the coast of Maine. He would pack what he could, bringing his video camera, warm clothes, and as much money as he had.

The useful details he had overheard were scant; it was mostly information about presentations and meetings and a ceremony on the last night.

He had kept listening in until the day before Christmas, when suddenly the connection went dead.

Patch knew he had no choice but to go. He had to find out what had happened to Nick, what had happened to Jared Willson and Alejandro Calleja, what had happened to his mother.

And he had to get more material for his show. Simone had made that much clear.

Patch had spent one night in a fleabag motel off the interstate outside Portland, and then he had managed to hitch another ride with a couple who were driving up the coast to visit their family. They agreed to drop Patch off at the ferry landing that went out to the islands.

The couple was already driving away by the time Patch was able fully to comprehend the schedule that was posted on the harbor master's announcement board; it was totally different from the information he had found online. A ferry ran to Caribou Island, which was five miles away from Isis, but no ferries ran directly to Isis. In the winter months, the service to Caribou Island was limited, operating only twice weekly.

Patch estimated that the next ferry would run—to the wrong island—three days from now.

He trudged the mile back to town, dejected and annoyed with himself for believing it would be this easy to get into the retreat. It was freezing out, he was hungry, and his fingers were numb. There was a diner, so he decided to grab a sandwich and some coffee.

It was one of those old-fashioned diners in a former railroad car, where all the booths are really close to one another. A few tables down from Patch, a group of guys was eating burgers and talking fishing.

Patch couldn't help eavesdropping; he gathered that they were going to take a lobster boat out. When he went to the restroom, he passed their table, trying to figure out a way to get their attention without being intrusive. While washing his hands, he looked at himself in the mirror. A day earlier, before leaving the apartment, he had cut off almost all his hair with a pair of clippers, leaving himself with a classic crew cut. He had put a Band-Aid over the tattoo of the ankh so it wouldn't be visible. After his second transformation in two weeks, he hoped no one on Isis Island would recognize him—assuming he ever made it there.

On the way back to his table, he decided to ask the guys where they were going. He figured he had nothing to lose.

"Why you want to know, kid?" the oldest man said to him.

"I—um, I'm looking to get to an island." He perched himself on the counter stool that was across from their booth. "It's nearby. Do you know it? Isis Island."

The four of them burst out laughing. There were two older guys, probably in their forties, and two younger ones. One of them looked like he was around Patch's age.

"What's so funny?"

"Isis Island—it's like a legend around here. I mean, it exists, but no one ever knows what goes on there. Rich people stuff."

"So how much would it cost for you to get me there? I know my way around a boat."

"Oh, do you, now?" The older one laughed again.

The kid who was his age spoke up. "Look, he knows *something*. He wouldn't be out here alone if he didn't."

"Come on, kid," the other old guy said. "Sit down with us. Maybe you can buy us lunch."

CHAPTER FORTY-FOUR

The morning that they were to leave Manhattan, Lauren packed carefully for the retreat. The instructions had said that most of the events would be casual and that they should plan to dress in layers, as it would be cold. Each person could bring no more than one small suitcase. Lauren couldn't wait for the whole thing to be over.

And to have Alejandro back again.

She had left two messages for his parents, but neither of them had been returned. She didn't know why. Maybe they saw her as an outsider who was prying into their business.

As she was packing, the Chloé bag caught her eye, flung carelessly on a chair. That bag, and everything that came with it, had brought her nothing but trouble. She took it with her, even though it wasn't appropriate to bring to some scrubby island in Maine.

After she had finished packing, Lauren rode the elevator down. Rory was on duty in the lobby. All month, the doormen had been collecting clothing for a charity drive that was organized by the building.

Lauren handed him the bag, explaining what it was for.

"Such a nice bag, miss—shall I leave a note, saying who it's from? You'll need a receipt, I imagine?"

"No," Lauren said. "I won't need a receipt at all."

An hour later, the three of them were at Teterboro Airport in New Jersey, waiting for the other Society members to arrive. As with many of the other events, each member arrived in a private car. Phoebe noticed how entitled some of the Initiates appeared, stepping out of their cars as if they owned them. Maybe that was part of Society membership, moving from fear into ownership.

The question was, ownership of what?

The jet they were flying on had a creamy leather and burlwood interior, and Phoebe wondered if it was owned by the Society. The class of Conscripts joined the group, and the twenty-eight of them took off together. Someone had a flask and started passing it around, and one of the Conscript girls pulled out a silver thermos filled with Manhattans. Thad Johnson was up front asking the pilots all sorts of questions about the plane, and they let him sit in the jump seat. Before long, it was like a rollicking party in the air. Phoebe, Nick, and

Lauren abstained from drinking. Phoebe knew she wanted to stay clear, at least in the beginning. She was determined to keep her guard up until she found out what was going on.

Nick wondered why he was supposed to go with the Initiates when his father, mother, brothers, and grandfather were all going to be traveling on their own to Isis Island. He figured that it was part of the bonding experience to arrive there with the others in his year.

When the plane reached the coast of Maine, Nick looked out the window. The islands were stunning, little gems in the dark blue ocean, surrounded by frothing whitecaps that swirled like frosting on a cake. He imagined they would touch down on the mainland and take a ferry over, but was surprised when the plane positioned itself for landing on a small airstrip at the tail end of the island.

After the plane landed, the twenty-eight members stepped onto the tarmac. Most of the ground was covered with snow. Seven hunter-green Land Rovers were waiting for the group, and everyone piled in, four to a vehicle. They drove in strict procession to the Great Cottage.

Nick had heard rumors about the Great Cottage, but he had never imagined it to look like it did. For one thing, it was hardly a cottage at all; it was a large building, three stories of stone and shingle and wood, with turrets and cupola windows cut into the roof. Over its pediment was a winged statue of the goddess Isis, mounted against the shingles. Pine and maple trees flanked the building on each side, standing guard.

All seven vehicles stopped on the main circle in front of the cottage. At exactly the same moment, each driver opened the car doors, allowing the Conscripts and Initiates to step out.

Waiting in front of the cottage, bundled in furs and top-coats, parkas and ski jackets, were the Elders of the Society, the two hundred of them attending the retreat. It was an overwhelming sight.

As the final Initiate stepped out, a drummer and a Scottish bagpiper in a kilt started playing a regimental march, an official-sounding tune that lasted for a minute as the twenty-eight of them stood wide-eyed in the gravel driveway. When they were finished, a cheer went up from the crowd, applause for the two classes, the Initiates and the Conscripts.

Some of the girls and their mothers started crying at the spectacle of it all.

Nick's family members rushed forward to him, crowding around him, hugging him and cheering. They pulled him and the other members into the Great Cottage's foyer, a vaulted structure with an enormous stag head as its centerpiece, its antlers appropriately garlanded for the holidays, and a grand Christmas tree, nearly twenty feet tall, in the middle of the room. The Great Cottage looked as if it had not changed in a hundred years. Its wide-planked pine floors were covered in worn kilim rugs of varying sizes, there were cozy club chairs by a walk-in fireplace, and the mantel was covered in conch shells and sailing trophies. Caterers in starched white shirts brought out silver trays of hot chocolate, hot buttered rum, and cider; on tables at each side and on passed trays were tarts and cookies, deviled eggs and bacon-wrapped shrimp. The entire thing was proceeding as if it were a normal cocktail party.

"What about our bags?" Phoebe whispered to Nick.

"I think it's being taken care of," he said.

"It is beautiful, I will grant them that. God, to think that all this is here, and it's used only a few times a year." She shook her head. "Bizarre."

"Phoebe!" Nick turned around to see his mother embracing Phoebe. "Darling, we are so happy that you are here. Don't you look pretty today! The Maine air suits you well. Come meet some of my friends." Gigi grabbed Phoebe and took her toward a group of women.

"Mom—Phoebe, you don't have to—"

"Nick, I'm fine." Phoebe smiled. "Don't worry about me. I'll see you a little later, okay?"

Lauren and three other girls were taken to their bunk by a valet in a ski parka. With the girls sleeping four to a room, the accommodations were a bit more Spartan than Lauren had imagined, but she didn't mind. While the Elders would stay in the Great Cottage's guest bedrooms, and in nicer accommodations in several outlying buildings, the Initiates and Conscripts were to stay in simple whitewashed cabins on the south side of the cottage, with multiple bedrooms in each, two bunk beds to a room. A bathroom down each hall was shared, with creaky plumbing and steam heat that rattled when it came on. There were banners on the walls of the bedrooms from various alma maters, left there as mementos from days past: Yale, Dartmouth, Harvard, Princeton. It could have been charming, like staying overnight in someone's college dorm room or going to summer camp again.

Except that it was the winter, and she had to find out what had happened to her boyfriend. Or sort-of boyfriend. Or whatever Alejandro had been.

That night, Lauren sat with the other Initiates at a casual seafood dinner in the main dining hall, which was a huge whitewashed space off the Great Cottage's foyer. It also had vaulted ceilings and its walls were covered with plaques and medals, symbols of past Society exploits, interspersed with colorful sailing flags, maritime paintings, vintage prints of seashells and coral. She saw Nick's family there, as well as friends of her mother's, people she had known since she was a child. It was all rather giddy, like running into people at an exclusive vacation resort and not realizing you had been planning to be in the same place at the same time.

Lauren looked across the room at Nick and Phoebe and how carefree they seemed. She was happy for them both but couldn't forget that she was alone.

CHAPTER FORTY-FIVE

Patch could barely believe that he had been able to get onto the island. He had started by going aboard with the Walker brothers and their two sons, who were going out lobstering on their boat, as they had for the past three years while their wives got some well-deserved time off between Christmas and New Year's. Patch almost wished he could join them, as it seemed like it would be a lot more fun. The guys played the Doors and Pink Floyd on the boom box they kept belowdecks, and they were particularly proud of the new GPS system they had recently installed. Patch even exchanged email addresses with the two cousins, promising he would look them up if he was ever in Maine again.

But that night, his goal was to get to the island.

While on the boat, Patch had come up with a plan.

According to the Walkers, a lot of local people were employed as part of the catering crew on Isis Island.

The Walkers' boat, the *Naugatuck*, approached the Isis landing. They followed Patch's instructions, seemingly amused at the little charade in which he had asked them to participate.

"Live lobster delivery for Palmer Bell?" said the older Walker brother, as the boat was pulling up against the dock.

A dockworker in a blue windbreaker checked his clipboard. "I'm not showing anything," he said.

The boat was moored against the side of the pier, the engines idling loudly. The two Walker cousins hoisted Patch up onto the dock, out of the worker's sight. Patch waved a quick good-bye to them before walking carefully toward shore. He could hear the voices in the distance: "You'd better check that list again. I know Mr. Bell wouldn't like it much if he didn't get his delivery. . . ."

At the end of a half-mile road leading from the dock was a large building, some kind of lodge or yacht club. When Patch arrived at the side door, he walked right in, asked someone where the uniforms were, and got to work, carrying crates of supplies, milk, and vegetables into the kitchen as directed. He hid his backpack in a storage room until he was assigned a bunk in the staff quarters, which were on a different part of the property. He hadn't had a chance to see much of the island at all; so far, it looked like a collection of stone and wood buildings, surrounded by trees.

He hoped he would have some time to think before figuring out his next move.

At dinner, Phoebe felt as if she were in a slow-moving, extremely odd dream. No one referred to Jared's death, nor Alejandro's disappearance, and certainly not to Patch. She saw Dr. Meckling, and Daniel as well, from across the room, though she was avoiding them both. Phoebe wondered what Daniel had told her mom he was doing during these few days.

After the main course, Phoebe got up, ostensibly to go to the ladies' room. She whispered in Nick's ear to meet her in the library. After using the restroom (it was the type where the plumbing and tile work, albeit in perfect condition, hadn't been updated since the 1960s), she found him in the dark, book-filled room that was down a corridor from the foyer.

"So what do we do?" she asked Nick.

"I don't know," he said.

In the dim, greenish light of the library's reading lamps, she looked at photographs of each class that were displayed. Captured in black and white, the members looked at the camera in stoic reserve, even though some of the photos were taken as recently as several years ago. There was something strange, though, that she noticed about the classes, aside from how stiff and posed the portraits were.

"Oh my God," Nick said. "I think this was my dad's class—look, here's my mom's class, and here's my dad. Wow." His mother and father looked so young in their portraits.

Phoebe examined two pictures, counting the members again. "Look at this," she said.

"What?"

"In some classes, there are fifteen members, and in others, there are fourteen."

"So what does that mean?"

Phoebe paused. "I don't know. I mean, it's not like there's a pattern to it. Here's the class of 1971, which has fifteen, and then the class of '72, which has fourteen, and then fifteen for two years, and then fourteen for two years . . . I can't really make any sense of it."

"I didn't think you would." The voice came from behind them, and Phoebe and Nick both started. At the entrance to the library was Parker Bell.

"Nick, Phoebe, I see you're doing a little bit of—what shall we call it—research?"

Phoebe faltered. "There's so much history here—we just wanted to see—to get an idea . . ."

"It's okay. You don't need to be afraid. You're curious. That's understandable. You've been part of the Society for nearly four months now, but you know very little about us. I, too, would be curious."

He walked over to a long green leather Chesterfield sofa

and sat down, crossing his legs. "Are there any questions I might be able to answer for you?"

Now, Phoebe thought, they were finally having the meeting they had wanted. Except this time it was on Mr. Bell's terms.

"Why are there fourteen members in some photographs and fifteen in others?" Phoebe said.

"Ah, the Power of Fourteen," Mr. Bell said.

"What's the Power of Fourteen?" Nick said.

"It will be explained in due time," Mr. Bell said. "Let's just say that classes with fourteen members are stronger. I myself come from a class of fourteen."

"But our class has fifteen members," Nick said. "Or at least, it did. Does what happened to Alejandro have something to do with this?"

"Just wait a few days," Mr. Bell said. "Everything will become clear."

"Dad, I think we're tired of these things constantly being kept from us."

"Nicholas, sometimes you have to wait. Especially for things that are important. Anyway, I need to be getting back to the dining room. I think they're serving coffee now. I suggest that you two do the same." He exited the room, leaving Phoebe and Nick to stare at each other.

"I want to get out of here," Phoebe said.

"Phoebe, how on earth are we going to do that? We're on

an island with spotty cell service, no ferry to the mainland, and a jet that no one has access to. We have to stay. Remember what Genie said, 'The best way to rebel can be from within'? You need to use that now."

She crumpled down onto an ottoman. It was all too much. Initiation rituals, the Great Cottage, the Power of Fourteen. The feelings of isolation and belonging at the same time. She started sobbing quietly.

"God, I'm not normally like this," she said. "I swear, the only two times I've cried in the last month have been in front of you. How silly is that?"

"It's not silly at all," Nick said. "I love—I love that about you. I love that you're honest. That you're real. It makes me feel like I, like I love—"

Phoebe held her breath, waiting for what Nick might say, but just at that moment, Nick was interrupted, mid-sentence, by an enormous crash in the hallway.

Nick jumped up and looked to the right, then to the left. At the end of the hall, a young man with close-cropped brown hair was quickly loading a pile of broken glasses onto a tray. Nick looked closer and it was—

Patch?

"Hey!" Nick said, before stopping himself. The young man put a single finger to his lips, grabbed the remainder of what had fallen off the tray, and scurried away.

Nick turned to Phoebe, completely forgetting the intensity of their moment together. "Okay, either I'm going completely insane or I just saw our missing friend. Carrying a tray of glasses."

"You mean, P—"

"Don't say his name," Nick said, coming closer to her and whispering. "I think it's better to be safe. We don't know who is listening."

"True," Phoebe whispered back. "But what the hell was it that your dad was saying about fourteen members in some classes? Nick, this is freaking me out."

"I know. We can't panic. We need to keep our heads screwed on."

He took her hand, holding it tight, and led her back to the dining hall.

CHAPTER FORTY-SIX

Patch had done his best to stay away from anyone he knew—the entire Bell family, other acquaintances, Phoebe and Lauren. Anyone who might identify him. But the next morning, he realized he was in trouble when he was put on breakfast line duty. The Society's Great Cottage served dinners with traditional table service, but its breakfasts and lunches harkened back to the days of prep school, which apparently many of the members enjoyed for its nostalgic value. Patch was stuck scooping out scrambled eggs onto people's plates as they went by his station in a long line. He was terrified Mr. Bell would look at him and identify him immediately.

The strangest thing happened, though: No one looked him in the eye. Nearly two hundred Society members passed by his station and mumbled that they would take some eggs or simply handed forth their plate. Some even thanked him, but few really looked at him. Even Parker Bell was too busy chatting with the woman next to him even to glance at Patch.

Nick, however, noticed him, but didn't let on. When his friend came by, he put forth his plate, giving Patch a meaningful glance.

Underneath it, Patch felt something, a piece of paper. He held on to it, handing the plate back to Nick, and deftly shoved the folded note into his pocket.

No one noticed a thing.

The note had said for Patch to meet Nick at two P.M., behind the tennis courts. Nick figured lunch would be finished at that point, and everyone would be in the afternoon session. Part of the Society retreat was a series of meetings, lectures, and seminars about finance, politics, the environment, and real estate. There were also lighter events such as wine tastings, discussions on art, a presentation on collecting vintage cars, and even a group that was putting on a short theatrical production. None of it was required, but it seemed to Nick that many used it as an opportunity—the information exchanged in these sessions could be invaluable, according to what his brothers had told him—while others saw the sessions more as social gatherings. The younger members enjoyed the wine tasting and the cigar seminar. And, of course, everyone was free to hang around the cottage, reading by the fire, chatting, enjoying cups of hot chocolate or spiced cider.

The crappy thing about all of it, Nick mused, was that he actually thought the retreat was pretty cool. When else did you get to talk to so many interesting people in such a relaxed and remote setting? When did you get to learn stuff for free, not because you had to, but because you wanted to? There was even a seminar by—and Nick couldn't believe this—Carlo Ferdinand, who, while not a Society member, had been flown in, signed a long nondisclosure agreement (as was the case with all the staff members, apparently), and was going to give a seminar on how to make the best DJ mixes.

Needless to say, in the freezing cold weather, no one would be at the tennis courts.

Nick trudged out in his fleece-lined L.L.Bean boots to meet Patch. He didn't want to look suspicious, so he put on his iPod and pretended he was out on a walk. He had asked Phoebe to meet him here, and he saw her up ahead.

"Is he around here?" she asked.

"I don't see him."

Nick motioned to her, and they went deeper into the woods behind the courts. "I didn't specify exactly which side of the courts," he said. "I'm assuming he'll pick the part that's not visible from the cottage."

Phoebe nodded.

Ahead of them, around the corner of the court, Nick saw some movement in the trees. Only a deer.

"Do you think he got held back?" Phoebe asked. "I think he was on clean-up duty in the kitchen, because I didn't see him serving."

"It's possible."

They heard a rustling behind them. To the rear of the cottage, on the hill where it sat, some of the Elder members were taking a walk. Dammit. This was not good. The Elders were too far away to see them through the woods, but they would certainly notice if Patch appeared in front of the courts.

"We can't let anyone see him talking to us," Phoebe said.

"Just stay still. I have a feeling he'll be here."

They waited for a few minutes. Phoebe's breath blew clouds into the chilly air. Nick loved how she looked in the cold, her nose slightly more pink than usual, her fair skin even more dramatic against her reddish-brown hair. It would have been romantic if they hadn't been so intent on finding—

There was a whistle. Nick recognized it: something Patch used to do, an annoying tune from some television show he would hum when they were walking along the dunes at the beach.

"Up here!" They heard a whisper and looked up, to see Patch waiting ten yards away, up a small hill that was covered in scrub brush and a thicket of birch trees.

Nick and Phoebe climbed the hill to meet Patch. It was strange seeing him, after all this time. His hair was completely shorn, like an army recruit. He wore the catering uniform under his snow parka.

"Hey," Patch said.

"We come all the way out here and all we get is a 'hey'?" Nick said. "Come on!" He stepped forward and offered Patch an awkward hug.

"Hi, Patch," Phoebe said.

"I guess we're in a bit of a sticky situation," Patch said.

"Yeah." Nick sat down on a tree stump. He hoped the Elders they saw didn't decide to go on some kind of nature walk. "We don't have much time."

"Are you okay?" Phoebe said. "Your grandmother is concerned about you. *We're* concerned about you."

Patch nodded. "I'm fine. Never washed so many dishes in my life. Do you have any idea how much food is wasted in this place? It's insane."

"All right, look," Nick said. "What's your deal? Are you here trying to spy on everything?"

"Hey, don't be a jerk about it. You know there's some messed-up stuff going on here. Someone needs to find out what it is."

"We know," Phoebe said. "We're trying to figure it out for ourselves. Something happened to Alejandro, but we don't know what."

"Might be the same thing that happened to Jared Willson," Patch said, looking at Nick.

"We don't know that," Nick said.

"What I'm saying is that I don't think Jared's death or Alejandro's disappearance were accidents. I think they were both planned. And I think the Society did it."

"We have no proof of that," Nick said. "We're trying as hard as you are to figure all this out."

Patch scoffed. "Oh, while you enjoy your wine tastings and cigar smoking and—oh, guess what—tonight there's a sundae bar. That'll be awesome. More plates for me to clean."

"Hey—you got yourself into this. I wasn't the one who asked you to sneak into the Night of Rebirth and film it."

Patch nodded. "I know. I sort of wish I had never planned the whole thing."

"Wait, what do you mean, *planned*?" Nick said.

Patch looked down. "Nothing. I just mean, I shouldn't have done it."

"No—you said *planned*. What did you do? How did you know—oh, my God."

"What?" Phoebe said. "Nick, what's going on?"

Nick looked at Patch. "You called the DJ. You told him not to come, or that the gig was canceled or whatever. You must have. That's the only explanation. It was too perfect: you being up in that booth, the only one with access to the air shaft. Admit it, you did it. Your grandmother must have told you about it beforehand."

"Patch?" Phoebe said. "Is that true?"

Patch said nothing.

"You son of a bitch!" Nick lunged at Patch, toppling him over. He punched his friend square in the face and then started wailing on his chest.

"Nick! Stop it!" Phoebe shouted. "Dammit, do you want to get us all in more trouble than we're in already?"

"Jesus Christ!" Patch said. "That hurt!"

"You deserved that," Nick said.

Patch's eye was red. "Here, take some snow," Phoebe said, making a snowball for Patch to hold up to his eye.

"Patch, you need to stop screwing around," Nick said. "We don't know what's going on with the Society, but you need to accept that you're not going to be the one who's going to figure it out. And you're certainly not going to be the next Michael Moore with your camera."

"I haven't done anything with my camera," he said. "I don't think I could get away with it. I still can't believe they didn't check my bags when I came in here."

"How did you get a catering job here anyway?" Phoebe asked.

"Long story," Patch said. "Or really, I guess, more like dumb luck."

The three of them stood there, not knowing what to do.

"Look," Nick said, "I don't have some great plan or anything."

Patch looked up through his injured eye. "Don't sweat it, Nick. You don't have a plan? Well, I do."

CHAPTER FORTY-SEVEN

Patch hadn't shared many details with Nick and Phoebe, but he told Nick to keep his cell phone on him, albeit hidden, at all times. He would let Nick know if and when he needed them. There was something strange he sensed in Nick and Phoebe: It was as if they suspected what was going on in the Society, whatever dreadful things it had accomplished, and yet felt completely powerless to do anything. It was like the Night of Rebirth, when his friend, the guy who would never join something like a secret society, so willingly had allowed the back of his neck to be tattooed.

The Society had that sort of control over people.

That evening, Patch had returned, after finishing work, to the caterer's quarters. There had been an awkward confrontation with his supervisor when he had asked Patch to verify the mailing address that they had on file for him. Apparently there was a "Jeb Elsdon" who hadn't shown up for work, and they were assuming that Patch was him. The trouble was, Jeb Elsdon (who had, thankfully, already signed the nondisclosure agreement) was forty-two years old. Patch assured his supervisor that it must have been a mistake and that the address in rural Maine was fine to send the check to.

Great, he thought. He was working for the Society, and he wasn't even going to get paid.

The catering staff all slept in a series of cabins downriver. The beds looked as if they had been installed a hundred years ago, and the staff was grouped ten to a room. There was a draft, and spiders and mice had made the rooms their home, crawling along the beams at night. Patch assumed the pay must be good or else no one would ever want to take the job.

Around one A.M., Patch woke up and crept out of bed, quietly putting on his clothes. The Great Cottage had a service entrance, and he wanted to take a look around. Before leaving that evening, Patch had made sure the door could be easily jimmied. The cottage didn't have an alarm system, and as far as he could tell, there were no surveillance cameras. It seemed that the Society was comfortable with old-fashioned lock-and-key security. Patch had noticed the two thugs in suits and a small group of guards on the daytime watch, but at night, there wasn't anyone on duty.

Or so he hoped.

The snow crunched in his ears as he walked up to the Great Cottage. His eye throbbed in pain and had swelled up to a nasty bruise; he had needed to make up a story for his supervisor about crashing into a doorframe.

He supposed that maybe he deserved the black eye from Nick. After all, he had nearly ruined Nick's club night, and he had been the cause of all this trouble.

But no, he decided he wouldn't see it that way. There was something going on with the Society, and Patch had to discover what it was. Surely the group was more than a bunch of privileged Upper East Siders who liked to hang out on an island in Maine, attending seminars and smoking cigars.

Patch was able to open the side service entrance with ease. It was a full moon, and he could easily find his way, but he had brought along a flashlight for inside.

The lower level of the Great Cottage was a labyrinth of tunnels, dumbwaiters, storage vaults, and service areas, all designed to serve the elaborate illusion on the upper floors that everything was running smoothly. The Society members had no idea how much went on down there to make sure their meals were delivered on time, that the cottage and cabins were kept clean, that there was always heat and hot water and freshly pressed linens.

One room, Patch had noticed earlier that day, was restricted. It was unmarked, at the end of a long hallway. Unlike the other rooms, its door was kept locked all the time.

He pulled out his file and started working away on the lock. The tumblers clicked, and the door gave way.

Once Patch was inside, he took a quick breath and let his eyes slowly adjust to the darkness. He switched his flashlight on. It was some kind of strange prop room; there were costumes on hangers, all along one wall. Against another was a rack of swords and weaponry. He walked forward and nearly stumbled into something, a large object on two sawhorses.

It was a giant wooden sarcophagus, one of two. On them were carved Egyptian-looking symbols.

Patch recognized them. They were from the Night of Rebirth.

What were they doing here? Hadn't they already used them back in September? Was this where they stored them? If so, then why were there only two?

Patch tried to open the lid on one, but it was sealed shut. No lock, no keyhole.

He flashed his light at the sarcophagus and took a cell phone pic. It was blurry, but it would be clear what it was. He quickly sent it to Nick's phone. He had two bars of service, just enough for the image to get through.

That was when he heard footsteps outside.

CHAPTER FORTY-EIGHT

The next morning after breakfast, Phoebe sat with Nick in one of the small, wood-paneled rooms off the cottage's foyer, next to a crackling fireplace. She had looked at the different staff members during breakfast, but didn't see Patch. Yesterday he had been on breakfast duty, so it was strange that he wasn't around this morning.

"He could be on cleanup," Nick said. "I need you to see something, though." Nick handed her his phone, displaying a picture Patch had sent to him. It showed the side of a sarcophagus, the same one that Phoebe now remembered as part of the Night of Rebirth back in September.

"He took this last night?"

"Look at the time on it." It was stamped from around two in the morning.

"So what do we do? More waiting?"

"We don't know what this means. This could be some storage area where they keep these when they're not using them." Nick shut off his phone.

"I'm not so sure about that," Phoebe said. "There could be people inside them. There could be—"

"Alejandro?" Nick said.

Phoebe couldn't say it.

"You can't be serious," Nick said. "You really think so?"

A shiver ran up Phoebe's spine as she heard a voice. Dr. Meckling was standing in the entrance.

"Phoebe," he said. "How are you feeling? I haven't seen you since our meeting last month. Your mother said you were doing better."

"Screw you," Phoebe said.

Nick looked startled and moved closer to Phoebe.

"Now," Dr. Meckling said, "there's no need to be rude. You know that kind of behavior isn't tolerated around here."

"You betrayed your profession," Phoebe said. "Saying you're a shrink and then being part of this."

He smiled. "I'm a board-certified psychiatrist. No question about that."

"You know what I mean," Phoebe said. "You're preying on innocent people. You're using your position to take advantage of them."

"Phoebe, that's not true. We're trying to protect you.

314

Which is why I think you should know that we're taking care of your friend."

"What friend?"

"Mr. Evans. He said he spoke to you yesterday."

"We don't know what you're talking about," Nick said.

"We suggest you lay off whatever it is you're looking for— if you want to see your friend unharmed," Dr. Meckling said.

"Don't you dare do anything to him," Nick said, standing up to meet his eyes. "I'll talk to my father—"

"I don't think you understand," Dr. Meckling said coolly. "You see, Nick, this message came from your father himself."

What had happened after he heard the footsteps was a blur to Patch. Some men grabbed him, possibly the same men from that night near the editing suite, but possibly different. He put up a fight, but was unable to break free. They took his cell phone and destroyed it. A man injected his arm with a needle, and he felt himself become faint before passing out.

Now he was lying in what felt like the inside of one of the sarcophagi. A needle that was connected to an intravenous drip bag ran into his arm. He had torn it out once, but they had opened the coffin again and stuck it back in. It was making him sleepy, as he drifted in and out of consciousness.

The odd thing was that the second time they stuck the needle in him, he realized he didn't want to take it out. It felt good.

He woke again as he felt one of the men lifting up his body and tearing away the Band-Aid at the nape of his neck. It didn't hurt at all.

"Bell should see this," the man said.

"Which one?" the other said.

"Both of them."

A moment later, Patch drifted off again.

Phoebe had said that if they were going to stick around, they should act as if they were normal Initiates, more like the other eleven in the group: drinking, playing games, hanging out, attending the occasional workshop, catching up on sleep. Nick wished he could be so relaxed. As they were sitting outside on the back porch of the cottage, their breath visible in the chilly air, he convinced her that they owed it to Patch to look for him.

"What are they really going to do if they catch us again?" Nick said. "My father isn't going to do anything to him. It's all just a big threat, to scare him into giving up that footage. My dad knows that I would never forgive him if he hurt Patch."

Phoebe stayed silent.

"What, you don't believe me?"

"Nick, your father and grandfather have lied to you before," she said quietly. "You don't really know what they're capable of."

Nick felt his brow furrow. He didn't want to believe that

what she was saying could be true, but he was starting to trust Phoebe more than anyone else.

"I'm sorry," Phoebe said. "I know it must be the strangest feeling in the world, to be betrayed by your family. I mean, with me, it's just my mom, and I know it's because she's confused by who Daniel really is. But with you, well, it's your whole—"

Nick looked at her, and she stopped talking. She didn't have to say any more.

"So what do we do?"

Phoebe looked out at the snow-covered treetops. "I say we look for him. Carefully. Very, very carefully."

CHAPTER FORTY-NINE

Lauren had felt distant from Phoebe and Nick since the start of the retreat. Although it was partly her own fault—she had been moody and withdrawn—it was as if they had been in their own private club of two. She knew they hadn't done anything deliberately to make her feel shut out— they had tried to include her in things, although she often declined. It was hard to be with them when all she could think about was Alejandro, about the night they had spent together, and the awful last moments when she saw him, being carried out of that club. She spent some of the first two days at the retreat trying to be sociable, but she found herself making every excuse she could to be alone.

On the third afternoon of the retreat, as she was leaving her cabin, Thad Johnson came out of his, bundled in a ski parka. He looked as if he had just taken a shower; his blond curls were frozen on his head, and he was carefully applying SPF lip balm.

"Hey," he called. "You going for a walk?"

Lauren nodded.

"No one our age really appreciates walks around here," he said, as he hurried up to her. "It's like they're all too busy making connections or racing from one seminar to another."

"Yeah, I know what you mean."

"Do you want company?"

Lauren was about to say no, but that would be a lie: She wanted company, but she wanted Alejandro's company.

"Okay," she finally said.

"Don't think about it for too long."

She smiled, realizing that he was teasing her.

"You seem a little down," he said.

"I'm just wondering," Lauren said, "if I'm the only one freaked out by this. I mean, we're part of this group, and two people are dead or missing."

"Alejandro," Thad said. "Have you heard from him?"

"No. And no one seems to know anything, not even his parents. Why would they do this to him?"

"What do you mean 'they'?"

"You know, 'they,' the Society."

Thad stopped walking. "You think the Society did something to Alejandro?"

"It's like they decide when they want to protect us and when they want to destroy us." She told Thad what she and Nick and Phoebe had discovered. "It's so screwed up, I feel like we're trapped here on this island, our phones barely work, we're all in this bizarre Stepford-country-club fantasy. I'm not sure I can handle it anymore."

Thad put a hand on Lauren's shoulder, and she flinched a bit. "Hey, I get what you're saying. It isn't exactly what I expected, either." He paused for a moment. "Listen, it's a bit chilly out. You want to go grab some hot chocolate?"

Lauren looked at him. It was sweet of him to ask her, but she wasn't sure if she should accept.

"Um, sure, but, Thad, you should really know, I'm not really in the market for—I mean, I don't mean to presume . . ."

"I understand—you're not looking to date anyone these days. That's okay."

"It is?"

"Sure. I'm, well—let's just say I'm not exactly into girls. At least not in that way."

Lauren laughed as relief flowed over her. Of course he was gay! How silly she had been not to see it—no decent guy would hit on her after what she'd been through. "Thad, you have no idea how happy that makes me. Because—" She realized what she was about to say and how childish it sounded, but she decided it didn't matter. "Because what I could really use right now is a friend."

Phoebe felt terrible about the whole thing with Patch, though, admittedly, it was his fault that he had given her the images that had started all the trouble. It was a sneaky thing of him to do, especially when he knew it could get her into such a mess. But she knew he was trying to do his art, and she was trying to do hers, and she couldn't really fault him. After all, wasn't art supposed to provoke?

While everyone was in the main seminar for the day, off in one of the auxiliary buildings, Nick and Phoebe made their way down to the lower level of the cottage. Employees were moving trays and carts of food and drinks, all in preparation for afternoon tea. No one paid them much mind, Phoebe noticed, as long as they acted as if they belonged there. Each door was marked with a specific label: MAIN KITCHEN, MEAT LOCKERS, WINE CELLAR, HOUSEKEEPING, LINENS.

"Do we check each room?" Phoebe whispered to Nick.

"I don't think we can," he said. "Too suspicious. We don't even know if he's down here. He could be in one of the out-buildings. Or at the athletic center—I mean, each one of those buildings has a basement. Not to mention about five hundred other rooms."

Phoebe heard the crackle of a walkie-talkie, and before they could react, Parker Bell came striding toward them.

"Nick, what is it now?" he said. "I had to leave the conference on global economic theory because I was told that my son and his friend were poking around in the basement."

"Dad, where the hell are you keeping him?" Nick shouted, his voice echoing down the hallway.

His ferocity startled Phoebe, but she realized that his tactic of causing a scene was working. Employees were staring at Parker Bell curiously and then looking away.

"You be quiet," Mr. Bell hissed. "Come with me." He took them to the end of the hallway, to an unmarked door. A security guard followed them.

"Do you want entry, sir?" the guard said.

Nick's father nodded. The security guard pulled out a ring of keys and opened the door.

"Come inside," Mr. Bell said.

Phoebe looked at Nick cautiously, but Nick nodded that it was okay. Phoebe figured Nick's father wouldn't do anything to her while his own son was around.

The guard shut the door behind them. Phoebe was startled to see the sarcophagus from the image Patch had sent to Nick, rigged up with an IV bag and a tube leading to it.

"Oh my God," Phoebe said.

"I'm bringing you in here as a courtesy," Mr. Bell said. "You two have caused enough trouble over the last few weeks and months, and I thought that by clueing you in to what is going on you might be willing to cooperate."

Nick said nothing, so Phoebe decided to do the same.

"Now, you're probably wondering who's in the coffins. The

first one contains your friend Patch."

"Dad, if you have done anything to him, I will make you regret it for the rest of your life," Nick said.

"Nicholas, relax. He's being monitored by a doctor. The IV tube is keeping him asleep, but feeding him vital fluids and nutrients. He's perfectly fine, probably healthier than half the people on this retreat."

"What are you doing with him?"

"That remains to be seen. I assure you he will not be hurt."

"How can I trust you? You've lied to me so many times before. How do I know this isn't just another one of your stories?"

"Nicholas, have some faith."

"What about Alejandro? What did you do with him? Is he in the other coffin?" Nick spat the words out at his father.

"No, he is not. The second coffin is empty. There is something you two have to understand. You were on the verge of discovering it the other evening. Each Society class is different. The ideal class, theoretically, is a group of fifteen members, all working harmoniously for the right goals. But sometimes members step out of line, members who do not reflect the highest beliefs of the Society."

Phoebe looked at Nick. His face was like stone.

His father continued, "You two, I'm sorry to say, fall into that category. It is not unusual—it's a recent trend, actually.

Youth today are so much less obedient. Even the best and the brightest, which you both certainly are, step out of line these days. It's part of your maturation process. And we understand that. But what we cannot tolerate is insubordination."

"Insubordination?" Nick asked.

"Disobedience. Not paying attention to the rules. Your entirely willful disregard for the rules is very troubling. And that is where the Power of Fourteen comes into play." Mr. Bell paused. "I am going to explain something to you before the other Initiates find out about it this evening. You must promise me that you will keep it to yourself."

Phoebe and Nick looked at each other. Nick gave her a shrug as if to say, *What choice do we have?*

"Good. So now we come to the matter of Mr. Calleja."

Phoebe felt a lump rising in her throat.

"In many classes, there is a weak member. It is almost unavoidable when you have to pick fifteen people. Sometimes they are legacies; sometimes they are people whose promise does not deliver in actualities. The weakest member is often not a threat. In Mr. Calleja's case, however, he was."

"How was he a threat?" Phoebe asked. Alejandro seemed harmless to her, much more harmless than she or Nick had been.

"You may not be aware of this, but Mr. Calleja had a serious drug problem. His behavior was out of control. His family had sought treatment for him multiple times, with little success. When he had his incident over Thanksgiving break and was quoted in several gossip columns making oblique references to the Society, we realized that something had to be done."

"So why not bring him in and talk to him?" Nick asked.

"We would have, if your class had been a normal class. But little did I know that my own son and his friends would be the insubordinates we always fear."

"What do we have to do with it?"

"It's the Power of Fourteen. If you would listen, you'll understand."

Nick stayed silent, as his father stood in front of the sarcophagus.

"Mr. Calleja is dead."

"No!" Nick shouted. "You did not do this!"

"You're exactly right. I didn't do this at all."

"Then who did?"

"All of you. You were the ones who let him die."

CHAPTER FIFTY

Nick looked at his father in amazement. "What the hell do you mean?"

"On the night Mr. Calleja was last seen, all of you were out partying with him—illegally, against the rules of your school and the laws of our state. He imbibed enough alcohol to black out, and he was carried away. All of your fingerprints are on the glasses that were found at the scene of the crime."

"Where is he now?"

"Mr. Calleja was taken to a facility where he was allowed to binge on drugs to his heart's content. He spent the last week consuming quantities of drugs that before he could only dream about."

Nick's father checked his watch. "If everything is on schedule, Mr. Calleja's body would have been deposited on the Lower East Side exactly fifteen minutes ago in an area, appropriately enough, known as Hell Square. He will be found, I imagine, by the authorities within the hour. When they examine him, they will find lethal doses of alcohol and other drugs, all consistent with the story that Mr. Calleja started partying on the nineteenth and went on a drug binge in the area. You see, sadly, people are almost always done in by their worst vices."

"How are you going to prove that? They'll know he was at your party at the club, won't they?"

"Oh, it was hardly the party that caused his death, but it started him on the downward spiral. His ATM card will show enormous withdrawals, enough to buy several hundred dollars' worth of drugs every day and to give him a place to stay, a flophouse in the neighborhood, the owner of which will verify his whereabouts. It's sad, but it happens."

"They would see it on tape, then. ATM machines have cameras, Dad."

"That's true, but unfortunately there's one at the corner of Rivington and Ludlow where the camera is broken. Mr. Calleja seemed to favor that one the most."

"So what does all this have to do with us?"

"That is the Power of Fourteen. The fourteen of you are now bound together with this irrevocable secret. Although you may not be convinced, the others will know that it was their enabling that started Mr. Calleja on this journey. Your class will be stronger than ever. You can't tell your families, you can't tell the police. You can only keep silent. We think it will put an end to all these shenanigans."

Nick sat down on a box, his head in his hands. He couldn't believe this. Finally, he looked up.

"You are an evil, vicious man," Nick said to his father, shaking as he uttered the words. "I can't believe I'm even related to you." He looked at his father, at his dad's turtleneck and blazer and duck boots, all the familiar trappings that clothed a person he barely knew. He couldn't fathom that this was the man who had raised him.

"I'd watch your words, Nick. All this has paid for everything you've grown up with. You can thank the Society for many of the comforts and privileges you enjoy. And I don't think you'd want that taken away, would you?"

"But why, Dad? Why would you want to do this?"

"Because it's so easy, Nick. People in the world see only what they want to see. We have a way of life to protect. It's unfortunate when it comes to this, but we are living in difficult times. Extreme measures must sometimes be taken. That's why we have the Guardians. Hector here is one of them." He motioned to the guard standing behind him.

Phoebe spoke up. "And this has been going on for how long?"

"Well, in recent years, it's happened more and more. The class of Conscripts, and the situation with Mr. Willson—that was unfortunate. But that class has bonded together in an incredible way. It seems most of them never liked Mr. Willson anyway. Once they realized he could potentially ruin their chances for future success, no one batted an eyelash when he was found dead."

"Jared died of exposure," Nick said. "Everyone knows that."

"Exactly," Nick's father said. "But the fourteen Conscripts know that they were with him the night he died. We have photo documentation of that rather lurid event, and you have to believe me, I don't think any of them want that getting out, particularly when they are waiting on college acceptances."

"When did this start?" Phoebe asked.

"In the 1960s was the first time," Parker said. "The Society started having problems. A few of the members tried to defect. A solution was found quite by accident, through an initiation ritual that has since been outmoded. Students had to hold their breath underwater in the Society's pool at the townhouse, for as long as they could. Fifteen of them, all at once. It was a way of creating unity. Little did they know that one of them had a rare condition that caused his lungs to collapse. It was a terrible tragedy, and everyone knew it was an accident. But what they found was that the class bonded together more strongly than ever before. Thus, the Power of Fourteen came into being."

"So you're saying this is our fault?" Nick asked. "That if

we hadn't messed with things, asked too many questions, whatever—that Alejandro might still be alive?"

"Maybe," he said. "Nick, you can't blame yourselves. On the contrary, I'm actually very proud of you and Phoebe."

"Why's that?" Phoebe asked.

"Because we have found in the past that those engaged in insubordination on the early side of their Society careers all turn out to be one thing."

"What's that?" Nick said.

"They make the best leaders."

Phoebe still couldn't believe what Mr. Bell was telling them. "So all this success, everything you've been offering us, it's all a charade?"

"Far from it," Mr. Bell said. "Phoebe, your paintings are good. Really, they are. But do you realize that ninety percent of them were purchased by Society members? You're in some of the most prominent collections in the city. But we can have those pieces put in storage, even destroyed if we want. Your work will never be seen again."

"Dad, that's absurd," Nick said. "Phoebe doesn't need your help to succeed."

"You may want to ask her how much attention was paid to her before we put in a special request at her mother's gallery."

Phoebe was silent.

"And what about me?"

"Nick, your future, whether it's club promoting or something else—and God help us if it is club promoting, but I guess we'll see—we can affect that just as easily. The same with Ms. Mortimer and her jewelry line. Sebastian Giroux isn't helping her out for his own health. With all the losses he's had to take on the line so far, he could easily pull it."

"So what if he does?" Phoebe said. "I know I'm stating the obvious, but none of that is worth you killing people."

"Of course not," Mr. Bell said. "That's why we engineered it so that the fourteen of you would be the ones doing the killing."

CHAPTER FIFTY-ONE

Lauren was waiting in her bunk, unsuccessfully trying to take a nap, when Phoebe and Nick came to visit her. They had a look in their eyes, a look of pity and shame.

"He's dead, right?" Lauren said, her voice barely a whisper.

Phoebe reached forward and embraced her. "I'm so sorry, Lauren. We're going to figure a way out of this. We don't know what it is. But we're going to, somehow."

"What about Patch?"

"They've got him hooked up to some kind of sedative, and they're holding him hostage," Nick said. "The room is guarded by two guys, around the clock. I don't think there's any chance of getting in there."

Lauren started sobbing. "Nick, they're ruthless—how do

we know they're not going to do something to Patch?"

"We don't," he said. "That's the screwed-up thing about it all: We don't."

Patch's body felt sore from being in the same position for so long. He had been in the coffin for nearly twelve hours. He was drowsy but otherwise fine—he wasn't hungry, he wasn't thirsty. It was as if all his emotions had been shut off. He had no idea what they were feeding him intravenously, but he had to admit that it was good stuff. Or so his muddled brain thought.

Several times in the afternoon, the coffin lid had been opened, and the two guards had stood over him while Dr. Meckling questioned him. They wanted to know where the footage was and how much of it there had been. The trouble was, in his drowsy state, he couldn't remember. The doctor made alterations in the IV, and Patch felt himself becoming more lucid.

Later, at a point that he guessed may have been early evening, the coffin lid opened, and Parker Bell stood over him.

"This is an unusual situation," he said. "I don't want to have to hurt you, Patchfield, particularly since we have a—what's the right word?—a *history* together. But there's a lot at stake here. You need to tell us where the material is that you shot of the Society initiation. It simply cannot be floating around. You tell us where it is, and when the time comes, we'll make sure you get home safely."

"I don't believe you," Patch said. "I heard about what you did to Alejandro and to Jared Willson."

Mr. Bell looked troubled. "Meckling, wasn't he supposed to be in a near comatose state?"

The doctor spoke from across the room. "Parker, it drifts in and out. I explained that to you. It depends on each person's metabolism, and we haven't had time to run adequate blood tests. I've been telling you for years that we need a proper medical clinic on the island."

"That's not important now," Mr. Bell said quickly. He spoke as if he were discussing a troublesome legal case rather than a matter of life and death. "Patch, what do you want? We could do away with you, as we have the others, but that doesn't serve us. And it doesn't serve—well, it doesn't serve my son. The material could still be floating around. We know about your production deal, and we have the power to kill it. Once we take a majority stake in Eyes Wide Open Productions, we could effectively squash the release of the material."

"You could never do that," Patch said. "Simone would never allow it."

"I wouldn't be so sure about that. She's much more interested in us writing a check so she can do hard-hitting documentaries than she is about your little high school television program."

Parker Bell was right. They had him in a neck hold and

weren't willing to let go. And yet, at the same time, they were asking him what he wanted.

Through the blur of the drugs they had been feeding him, he decided to tell them.

That evening, Nick sensed a grim reality settling in over himself and Phoebe and Lauren. They knew about Alejandro, they knew where Patch was being held captive, and they had no control over any of it.

It was the last evening of the Society's retreat, before the Elders would leave to spend New Year's Eve with their families. The Initiates and Conscripts were to stay behind and be fêted at a private bash in the cottage, which Nick wasn't particularly thrilled about. It seemed like every move was a game, every event an opportunity for exploitation.

There was an enormous banquet that evening in the dining hall, and everyone was dressed up smartly—dresses for the girls and khakis and nice shirts for the guys. After dinner, everyone except for the Initiates put on their coats and went outside. Through the windows, they could see that lit torches lined the pathways in front of the main entrance to the cottage.

The Initiates were asked to stay back and convene in an upstairs room. Called the game room, it was a meeting room on the second floor, at the top of the cottage's grand staircase. At first Nick thought it might be a room for people to play chess or checkers or poker. Instead, it was a room filled with wild game: mounted heads on plaques; lion, zebra, and even a polar bear skin on the floor; a chandelier made of antlers. The room was dimly lit, flickering candles on the wall sconces the only illumination.

Nick's father stood in front of the group of fourteen. He started speaking slowly, about the power of commitment to the Society, of responsibility, of bravery in the face of adversity. Then he started talking about Alejandro.

"You all know by now of the disappearance of Mr. Calleja. Sadly, Mr. Calleja was not cut out to be a member of the Society. He was the proverbial bad seed, the rotten apple in the barrel. Mr. Calleja had a difficult night during your last Initiate gathering. The party triggered off a drug binge for him, an addiction he had tried to control for many months. Tragically, it got the better of him: He was found dead on the Lower East Side this morning."

People in the room gasped. Nick saw Phoebe holding Lauren tightly.

"It is absolutely imperative that none of you mention to anyone the Society event where you last saw him," Nick's father said. "It could jeopardize everything you've been working for."

"Why not?" Thad Johnson said. "Shouldn't the police know about it?"

"Thaddeus, you must believe me when I tell you that the

authorities should not be contacted. You see, all of your fingerprints are on the glasses from the party. The police will want to question each one of you. It will be in the newspapers, your parents will find out, and so will your schools. Believe me, it is not the kind of publicity that you want to have. The media feasts on this kind of news like vultures. All of you would be in the papers for months." He paused for a moment before continuing. "You are now all bound together by this secret. If one of you tells, you put at risk not only yourself, but the entire group."

Lauren felt numb with pain as Phoebe gently led her outside with the others.

"We don't have to do this," Phoebe whispered. "We can go back to the cabins and talk about it."

"It's fine," Lauren said. "I need to see what this is all about." That Alejandro was dead had been the worst possibility, but she had suspected it all along, a horrible, awful sensation that she had tried to push from her consciousness. Now it was a reality, confirmed not only by Nick and Phoebe, but also by Parker Bell. She felt an icy chill in her heart, the truth of him being gone, of being betrayed, of having been so foolish as to cling to any hope that he might have been alive.

How stupid he had been with his life, and how stupid she had been to follow him.

Ahead of them, outside the cottage, the entire group of

Elders was gathered. In the center of the main clearing stood a wooden platform with a podium. To the side of the platform, ten yards away, a crackling bonfire reached two stories high. The Initiates were herded to the front of the group, where they were made to stand in front of the platform.

Parker Bell now walked up the staircase to the structure, his breath visible in the cold air. Behind him sat Palmer Bell and the members of the Council of Regents.

At the side of the Great Cottage, there was a commotion. A group of men carried two different sarcophagi on pallets, moving them toward the fire.

"No!" Phoebe screamed. She tried to push her way through the crowd, but the Elders stopped her.

"Settle down, young lady!" an older man said. "They're empty!"

Parker Bell spoke into a microphone. "Tonight, at the final evening of the Bradford Trust Association, these symbolic sarcophagi are burned in memory of the lives of Jared Willson and Alejandro Calleja, two of our youngest members whom we lost this year. It has been a time of sadness for many. We must remember, however, that there has been light as well."

A group of men brought a figure, all in black and wearing a hood, up the stairs to stand next to Mr. Bell.

"Oh my God," Nick said. He appeared to be readying himself to jump up onto the platform.

"What is it?" Phoebe said.

"Rather serendipitously, we have a new member of the class of Initiates this year," said Parker Bell.

The hood was lifted from the figure. In front of them all stood Patch.

CHAPTER FIFTY-TWO

His eye was still purple and swollen. With his shaved head and newly toned body, he looked like a prize fighter after a tournament. He was blinking wildly, as if he hadn't seen the sun in days. A bright spotlight slowly came on from behind them all, giving everyone on the platform the appearance of gods.

"Patchfield Evans III has gone through an unusual and nontraditional initiation this fall, but the Council of Regents has voted for him to take his place among the class of Initiates."

Nick's father handed Patch a list of rules, one Nick recognized as the same they had all been given on the Night of Rebirth.

"Patchfield, do you accept these rules as the tenets for membership?"

"I do." He nodded, but his voice was weak.

"Patchfield is a promising young filmmaker, and we are delighted to have him as part of our group. Patch, you may now join your class."

Patch was led down to stand next to the group of Initiates. Nick looked at him, hoping he was okay.

"And now, by the power of the *crux ansata*, I pronounce all the Initiates as having advanced to the level of Conscripts."

A cheer rose up from the crowd as the Elders rushed toward the group. Everyone popped open bottles of champagne, spraying them in the air, and the somber event became a party once again. Nick left Phoebe and rushed over to Patch, two stoic figures amidst the pandemonium. He didn't know what to say to him.

Nick reached forward to embrace Patch, hugging him tightly, making a silent promise to his friend that never again would he let him go.

ACKNOWLEDGMENTS

Secret ankh tattoos to everyone who has supported me during this novel's creation: friends, colleagues, and mentors.

To my agent, Kate Lee at ICM, who championed this idea from its inception.

To my editor, Brenda Bowen, whose passion for this series has inspired me.

To Sarah Shumway, Katherine Tegen, Molly O'Neill, and everyone at HarperCollins who has worked on this book.

To my assistant, Susanne Filkins, who has proven herself to be a crack researcher.

To Melissa de la Cruz, who never doubted for a moment that I could write fiction for teens.

To Tom Williams and Corey Lambert, born and bred Upper East Siders, for their insight.

To the Dolby and Frist families, for their encouragement.

And of course, to Drew Frist, who knows where all the bodies are buried.

Secret Society

An Investigation into the Archives
of the Bradford Trust Association

Confidential Files on Nick, Phoebe, Lauren, and Patch

A Preview of *The Trust*

An Investigation into the Archives of the Bradford Trust Association

The Bradford Trust Association Archives
44 East 66th Street
New York, New York 10065

A Note to Visitors

Access to the Bradford Trust Association archives is granted on an exceptional basis to Society members by Miss Katherine Stapleton, administrator and archivist of the BTA, on the sole advice of the Council of Regents. Respect for the Trust's materials is paramount. No recording devices are permitted into the archives, nor are writing implements. Under no circumstances may material be copied or removed from the archives, and visitors agree that the contents of these materials may not be published, broadcast, or quoted from in any way.

I understand these rules and will abide by them.

Signature: _____

Date: _____

BTA-248
A Letter from William Bradford to His Brother, Edward

New York City
January 14, 1802

My Dear Brother:

After much reflection, I have concluded that the city would benefit from a benevolent organization with the express purpose of bringing together those of like countenance & spirit. After one is graduated from college, while there are numerous social clubs & organizations, many feel little there that attracts in a genuine manner. My colleagues sense a yearning for a deeper connection among men, for a fraternal organization that would forge business associations & possibilities for future expansion of mind, body, spirit, &c. I believe that the creation of this organization is in our hands.

I propose a Society, clandestine in nature, for us, these sons of privilege, with a fixed meeting place in New York City—a space in which

4

men can feel free to act as they wish. Naturally, a strict code of conduct would be applied. It is my experience that men do best when given boundaries within freedom. Secrecy will be of the utmost concern; it is in secrecy that the group's strength will lie.

For the group's symbol, I propose an ankh, the Egyptian symbol for life, for immortality, & for good fortune & protection from evil. Much has been made of the Egyptians & their unique & curious culture. We have much to gain by selecting an abstruse image such as this one to serve as our insignia. The crux ansata is a design of much beauty, simple in form, reproducible in multiple formats, & still entirely ineffable in its meaning.

Would you join me in this fledgling effort? I believe much good could come of it. Let us dine soon & reflect on the best course of action, &c.

Yours faithfully,
William Bradford

A Selected Chronology of Significant Events in the History of the Bradford Trust Association

1802: Bradford Trust Association founded by William Bradford and his brother, Edward, as a benevolent social organization known to most members as "the Society."

1871: The Bradford Trust has developed into a significant force in the social and philanthropic life of the city. When the Metropolitan Museum is founded in New York City, Society members fund several significant galleries.

1881: Cleopatra's Needle erected in Central Park by William Vanderbilt. Society members assist in financing its installation. Increasing American interest in Egyptology causes Egyptian rituals to be incorporated into the group's traditions.

1922: Howard Carter discovers King Tut's tomb in Egypt's Valley of the Kings. Society members are concerned that "Egyptomania" in the United States will necessitate the group going further underground. Proposal of the abolition of the ankh is overruled by the Council of Regents.

1929: Wall Street crash occurs. Society members group together to help one another financially.

1941: During wartime, secret societies at Ivy League colleges are disbanded while the Bradford Trust continues to flourish. Palmer Bell, future Chairman, is drafted into the military and becomes an active member of the Society two years later.

1958: Due to youth culture explosion in United States, Society membership is now offered to males sixteen years of age and older.

1963: The Power of Fourteen discovered through tragic accident during swimming-pool initiation ritual.

1977: Women permitted to become members of the Society.

1978: Palmer Bell becomes Chairman of the Society.

2000: Parker Bell becomes Chairman of the Society. Palmer Bell becomes Chairman Emeritus.

2009: Admission of Nicholas Bell, Phoebe Dowling, and Lauren Mortimer among others in the class of fifteen members.

Confidential Files
on Nick, Phoebe, Lauren, and Patch

BTA-5497 to BTA-5501
Excerpts from a Selection of Individual Dossiers
BTA Admissions Committee—Internal Documents
Confidential and Proprietary

Candidate: Nicholas Bell, 16, male

Society legacy. Son of Parker and Georgiana Bell of New York City, and grandson of Palmer Bell of Palm Beach. Siblings: Henry Bell, 21, and Benjamin Bell, 19. Parents upstanding members of BTA. Father is chairman of Bell Trading Company. Candidate attends the Chadwick School. Quality of academic transcript is adequate. College prospects include Yale, assuming trustee recommendation. While Mr. Bell has not yet distinguished himself academically, he displays unique gifts for social leadership. Mr. Bell exhibits potential for maturity, and great motivation when he chooses. Past disciplinary actions include a questioning by the Southampton police after a party involving alcohol, though Mr. Bell was released without incident; two detentions and one suspension at the Chadwick School, though the marks were expunged from his official record.

It is the opinion of the BTA admissions committee that Mr. Bell should be admitted as a legacy. Through time and grooming, he will prove himself an asset to his class. He has potential to be a leader, either socially or politically.

Decision: ACCEPT

Candidate: Phoebe Dowling, 16, female

Daughter of Preston Dowling of Los Angeles and Maia Dowling, soon to be of New York City; parents divorced. Father is a venture capitalist. Mother is a fine art photographer. Candidate attended St. Catherine's School in Los Angeles; admitted to the Chadwick School for the fall. Quality of academic transcript is outstanding. College prospects include Brown, Yale, and Williams. Miss Dowling displays interests in visual art, photography, and writing. She exhibits excellent levels of motivation and maturity for her age. She has no past disciplinary actions, according to St. Catherine's records.

It is the opinion of the BTA admissions committee that Miss Dowling should be admitted in order to increase the diversity of the class. The candidate is from the West Coast, is an artist, and would contribute much to the liveliness and energy of her class. She has potential to be a successful visual artist, a community leader, or a writer.

Decision: ACCEPT

Candidate: Lauren Mortimer, 16, female

Daughter of Trevor and Diana Mortimer of New York City; parents divorced. Sibling: Allison Mortimer, 14. Father is an investment banker. Mother is an interior decorator and community fund-raiser. Candidate attends the Chadwick School. Quality of academic transcript is good. College prospects include Brown, Rhode Island School of Design, and Fashion Institute of Technology. Miss Mortimer displays interest in fashion and design, though she has yet to express these talents publicly. She is a social leader in her class and among her peer group in the city. Miss Mortimer displays strong levels of motivation and maturity for her age. Unfortunate disciplinary action includes two detentions for smoking in the restroom at Chadwick; no other incidents recorded.

It is the opinion of the BTA admissions committee that Miss Mortimer should be admitted as a strong social leader in her class. The candidate has been noted for her personal style and charisma, and would contribute much to the social standing of her class. She has potential to be a fashion designer as well as a social or community leader.

Decision: ACCEPT

Candidate: Patchfield Evans, III, 16, male

Son of Patchfield Evans, Jr., deceased, formerly of New York City, and Esmé Evans of Ossining, New York. Parents former members of BTA. Father was a banker. Mother is non compos mentis and resides at Stoney River Psychiatric Hospital. Candidate lives with legal guardian, his grandmother, Eugenia Madison of New York City. Attends the Chadwick School. Quality of academic transcript is excellent. College prospects include Columbia and Princeton. Mr. Evans displays interests in filmmaking and photography, as well as the development of his personal website, PatchWork. He exhibits great potential for being a leader in the area of online social networking. Overall, Mr. Evans shows outstanding levels of motivation and maturity. Past disciplinary actions include a citation for underage drinking while at a party with Nicholas Bell in Southampton. Candidate was given twenty hours of community service. Unbeknownst to Mr. Evans, Parker Bell succeeded in having the record expunged, given that the young man was a minor. Mr. Evans has no serious disciplinary actions at the Chadwick School.

Mr. Evans is a difficult case. He would have much to offer the current class of Initiates, but given his family history, he is a risky choice. His mother is no longer a member of the BTA in good standing, and the BTA is well aware that Mr. Evans's grandmother does not hold the BTA in high regard. While Mr. Evans is eminently talented, it is the opinion of the BTA admissions committee that Mr. Evans should not be offered admission to the current class of Initiates.

Decision: DENY

A Preview of

The Trust

A SECRET SOCIETY NOVEL

PROLOGUE

NEW YORK CITY, 1992

Outside the Metropolitan Museum of Art one cold February evening, photographers swarmed around the entrance, pushing and jostling, angling for the perfect shot. The Met's grand staircase, swathed in black carpet and dotted with snowflakes, was the runway for a flock of Manhattan luminaries who ascended the steps to the museum and into the event of the winter season, the Dendur Ball. Most posed and preened for the cameras, savoring their moment in the spotlight before they were ushered into the museum.

An exquisitely beautiful woman in her late twenties, with long dark hair, fair skin, and a thin, regal neck, walked across the street with her husband, dodging the limousines and town cars that were stacked three deep on Fifth Avenue. She clutched her dress so it wouldn't catch on her heels, and held her petite handbag in one hand and a sheer wrap that fluttered in the wind in the other. She didn't come in a chauffeured car or a taxicab like the other guests at the ball. She didn't need to, for she lived right across the street.

The crowd parted ways for the two of them, as if they carried an electric charge, an irresistible field announcing to all that she was in their path. He was handsome and dressed in a classic black dinner jacket, but it was she who commanded attention as she ascended the staircase, photographers and reporters shouting her name. She appeared barely to hear them as she climbed slowly and carefully. At the top of the steps, she turned around and glanced not at the crowd, not at the white-hot flashbulbs, but at the swirling snow around her.

She delicately stuck her tongue out and caught a snowflake on it, closing her eyes, as if to make a wish.

Her name, photographers whispered to the uninitiated, was Esmé Madison Evans. She was wearing an ivory column dress that had been designed by Sebastian Giroux, the up-and-coming young couturier. Around her neck was an exact replica of the new jewel of the Met's Egyptian wing, an artifact temporarily on loan from the Museum of Egyptian Antiquities in Cairo for a special exhibit. Around the neck of Esmé Madison Evans, wife of Patchfield Evans, Jr., was a replica of the Scarab of Isis, a necklace that, until tonight, had never been viewed in New York City.